A raw string of Tenctonese expletives assaulted George's ears

It was startling b[...] [...]san exercise that por[...]

He looked into th[...] [...]san standing before Vessna's cri[...] [...]re something wrong?" he asked.

"Think, George," she commanded, her voice cold yet frightened. "Is there something you've forgotten?"

"That's odd. I was just thinking that, but I simply couldn't imagine what it was."

"Look into the baby's crib. Maybe that will refresh your memory."

George glanced into Vessna's crib, and caught his breath. Partially hidden by the baby's pink and white blanket was the grip of his .38 Smith & Wesson revolver.

The weapon was fully loaded and the hammer was fully cocked. That was curious too, because the gun had a hair trigger. Simply brushing against it, the baby could have fired it, which would have been unfortunate, since the barrel appeared to have been aimed at Vessna's head.

He pushed the blanket aside, picked up the weapon, and held it in his hand. Susan kept staring at the gun, saying nothing, which was good, because George was fresh out of responses . . .

Published by POCKET BOOKS

#4 ALIEN NATION™

THE CHANGE

THE NOVEL BY BARRY B. LONGYEAR
BASED ON THE SCREENPLAY BY
STEVEN LONG MITCHELL & CRAIG W. VAN SICKLE

POCKET BOOKS
New York   London   Toronto   Sydney   Tokyo   Singapore

An *Original* Publication of POCKET BOOKS

POCKET BOOKS, a division of Simon & Schuster Inc.
1230 Avenue of the Americas, New York, NY 10020

ISBN: 0-671-73602-7

First Pocket Books printing March 1994

10 9 8 7 6 5 4 3 2 1

POCKET and colophon are registered trademarks of
Simon & Schuster Inc.

Cover art by Dru Blair

Printed in the U.S.A.

*To Isaac Asimov,
who didn't need a* Hila
to understand this.

THE CHANGE

CHAPTER 1

China Lake Federal Maximum Security Facility

Hardened steel locks clicked open and slammed shut, heavy metal doors hissed on their pneumatic hinges, silent lenses studied long, sterile passageways. Despite the air circulation system, the slight odors of machine oil and disinfectant hung in the air. The disinfectant killed germs. The machine oil helped the bars and locks keep the prisoners behind them from killing each other and the public at large.

The Newcomer's face appeared on the screen set into the steel wall, his hairless, spotted scalp covered by a guard's cap. "Just a moment, Warden," crackled the monitor's tinny speaker. Warden Tom Rand tapped the letter against his fingers as he waited for the guard to open the security doors to the electronics shop checkpoint.

Servo-mounted security cameras examined the warden and his surroundings from three different angles. They saw an athletically built man who kept

1

that way by pumping iron with the yard monsters in the prisoner's weight room. Rand was comfortable with the prisoners. The cons at China Lake, if they had the capacity to like anyone, liked Warden Rand. He was strict, intolerant toward rule breakers, but honest to the point of political stupidity. Respecting punishments, rights, opportunities, and privileges, it was Tom Rand's mission in life to see that his charges always got what was coming to them. He had no family, no church, and no political affiliations. He believed in China Lake, rehabilitation, the L.A. Dodgers, and his own mission, in that order.

As a concession to his fiftieth year, his hair was thinning, revealing a nine-centimeter-long scar on the back of his head, compliments of one prisoner who hadn't liked him. That had been shortly before the alien ship crashed in the Mojave Desert. Warden Rand was rather proud of his scar; proud of the con who had given it to him, rather. The fellow had gone on to receive his masters in clinical psychology, and upon his release from China Lake, had received his doctorate. He was now a prison psychologist in Oregon, and he had asked Tom Rand to be the best man at his wedding. Partly as a joke, mostly because they meant it, the yard eagles had nicknamed Warden Rand "Saint Thomas of the Crowbars."

"Enter your card now, sir."

Warden Rand removed his specially encoded identification card from his breast pocket and shoved it into the slot next to the monitor.

"Thank you, sir."

As the card emerged from the slot once again, the remote-controlled locks on the steel door behind Tom slammed shut while the locks on the door before him clicked, allowing the barrier to hiss open. Tom Rand shivered at the sounds. A wry expression crept onto his face as he removed the card and replaced it in his breast pocket. He had just realized something: China Lake gave him the willies. Perhaps it was the oppressive security. Perhaps it was the ever-present possibility of having to be ready to kill or to die to maintain control. He shrugged off the feeling. The guards were prisoners too. The willies didn't have to look any further than that for a cause.

Warden Rand went through the door and stopped before a booth faced with a three-inch-thick plate of bullet-proof glass. Behind the green-tinted barrier, the guard who controlled the checkpoint examined directly with his eyes what had already been examined electronically through the security cameras. "Very well, sir," the guard said as he threw a switch that closed and locked the door behind the warden.

Newcomers made excellent prison guards. They were intelligent, patient, attentive to detail, and able to adapt to changing conditions. That, and they all had lifetimes of experience as either prisoners or keepers. Many humans hated the coming of the Tenctonese, but Tom Rand didn't number himself among them. The Newcomers had been a boon to the entire prison staff, not to mention bringing variety to the prisoner population. Prisoner Maanka Dak, aka Pete Moss, was a primary case in point.

"Going to Dak's place, Warden?"

"As usual," Rand answered with a smile. "Everything quiet, Hobbs?"

"Like a tomb." The guard turned from his monitors, where he'd been examining the opposite side of the door through which the warden was about to walk.

Hobbs nodded toward the letter in Rand's hand. "Good news for Dak?"

"It certainly looks that way. Don't be surprised if you see him walking out of here soon."

"Good. Someone with his gifts really doesn't belong in here."

"That's the honest truth. My guess is that the next parole board will see it that way too."

"That's terrific, Warden."

Tom Rand smiled, raised his brows and pointed at the door with his thumb. "I know you're lonely, Hobbs, but I can't spend all day getting through your checkpoint."

Hobbs's eyes changed color as he grinned. "Yessir. Sorry. I guess it does get a little too quiet at times."

"That's just the way I like it."

The door swung open and Tom Rand waved at the guard and entered the guard room for the prisoners' electronics complex, nicknamed "Button Row." He waved at the human guard behind the glass and continued through the door the guard automatically opened.

Everyone on staff knew Warden Rand liked to spend time with Maanka Dak. Everyone else did too. Dak's obvious brilliance and good nature combined to make you feel good just to bask in his intelligence and wit. By himself, Dak had vindicated Tom Rand's efforts to get the educational facility for his occupational rehabilitation program.

It was the most advanced rehabilitation facility in the nation, if not the world, for instructing inmates in electronics; computer programming; industrial, home, and computer electronics design, calibration, and repair. Because of prisoner Maanka Dak's experience and special aptitudes, the facility was rapidly developing its own medical electronics division, as well. While behind bars at China Lake, Maanka Dak had been granted over thirty patents on his inventions, several of which were already in hospital operating and therapy rooms saving lives. His holographic high-density imager had virtually revolutionized diagnostics. One could only imagine what the Newcomer would accomplish if he were on the outside with the proper funding and support facilities.

After the locks on the final door slammed shut behind him, the warden inhaled the mysterious smells of electrical equipment, hot and hard at work. Humans and Newcomers alike were seated and standing before banks of equipment at workbenches, totally absorbed in what they were doing. Here and there a prisoner's hand waved in greeting. Tom always waved back. The voices of visiting instructors in basic and advanced electronics could be heard coming from the separate classroom facilities on the other side of one of the security barriers.

In the back of one of the workshops was "Dak's place," as it was known to guards and yard eagles alike. To Tom Rand, the racks of equipment there, half of it designed and built by Dak, looked like the bridge of a spaceship. Maanka Dak was bent over a computer keyboard, entering some calculations, while his Newcomer assistant, Sing Fangan, looked on over his shoulder. Sing noticed the warden first and smiled as he straightened up. "Hi, Warden."

"Hi, Sing." He nodded toward Dak's upturned face. "Hi, Maanka. I hope I'm not interrupting anything."

"Have a seat, Tom. Always glad to see you," said

Dak, reaching out his hand. Warden Rand shook hands with the Newcomer and pulled up a chair from the end of the workbench. Dak nodded toward his computer's monitor screen. "Sing and I were just double-checking some calculations on the neural transmitter experiment series we completed last week."

"How do they look?"

A slight frown crossed Dak's face. "The results are very promising; better than I had hoped, really."

Tom Rand pointed his finger at Maanka. "Then why the long face?"

Maanka Dak glanced at Sing Fangan, his assistant shrugged, and Dak looked back at the warden. "Tom, it's just that Sing and I have pushed this thing about as far as we can in here with these facilities. I'm certain now that the neural transmitter for humans is feasible. After all, the medical technicians on the ships used to use something similar to diagnose and treat certain disorders as a matter of routine."

Sing's face grew grim. "They were also used to control and torture, as well."

Dak nodded and continued. "Be that as it may, I'm certain that with the adapted implant technique and different programming, the thing can work on humans. It's just that we can't prove it here."

"What is it?" the warden asked. "Is there a piece of equipment you need, materials, what?"

"What I need, Tom, is a complete zero gee lab."

"A zero gee lab?" Warden Rand held up his hands. "That's something I can't get you." He paused as he saw the letter in his hand, and remembered why he'd come. "Perhaps I spoke too soon."

"What is it?"

"Maanka, I've gotten a letter from Dr. Norcross."

"Oh? Has she gotten the funding for her xenoneurology institute?"

"There's nothing new on that."

Maanka nodded. "One wonders if the peace dividend is ever going to pay off. What's the letter about?"

"You respect Carrie Norcross a great deal, don't you?"

"She's supplied the funding for a good bit of my work here, Warden, and I've consulted with her a great deal in designing the adaptation programs for the neural transmitter." Dak pointed toward the letter. "Does that have something to do with the application for the new equipment we were hoping to get here?"

"It's a letter from her to the parole board." He withdrew the letter from its envelope and looked down at it. "In here she describes your work and its value to the medical profession, and in particular points out the potential for your work in addressing an entire host of mental and neurological disorders, particularly the ones clogging the courts and prisons right now. Listen to this: 'Imagine being able to cure an alcohol, crack, or heroin addict with a simple outpatient operation that would cost less than it takes to support the same addict for one day at a medium security prison.' She goes on to urge the board to grant your parole, and the letter is signed by a virtual medical and political who's who."

He held out the letter, and Maanka Dak took it and began reading, Sing Fangan looking over his shoulder. "The surgeon general?" Sing exclaimed. He pointed at the letter. "Look at this. L.A.'s chief of police."

"And the mayor," the warden added. "If I was a betting person, Maanka, I'd say your next parole hearing was a done deal."

"How about that?" Dak said, beaming at the warden. He turned his head and looked up at Sing. "Maybe in another few months we'll be out of here."

Sing frowned and studied the letter. "I don't know if I'm included." He looked up at Tom Rand. "Warden?"

"The charges of bank robbery and attempted murder were the same for both of you, as well as the circumstances. In addition, Sing, I think everyone is aware of how valuable your skills and experience are to Maanka's work. I don't see how the board could parole Maanka without paroling you, as well. I will insist upon it, and I know Dr. Norcross will, as well."

"You'd go in front of the board for us?" Dak asked.

"I've done it twice before. Why would I stop, now that wanting you out from behind crowbars is getting chic?"

Maanka placed his hands on the warden's shoulders and said, "I guess what you told me the day I first came through the gate six years ago is true. The good things come for those who work for them." He smiled sheepishly. "I guess I was pretty angry back then."

"Ancient history," the warden answered.

Maanka removed his hands from the warden's shoulders and favored Tom Rand with a proud grin. "Well, would you like to see the latest?"

"You bet."

"It's a bit crude, of course, but it's a fully operational unit." He glanced at Sing and nodded. Sing Fangan went to the tiny refrigerator, opened the door and reached inside.

"How come you keep it on ice?" the warden asked.

"It's powered by a thermocouple, so once it gets to a certain temperature, it turns on. The only way to keep it off is to keep it cold."

8

Sing closed the refrigerator door and walked over to Maanka and the warden. He bent down and held out a small white foam block in the center of which was a stubby needle a little over a centimeter long and almost a millimeter thick. "The production models would be much smaller," he said, holding out a magnifying glass.

Warden Rand held the magnifier close to his eye and studied the needle. "Maanka, you showed me the schematics for this, but it's hard to believe you and Sing managed to get all that in something the size of a piece of pencil lead."

"Once we have the facilities, we can make that capsule thinner than a hair."

"Amazing." The warden looked up and frowned. "The operation itself . . . how is the transmitter implanted? One of your goals was to be able to implant the transmitters on an outpatient basis."

Dak held up an instrument that resembled a curved stiletto with a grooved blade. "This is all it takes. We call it the ice pick."

Tom Rand took the instrument and examined it. "Wicked-looking thing. How do you make the implant without actually making an incision?"

"Here, Sing, show him the book."

Sing Fangan reached across the warden to a shelf and removed a thick volume from between two pieces of test equipment. As Dak fitted the neural transmitter to the grooved blade of the implantation awl, Sing's nimble fingers flipped through the pages until they stopped on a transparency set showing cutaway views of a human head. "In reality, it is an incision," he said. "It's just not a visible incision. After using a local anesthetic to desensitize the eye and eyelid, the eyelid is lifted, the top of the eyeball is depressed slightly, then the awl is inserted and punched through the—"

"I think I've heard enough," Tom said, only half joking.

Maanka laughed as he patted Sing's shoulder. "Let's not spoil Tom's dinner." He held the awl toward the warden. "See how it locks into the grooved end? It stays locked until the awl is withdrawn. Once the transmitter is implanted, the biofilaments begin growing, attaching themselves to the appropriate neurons."

The warden studied the end of the awl as he asked, "How long does it take for the filaments to begin functioning?"

"Almost right away, although they continue growing until they run out of medium, unless arrested. We can do that with the controller."

Tom shook his head and grinned. "I don't know much about these things, but I know you're going to have to come up with another way to implant the transmitter. That under-the-eyelid method's never going to get past the description."

"Well, there is another way," Sing Fangan said, and he placed his hands on the sides of the warden's head, holding it in an iron grip.

Tom instinctively reached up, but before his fingers could get to Sing's powerful hands, Maanka Dak shoved the tip of the implantation awl through the top of the human's left eyelid and deep into his brain. The universe filled with bright flashes as what felt like enormous electrical shocks paralyzed every muscle in Tom Rand's body.

"Actually, Tom," Dak said, "there are a few problems with the neural controller I hadn't mentioned." He nodded, and Sing released the warden's head. Tom tried to move, but motion was impossible. His open right eye could see the handle of the awl sticking out of his own face. "We haven't figured out how to arrest the biofilament growth in humans. In the interests of science and entertainment, we tried it out on two inmates. You remember Conner and Beckman? Beautiful boys. We were able to achieve remarkable motor control over them for a few hours, then unfortunately they went quite homicidal. You must remember that ugly scene in the yard last month when Conner took that homemade sticker of his and perforated those three inmates and the guard? When Beckman went homicidal, Sing and I took care of him ourselves by staging his suicide. After all, we couldn't afford an autopsy discovering Beckman's brain half strangled by the filaments on my little toy."

"Maanka?"

"Yes, Sing?"

"If we were getting out soon anyway, brother, why are we doing this?"

"Don't be absurd. We have to get out now if we're to finish with our brother Nicto by the next *mitr*. Dr. Norcross will understand. Believe me, she will understand."

"It is the *vikah ta*? It is all the *vikah ta*?"

"Samuel Francisco." Nicto's immigration joke name passed though Maanka's lips like a curse, the venom dripping from every syllable. "Warden Rand will be the beginning: the first abscess removed in executing the *vikah ta* against our former brother."

"All these years? All our work?"

Maanka Dak glanced around the shop, checked his watch and nodded at Sing, all emotion removed from his voice. "That ought to be enough time."

Sing Fangan frowned and gripped Tom Rand's head

as Dak slowly withdrew the awl from the warden's eyelid. Blood streaked down Tom's face, and Sing caught the flow with a gauze pad just before the blood dripped onto the warden's shirt. "Maanka! There's too much blood!"

Dak frowned at his partner. "Keep the urgency out of your voice and facial expression, Sing. Remember, we always risk being under surveillance."

"What about the blood? It's not clotting. Look how dark it is. He's a bag full of scarlet dye. He can't have a bandage over his eye when we go back through the checkpoints. The guards will remember that he was wearing no bandages when he came in. If they stop us to question the warden, what then? That crude little program in the implant can't handle very much in the way of questions."

Maanka reached out his hand, lifted the gauze square, and watched a fresh trickle of blood begin flowing. "I hadn't thought of this. He's on a blood thinner." Maanka looked into the warden's unblinking stare. "A heart problem, Tom, old friend? Doing your aspirin a day like a good boy? Who would've thought?"

Replacing the gauze, Dak thought for a moment, turned to his workbench and picked up his soldering gun. Depressing the trigger, the tip immediately began smoking. "This is going to be a little uncomfortable."

Thrusting the point of the gun into the wound, he seared it shut as the smell of burned flesh crept into the air. "That ought to do it." He removed the gun and replaced it on the workbench.

As Sing cleaned up the warden's face and Maanka placed a red plastic container into his jacket pocket, Tom Rand neither moved nor cried out. He was not in command of those motor abilities. Inside, however, he screamed in silence at the puncture behind his eye, at the pain of the filaments wrapping themselves around his nerves one at a time, strangling his will into submission.

"And now, Tom," Maanka Dak said, picking up a small box resembling a remote control for a VCR, "it's time for you to take Sing and me through the checkpoints and then drive your new van to the loading dock so that we may pack my equipment. Then you may drive us through the gates." He pressed a button, the transmitter's preprogrammed instructions began running, and Warden Tom Rand laughed out loud, stood, put his arm across Dak's shoulders, and led Maanka and Sing toward the first checkpoint.

"I can't tell you two how proud I am of you," the warden said as they approached the first checkpoint's cameras.

Maanka Dak grinned and changed eye color as he shrugged, looked at his feet, and put on a credible "aw shucks" performance for the guard watching the monitor and listening to the audio pickups. "We owe it all to you, Tom. To you and to your faith in us."

CHAPTER 2

THE GHOSTLY RED numbers of the alarm clock's read-out cast an eerie glow over the entire bedroom. Matt Sikes groggily burrowed his head into his pillow, shut his eyes, and flopped his forearm over his face as he chased elusive sleep into its labyrinth. The detective in the back of his head impeded the pursuit. It had questions without answers. They were life and death questions—mostly death—about the Thunderbolt Poet, the current serial killer feasting upon Matt's time and peace of mind. Matt had refused to allow the little detective in the back of his head to think about the Thunderbolt, because he desperately needed some sleep. Forbidden to think about the Thunderbolt, the little detective picked at other questions.

That clock was wrong. Not the time, which read seventeen after four in the morning. The clock itself was wrong. Matt liked a bedroom as black as possible. Who had set up a bloody red searchlight to burn out his retinas? He rolled over, his back to the offending glare, and felt his awareness drift into soft nothingness. Perhaps sleep would return. It was possible.

There was more to the clock than it being red and very bright, announced his little detective to the rest of his brain. Matt didn't own an alarm clock with a red LED readout. There had been no birthdays, Christmases, or other gift days. There was no reason why that clock should be shedding its red light upon Detective Sergeant Matthew W. Sikes. He opened his eyes and saw the back of a bald, spotted head on the next pillow. Cathy Frankel. He was in her bed.

There were several automatic bolts of electrifying guilt, apprehension, self-doubt, and censurable memory that coursed through his mind, ending for the night the prospect of further sleep. Of course, he knew that sleeping with a Tenctonese woman did not make him a pervert, and that his guilt and apprehension had more to do with his problems regarding self-esteem than with having done something wrong. He knew all these things, but the knowledge was part of thinking; reasoning things out; gathering the facts and forging a conclusion based upon those facts.

There was old knowledge, nonetheless; other knowledge, rooted deep within his being, that said that Cathy Frankel was not one of "us." She was one of "them"; a rubberheaded space freak. Hence Matt Sikes was some kind of major degenerate for having made love to her. He allowed his memory to flash back upon the previous evening's erotic experiences, and his recollection threatened to make his eyeballs explode. That, too, he forced out of his mind.

Everything out of his head. He commanded the little detective to shut up and go to sleep, he pulled the covers over his eyes to cut off the light from the clock, and he avoided reaching over and caressing Cathy's mind-battering buttocks. He avoided even thinking of them. Their smooth contours, the way her cheeks glided up and down against each other as she walked naked across the floor, the way her spots tapered down her neck, coming to a point at the small of her back, combining with her cheeks to make a heavenly exclamation mark—

He shook the image from his head. Everything had to be exiled from his mind. Once the mind was blank, sleep would come. After all, Cathy was a biochemist. She spent her days mucking about in icky, stinky substances and piles of printouts choked with numbers. For the moment, at least, he could put Cathy out of his mind.

But there was one little thing more. Everything could have been put aside in the interests of further sleep, save the pressure on Matt's bladder. One of his eyes opened.

"Nuts," he muttered as he sat up in bed, scratched his knee and glared at the clock. Grabbing Cathy's bathrobe and putting it on against the air-conditioned chill, he stumbled into the bathroom, turned on the light, and relieved himself. When he was finished, he looked into the mirror and studied with disgust the image before him. His almost baby-faced features combined with sleep-puffed brown eyes and unshaved stubble to produce the image of a debauched, world-weary infant.

It was the negative view, he knew. Over three dozen or more Thunderbolt victims kept his view negative. He knew that the view would remain negative until the Poet had been taken down. Matt glanced through the bathroom door at the top of his notebook, sticking out from the clothes he'd tossed on the couch the night before. The sight of the notebook drove from his head the recollection of how his clothing had gotten tossed there. He faced the sink and turned on the water.

He shaved and showered, and when he was done, it was still before five. Sleep was impossible. Matt went into Cathy's tiny living room and picked up the remote to turn on her television before realizing he didn't want to turn it on. He didn't want to hear any news or even watch any movies that might be interrupted with a special eyewitness report about the discovery of yet another damned victim of the Thunderbolt Poet serial killer.

"It's really getting to me," he said aloud. "Now I'm afraid to turn on the damned TV." He pushed his discarded clothing aside, flopped down on the couch and looked disgustedly at the blank screen as he nervously slapped the remote against his palm. "Green stars weep no more," he muttered. The line had been on the message at the most recent of the Thunderbolt killings. Green stars weep no more. It sounded like the end of something. Maybe nothing.

Matt fished among his clothes for his notebook. He turned the pages until he came to the last few lines of the Thunderbolt's alleged poetry.

> Blade Of Victory
> Climb This Mountain
> Death Holds Sorrow Naught
> Reach The Sun
> Cry The People
> Green Stars Weep No More

There were several pages filled with similar nonsense. Captain Grazer had gotten poetry professors from several universities as well as professional poets from around the L.A. area to read and comment upon the Thunderbolt's lines. The order of the lines was taken from the order of the victims' deaths. All that remained was what the lines meant.

Grazer's poets had been prolific in their interpretations. Sikes had waded through the mountains of commentary they had produced at taxpayer expense regarding Christ symbols, phallic emblems, death motif, and ultraprimitive horseshit slinging. In other words, Grazer's search had been an enormous waste of time. One curious thing Matt had noticed: poets who had been following the Thunderbolt killings in the news found the killer's poetry negative, morbid, depressing. The few ivory-tower types who had never heard of the Thunderbolt, found the killer's lines generally uplifting and life-oriented.

"What crap!" Matt muttered.

"Darling?" said a soft voice from the shadows. "What's the matter? Can't you sleep?" Cathy came into the light from the darkness of the bedroom, her nakedness almost covered by a turquoise afghan.

"Sorry. I didn't mean to wake you up. I just have a lot on my mind."

"You promised you wouldn't think about it tonight."

Matt shook his head as he held up the remote for the TV set and said, "I wish I could turn myself on and off like that." He pushed the power button on, and a picture leaped upon the screen. Before the sound came on, Matt punched off the power and the picture died.

Cathy walked over and took the remote from Matt's hand, her expression troubled. "You don't want that, darling. Believe me." She dropped the remote on an end table and looked down at Matt. "I've seen men and women controlled like that. You don't want it." Her troubled expression melted into a smirk as she looked at the human. "You look silly in my robe."

"Should I take it off, then?" Matt joked.

The biochemist allowed the turquoise afghan to slip to the floor as her eyes fixed him with a hooded stare. "Yes, Matt. I think you should take it off."

Matt stood, hesitated for a second, then let his notebook fall to the couch as he removed Cathy's robe. Picking up the Tenctonese woman, he carried her into the bedroom.

Even as they made love, even as Matt began drifting off to sleep, the little detective in the back of his head was still worrying over all of the questions that still had no answers.

CHAPTER 3

IT WAS AS though he was a tiny insect commanding the cranial operations center of an enormous robot. With his many arms and legs, he operated the complex banks of switches and dials. A tiny leg would trip a switch, and suddenly the tiny, helpless insect had power: power to feed, to defend, to avenge.

Through the robot's stereo screens the insect saw a Newcomer girl standing behind the counter. She was wearing orange slacks and blouse, and an electric-blue furry pillbox hat. On the hat was mounted a cartoon image of a buck-toothed rodent with crossed eyes and a silly grin. "Welcome to Bucky's, sir. May I take your order?"

"Order?" The insect felt incredible itching fill his brain, then devilish pain made him swoon against the controls as the robot asked again, "Order?"

"Yes sir. May I take your order?" The girl's smile

evaporated as she mugged at her supervisor and cocked her head toward the robot.

"Take my order?"

The insect twisted a servo control, and the robot's head rotated to the left and to the right. The establishment was crowded with Newcomers. Only a few humans. Night owls and early risers. Street walkers, dealers, users, the morning shift, the unemployed, the unemployable. Most of them were eating breakfast. Icky, disgusting things. Tenctonese fast food. There were humans who could eat the stuff. It just went to show how hungry some people can get. How hungry and how low.

The insect twisted another servo control and the robot's head looked up. Behind the girl's head, high on the red-tiled wall, was mounted a row of video screens that listed the sandwiches, dinners, beverages, and side dishes available at Bucky McBeaver. Weasel jerky, the Big Buck Beaverburger, tofu fries, snail yogurt.

The insect looked at the rising pain monitors on his panel, reached out its legs, and shut down more circuits. The insect nodded as it accepted fully how much he hated things that walked upon two legs.

Hate.

It was a living, walking power: hate. He couldn't understand why he had never seen it before. How blind could he have been? It was all around him. The universe was dipped in it. Hate is God. Hate is love.

"Warden? Hey, Warden Rand?"

The insect was confused as familiar audio vibrations stimulated his receptors. Again he twisted the servo control, rotating the robot's head. The video sensors displayed the image of a dark-complexioned

Tenctonese male who appeared to be in his late forties.

"I'm sorry," said the insect into his microphone. "I don't remember your name." The insect frowned at the sound of its own words, for it knew he wasn't sorry. There was the danger panel that controlled the man; the man mind. Through cracks in the panel the insect could see eyes wide with terror, teeth and flecks of saliva as they framed silent screams. The insect turned a knob, and the eyes, the teeth, behind the panel faded.

"Rorik Ifan, sir." The face grinned. "With forty thousand residents at China Lake, I don't expect you'd recognize me. We only talked once or twice, but I sure remember you." The smile faded and was replaced by a frown. "Are you all right, Warden? You look ill."

"All right?" repeated the insect into the microphone. It turned away from the controls and pondered the concept of "all right."

Certain things had to be taken care of before he could be "all right." His house was very large. It was full of broken men, broken women, and broken children. They could have jobs, but government taxation, safety, age, and insurance regulations made it impossible for anyone who was not a megabuck industry to hire anyone.

They get hungry, cold, full of fear, locked into despair. Usually drugs came in, or were already there from birth, and the government was again driving the nation insane. The President of the United States at a reception, videotaped answering a question, saying, "This president is serious about doing something about the drug problem," and saying it with a double martini in his hand.

All right?

The insect went back to his controls and said, "Rorik, I make pretty good money as the warden at China Lake. Pretty good."

"Yessir?" Rorik Ifan frowned as the counter girl cocked her head and made like she was telephoning with her hands. He nodded and looked back at the warden. "It's a big job you have, Warden. I expect the pay would be right up there."

"There are things I'd like done around the house; out in my garden; things to clean up; fences to paint. I could hire maybe three or four kids—high school, college—three or four. Keep 'em on for the whole summer. I can afford it, and I'd rather let some kid get a break to get the work done than to take time from my work and do it myself. Do you understand?"

"Sure." Rorik Ifan made a hurry-up motion with his hand at the counter girl.

The insect shook his head as the tears rolled down its cheeks. "I never forced inmates to do slave labor around my house. I treated everyone with respect. I paid for everything I ever had done. If someone was going to work for me, I'd pay them. That's why I can't have anybody work for me."

"Sir? Warden, I don't understand."

The children. All of those broken children.

"Those three or four kids I could've hired. Instead of working for me, they're out there on the streets, getting into trouble, mugging, taking down their despair with chemicals, killing to get more, lashing out in frustration and hate against the universe! I can't hire them! I can't screw with W-2 forms, withholding, child labor laws, liability insurance, worker's comp, fucking bureaucrats, goddamned lawyers, idiot after idiot after idiot! No! I'm not all right! I don't know anyone who is all right. I cannot even conceptualize a being in the entire universe who is all right."

The Rand panel was acting up again. The man mind. The insect gave the knob another turn, but all of the safety interlocks had melted. The video monitors showed the convict, the counter gang, all of the ones in the place, looking at him. Looking at the shell. Seeing only outside. The universe of creatures is made up of countless insides. The universe of perceptions is made up of countless outsides. How could they ever understand?

"Can't you see it, Rorik? It's all a cesspool: courts, bureaucrats, politicians, lawyers. It's the wrong kind of people, their heads filled with the wrong kinds of ideas, killing the country by sucking it dry to implement unworkable solutions!"

The customers screamed as the robot lifted its arm, took an assault rifle from beneath its coat, and jabbed the muzzle into Rorik Ifan's chest. "Kill a lawyer for Jesus, Rorik! Say it! Kill a lawyer for Jesus!"

"Kill—kill, kill—"

"Say it, you fucking convict piece of nigger slag! That's what they used to call you until I stopped them: nigger slag! Say it!" He pulled a machine pistol out of his pocket and waved it around at the customers. "Everybody! Kill a lawyer for Jesus! Kill a lawyer for Jesus!"

"Kill a lawyer for Jesus," whimpered a few voices. "Kill a lawyer for Jesus."

"Louder!" screamed the insect. "That was terrible! Shout it! Let's hear it again! Kill a lawyer for Jesus!"

"Kill a lawyer for Jesus!" screamed the customers and staff.

Three patrons tried to sneak through one of the glass double doors. The motion detectors in the robot's control room sounded the alarm, and the insect pulled levers, twisted servos, and pressed the fire button. The robot squeezed the trigger on the machine pistol, stitching the three across the back. The screams through the control room's speakers were deafening. The insect reached out a leg and turned down the volume.

"Now," he said finally, "that was what I call the wrong kind of idea." He looked up and saw the counter girl whispering hysterically into a telephone. The insect pushed the fire button again, sending a .30 caliber lump of steel-jacketed lead from the assault rifle through the counter girl's spotted head. The contents of her cranium spattered the video screens behind her.

It's so hard, thought the insect. Doing the right thing is so hard. Some people have relatives that are lawyers. Every now and then you run into a lawyer that seems like a pretty good sort. Once in a while a day goes by when you don't get screwed by a lawyer, or at least you don't know about it until it's too late. You get lulled into this false sense of security; like lawyers are just like any other working stiff, putting in the time, hauling it home, catching shit about forgetting the anniversary. It makes you forget they're aliens; hideously fiendish monsters from Hell's last dimension.

"It's all smoke, Rorik," said the insect into the microphone. "Lawyers, even the ones with a streak of goodness, have a terrible disease of the conscience and soul. They're like addicts and little, abused infants whose minds have shut down, who cannot afford to admit to the too painful truth."

The robot lurched over to a booth and bent over as it waved the assault rifle at the three persons sitting there. "I have proof! I have proof!" He looked down at the table. In its center was a candy-striped bucket half filled with greasy lumps of breaded something.

"What's that?" He looked up at the faces one at a time. "What is that shit?"

"Sq-sq—" stuttered one.

"Nuggets," said the one on the right. "Squirrel nuggets."

"Squirrel nuggets!" screamed the insect. All of the pain monitors were pegged. There were no more circuits to shut down.

There was that tiny baby squirrel little Tommy Rand had found beneath a tree. Tommy had taken it home and kept it in a shoe box. He had fed it milk with a dropper until the furry little thing opened its beautiful eyes. It had such a soft, pink little tongue. It used to lick peanut butter from his finger. "His name was Rocky."

A bucket of squirrel nuggets.

"You bastards!" The robot swung around and screamed, "His name was Rocky!" The insect threw all of the firing switches and watched the monitors as the bullets ripped through the people, the gang behind the counter, the video screens, and the gaudy plastic furnishings. One clip emptied, the insect had the robot fit a fresh clip into the weapon. The bolt was thrown, and again he greased the squirrel eaters, the lawyers, the pain givers, the pain oceans, the early risers and whores.

"Kill a lawyer for Jesus!"

He loaded the weapon again, chewed up more bodies, and then the assault rifle jammed. It was silent in the restaurant except for the whimpering and moaning of a few customers. There was someone talking, though. The insect turned up the volume and heard a voice from outside the building. It was a woman's voice speaking through a bullhorn. He dropped the assault rifle and checked the machine pistol, noting that its clip was still three-quarters full. With his left hand he pulled a loaded revolver from his pocket. Holding a weapon in each hand, he tried to look though the windows at who was calling him.

The insect frowned as it realized that the robot was standing in probably the only place in the restaurant's customer area that couldn't see through the windows. The woman on the bullhorn spoke again, this time the voice more urgent. The insect shook his head in frustration. He never could understand anyone speaking through a bullhorn.

He saw Rorik Ifan on the ceramic tile floor, his pale pink blood spreading out on the squares of white and tan. "Blood like that," said the insect, "it's not like killing a man at all. It's more like squashing a bug."

That Dr. Norcross. What was it she'd expected from Maanka Dak and Sing Fangan? She'd sent money, she brought authorizations and blessings from the Surgeon General, the Justice Department, and the Bureau of Prisons. Everybody seemed to think Maanka Dak was the best thing since the microchip. There was something wrong, though.

But the new thing wrong is not with Maanka, thought the insect. Everybody knows what's wrong with Maanka. What's wrong is with the other one.

The insect looked at the Rand panel. It was in there. What was wrong with Carrie Norcross was in there. He'd have to let Rand out from behind his panel, though, and that he wasn't allowed to do. There was something wrong, though. Something terribly wrong.

He took a step toward the former inmate's inert form, and in the space of less than half a second almost two dozen high-powered slugs flew through the windows, shattering them, and into the robot's torso, splashing the floor and the walls with red.

The insect nodded as the sensors dimmed and went off the air. "Now that," said the insect, "is blood."

CHAPTER 4

GEORGE FRANCISCO OPENED his eyes to see the shadowy figure silhouetted by a ghostly glow. It was too soon for the pain minister. It was too soon.

That was the past; other times, other planets, other solar systems. He tore himself from the ship, from the treatment bay, from the past. Overseers, pain ministers, slavery, were things of long ago.

Still, the figure stood in the door of the bedroom; his bedroom, on Earth in Los Angeles.

The Thunderbolt Poet Killer. Did the killer know George was on the trail? Soon his blood would soak the bedclothes, and the Thunderbolt would leave another drawing of lightning coming out of a rain cloud, another cryptic line of poetry.

Overwhelming dread vibrated every fiber of his body. There were a lot of sick individuals on Earth. Many of them had turned their sicknesses against the Newcomers. George could tell from the smooth silhouette of the *large head that the person in the door was a Newcomer. The Thunderbolt only killed Newcomers, hence the police psychiatrist's profile listed the killer as a human.*

This was a Newcomer. A female. Yet, the dread remained.

"Susan?" he called. "Odrey, kak t'avee?" he asked in Tenctonese.

"Nicto, t'vot," answered Susan's voice. "Nicto, it's you."

The figure came closer, and George sat up in bed and raised his hand to stroke her temples. She did not bend down for the caress. "Susan, what is the matter?"

"It's you, George. It's you. It's always you. It's always been you. It's you now. It always will be you." Her voice was dull, but charged somehow with cold, raw hatred.

George lowered his hand and pushed himself back against the bed's headboard. "What are you saying?"

"You're less than enough. You're nothing, George. You were genetically designed to be nothing, and there's no fighting genes, George."

He was struck speechless, his universe a fiction, his life a revealed fraud. Devastation crushed his hearts as he finally found his tongue. "I don't understand. I've fought. I fought for us, our children. Itri Vi. Don't you remember Itri Vi? What about our love, our children, our home, our—"

He cut off his words as he saw the flash of the blade in her hand. It was a kitchen knife with a ten-inch blade. She swung down the blade, and George threw up his arms to protect his face. The point of the razor-sharp blade cut through his hand and struck deeply into his head through his right eye—

"Aaaaaaa!"

"Daddy?"

*Emily's voice came to him as though through a fog.
"Run, Emily! Grab Vessna and run, darling! Your
mother's got a knife! Warn Buck!"*

"Daddy? Wake up. Are you all right? Daddy?"

George opened his eyes, his throat constricted with
panic. It was full daylight. He was in bed alone, the
covers wrapped about his head. Standing before him
was his daughter. "Emily? What is it?"

His daughter held out her hands, dropped them to
her sides, and rolled her eyes in a show of exaspera-
tion. "Nothing. Nothing's the matter. It's almost
seven-thirty, you're still in bed, and you were screaming your head off."

"Seven-thirty? Nonsense." He took a deep breath,
let it out, and tried to chase the dream shadows from
his mind. "The Wexler cat kept me up all night. I set
the alarm for six-fifteen. I know I did because I have to
take Vessna to day care today."

"Daddy, Polly Wexler's cat doesn't bother anyone
except Ramon, and he only complains so he can see
her. I think he's in love."

George looked at the clock and pushed the alarm
button. The readout showed the alarm set for seven-
fifteen. It also showed that the alarm button had been
disengaged. "I don't understand. I'm certain I set the
alarm."

"I'm guessing you forgot." His daughter grinned
wickedly and asked, "What was your dream about,
Daddy?"

"Nothing."

"Nothing? You sounded as though every Halloween
slasher since the landing was after you. Was it about
the Thunderbolt? Was Mom in it?"

"Child, you are developing an unhealthy interest in
the morbid."

"Maybe I just want to follow in my daddy's footsteps."

George scowled as he turned and looked up at Emily. He saw that she was wearing her usual designer-shredded jacket and electric-blue leotards, but there was a new touch: hair. In Technicolor. Reds, golds, oranges, greens, blues. "What's that on your head?"

Emily touched her hand to the tie-dyed fall that covered the right side of her spotted scalp and was gathered into a hot pink curl on her shoulder. "Isn't this the tot's spots? It's called a woobie."

"Woobie? It's hair! I won't have it! We've been through this before. You're not a human, and you're not to make yourself up like one. Do you think any self-respecting Tenctonese boy will find that demeaning display attractive?"

Emily stood and fumed for a moment, then tossed back her hair and said, "First, I'm not responsible for what nice Tenctonese boys think. Second, Ricky Martin thinks I look just fine. There're lots of girls in class, but I'm the one he asked to help him with his part in the school play. Third, Mom thinks I look just fine, and she already said I can wear my woobie. If you have a problem with that, you have a problem with Mom, not with me." Emily abruptly turned on her heel and left the room."

"Woobies," George grunted disgustedly, confused at how much Emily's attire seemed to threaten him. Nonsense, he thought. I'm not threatened; I'm offended by this unthinking racial outrage.

George put his feet on the floor, stood, and faced the empty door. He frowned as he remembered something. "Now, just one minute, Emily. Who is Rick Martin? Are you dating a human? I—"

George's words were cut short as a wave of dizziness and nausea struck. He sat back on the bed, his head still spinning. "What's happening to me?"

When George at last dressed and made it to the kitchen, the television was on. Susan was frantically finishing up breakfast dishes and cleaning Vessna's face while everyone seemed to be talking at once. George attempted to wish his wife good morning, but the chatter in the room in combination with the noise from the television seemed to overwhelm him. Dropping into his chair, he looked at his watch and said, "I'm sorry. The alarm didn't go off. I won't have time to take Vessna to day care."

"I certainly don't have time," Susan retorted. "Why did you stay in bed so long?"

"The alarm didn't go off."

"It didn't go off," Emily explained, "because Daddy forgot to set it."

George's fist came down on the table. "I told you about that hair!"

Emily's eyes went wide with fright. Susan picked up Vessna suddenly, frightening the child into screaming.

"Mom!" Emily shouted. "It's not okay for Daddy to talk to me that way!"

"Quiet!" Susan shouted. "Everybody quiet!" She took a deep breath, calmed down, and stroked Vessna's temples. After a moment the child's cries were lulled to sobs, then Vessna lost interest in crying and reached out her arm toward an electric-green ski mask on the end of the kitchen counter next to the small-screen TV. Susan allowed Vessna to pick up the ski mask and placed her on the floor. "Now, George," she said, her syllables held artificially calm. "What *is* your problem?"

"I don't know."

George held his hands to his head as he looked at his son, Buck, entering the room. Instead of his usual jeans and bomber jacket, Buck was wearing a dark brown hooded poncho over similarly colored shirt and trousers. George averted his eyes and saw Vessna pulling the ski mask over her head. Once she had it on, blinding her eyes, she stumbled into the table leg and knocked herself to the floor. The crying resumed.

"What's going on?" George demanded quietly. "When I went to bed last night, my life seemed to make some sort of sense. Now Emily's sprouting neon hair, my son is dressing like some kind of mad monk, somebody turned off my alarm, and why is the television on?"

Her eyes flashing, Susan placed her hands on her hips. "We discussed Emily's current fashion statement days ago, when you went into a snit about the mess she'd made in the basement with her old toys." She turned toward Emily. "A matter that still needs to be taken care of."

"Yes, Mom."

Susan faced George. "Buck looks just fine, no one but you touches your precious alarm clock, and there may be rain this afternoon. The television is on because I was hoping to hear some weather. Is there anything else you need to know, overseer-in-training?"

In the ensuing embarrassed silence, George looked down at his bowl of Roach Toasties and pushed it away. Susan turned down the volume on the television, came over to her husband's side and said, "What is it, George? You're acting very strange and you look terrible."

"Thank you for that," he answered sarcastically.

"This day has been going so extra specially well, the only thing I needed before going to work was to have what little self-image I have remaining pulverized—"

He cut short his tirade when he realized he was in the midst of yet another embarrassed silence. He glanced at his wife and children, absorbed their looks of injury and concern, and looked back down at his breakfast cereal. "I'm sorry, Emily. Buck." He glanced at Susan. "I'm sorry. I can't imagine what's come over me. When I came home late last night, Mrs. Rothenberg's pit bull went after me. I had a crazy nightmare, and I've been dizzy and sick to my stomach all this morning. I couldn't even figure out what necktie to put on."

"We noticed," Emily said, grimacing at George's bright purple tie. At the look from her mother, Emily said, "Sorry."

Susan brushed George's temples with her knuckles. "Perhaps you have a touch of *nia.*" She held her fingers beneath his jaw and felt around his jawline to his neck. "Your *nemeh* glands are a little swollen."

"They are?

"I think you should have a doctor look into it, George. It might be *nia,* but it may be something more serious."

"I don't see where I'll find the time," he answered, shaking his head. He pulled down his tie and unbuttoned his shirt collar. "I'm sorry. I know I said I'd take Vessna to day care today. I'm running so late I just can't see how I can. Matt and I are up to his ears with a case."

"The Thunderbolt Killer?" Emily asked.

"Yes."

"I can take Vessna, Dad," Buck said.

"You? The mad monk? You've only had your license for a year. It was only a few summers ago you got your head stuck in that storm drain in back of the house. And that car—"

"You let Buck drive *me* to school," Emily said. "If he and the car are so unsafe, why—"

"Very well," George interrupted. "My inconsistency. Yes. By all means." George waved both his hands in angry resignation. "Yes, Emily, I value you as highly as I value Vessna, despite the fact that the frying pan you were playing with five days ago is still sitting on the front steps, getting rustier by the hour." He held up his hand to stifle her protestations of innocence and shifted his gaze to Buck. "Yes, Buck, you may bring Vessna to day care. Be sure to get the car seat from your mother's car. Thank you so much for offering. Have a successful day. Now, are everyone's sensibilities adequately soothed?"

"Not quite everyone's," Susan said, looking down at George.

There was a moment's silence, then Buck said to Emily, "We'll be late. Take care of the skillet after school." Buck picked up Vessna and, carrying the child, followed Emily out the kitchen door.

Susan looked at her husband's dejected expression and said, "Would you like me to fix a few beaver strips for you or toast up a moth tart?"

"No, thank you. Just some tea, and I'll get it. You're running late too."

He walked over to the stove and picked up the teapot. As he filled it at the sink, he glanced at the television screen. On it was the image of a familiar face. "Susan, turn up the sound. That's Thomas Rand." Susan dried her hands and touched the remote.

"*—eleven killed and at least fourteen wounded. The*

gunman was killed by police officers at the Bucky McBeaver's near Marengo and Soto shortly after seven this morning. Acting Police Chief Marcus Steadman said there is no connection between this incident, the Black Slayer, or the Thunderbolt Poet Killer, and—"

"Nos dessa!" George swore. "Susan, it's Tom Rand. He's been either wounded or killed in some crazy mass slaying."

"Tom Rand?"

"The warden at China Lake. You remember. He's the one who addressed our quarantine group before we were released. He's—"

"Yes, I remember now. He spoke to us about human law and law enforcement." She went to George's side and placed her arms around his waist as she looked at the screen.

"A great man. He's the one who taught us to be men and women instead of slaves. Pride." George nodded. "He taught us to have pride. Now he's been killed in some senseless slaughter. What are humans, that this kind of madness keeps happening?"

He shook his head as the image showed the camera panning the carnage at the Newcomer's fast food franchise in the pit of Slagtown. The image rack focused down until it filled the window above and to the left of the anchor's shoulder. The person on the screen was the Newcomer queen of the Slagtown news beat, Amanda Reckonwith.

"To repeat, a gunman armed with a revolver, a machine pistol, and an assault rifle entered the McBeaver's near Marengo and Soto this morning and began peppering the patrons with automatic fire. The latest body count has risen to at least eleven dead and fourteen wounded. One of the dead and two of the wounded are humans. In an astonishing recent devel-

opment, the gunman's identity has been confirmed by federal authorities to be Thomas J. Rand, warden at the China Lake Federal Maximum Security Facility. The spokesman for the Bureau of Prisons could shed no light on Warden Rand's possible motives or mental state. However a thorough investigation—"

George punched off the TV's power button, stumbled over to the counter and hung on as another wave of dizziness washed over him. "I don't understand." He looked into Susan's eyes, searching for answers she didn't have. "I don't understand it at all."

He pulled his necktie off and thrust it into his coat pocket, took a deep breath, and nodded. "I have to get to work. This business will have the entire department in a turmoil." He removed his suit jacket and draped it over the back of a chair.

Susan placed her hand on George's arm. "I'm sorry about Tom Rand. I know what he meant to you."

"Feel sorry for the twenty-five dead and wounded down in Hollenbeck he left behind on his way to oblivion." He brushed her temples with his knuckles, "We both need to get to work."

"Please see a doctor, love."

George frowned at the human term of endearment. He didn't think he objected to it. For some reason, it just struck him as very very strange. He seemed somehow loosely connected to reality.

"I will." Before Susan turned to go into the nursery, George looked into her eyes, and for the first time noticed that they were deep maroon in color. This was strange to him, as well, for he knew they were blue. At least, he thought he knew they were blue. He was beginning to doubt everything.

It was like the doubtful Descartes joke Buck had

brought home shortly after he had begun college: "I think, therefore I am, I think."

George stood for a long moment, feeling as though there was something he had forgotten, and strained his mind trying to remember what it was. For some reason, he felt it was quite important. He went to the closet, pulled out his old weekend windbreaker and put it on. Suddenly, a startlingly raw string of Tenctonese expletives assaulted George's ear folds from the direction of the nursery. It was startling because George had never heard Susan exercise that portion of her vocabulary.

He looked into the nursery and saw Susan standing before Vessna's crib, her back to the door. "Is there something wrong?"

"Think, George," she commanded, her voice cold yet frightened. "Is there something you've forgotten?"

"That's odd. I was just now thinking that, but I simply couldn't imagine what it was."

"Look into the baby's crib. Maybe that will refresh your memory."

Quickly George mentally raced through the diaper changing, bottle preparing, toy selection, and toy placement baby maintenance chores that he was supposed to have done, but he could clearly remember doing them all, and doing them well. He took three steps into the room, glanced into Vessna's crib, and caught his breath as he instantly remembered what he'd forgotten. Partially hidden by the baby's pink and white blanket was the grip of the .38 Smith & Wesson revolver he'd been awarded for graduating at the top of his class at the police academy. The weapon was fully loaded and the hammer was fully cocked. That was curious too, because the weapon had a hair trigger. Simply brushing against it, the baby could have fired it, which would have been unfortunate, since the barrel appeared to have been aimed at Vessna's head. There was good reason to believe that the baby had tried sucking nourishment from the barrel at some time during the night.

George looked dumbly into his shoulder holster and was crestfallen to find it empty. Before he found the empty holster, he had entertained a split-second fantasy in which the gun belonged to someone else, which would have created another set of problems. He pushed the blanket aside, picked up the weapon, and held it in his hand. Susan kept staring at the gun, saying nothing, which was good, because George was fresh out of responses.

CHAPTER 5

"DID YOU HEAR about that freakout over in Hollenbeck Division?" Sergeant Dobbs asked as he poured himself a cup of coffee. Detective Sergeant Matt Sikes reversed his feet on the edge of his desk and punched at the keyboard he had perched on his lap.

"Everybody's heard about it, Dobbs," Sikes answered as he smacked the keyboard and snorted a breath of frustration through his nose. "Dobbs, have you seen George? My PC is jammed tight. Did George decide to rearrange everything again?"

"I don't know, man. It wasn't my turn to watch him."

"Hasn't he come in yet?" asked Mark Diaz from his side of Dobbs's desk.

"Would I be looking for him if he was here?"

"Who can say?" answered Diaz. "Sometimes when George is here, he's not all here. Know what I mean?"

"No, Diaz. I don't know what you mean."

"Like yesterday, Sikes, when he emptied all the paper clips into his tea—and drank it."

"I've got a lot of work to do and George is late, and that's all I'm talking about."

Dobbs shook his head. "George Francisco can't be late. He hasn't been late once since he came out of the academy. The man has a punctuality fetish."

"There's just no respect for tradition anymore," Diaz added.

"You two've been overdosing on jerk pills again." Sikes removed himself from the conversation, punched at the keyboard once more, and sighed. "All I get on this piece of junk is squat and squat squared."

"Who's popping idiot capsules, now?" asked Diaz. "I mean, my terminal works just fine."

"A poor detective blames his keyboard," Dobbs chimed in, then fell silent. After a stunned moment he said, "Holy shit. Check out the seven-day lost weekend."

Sikes looked up and saw his partner virtually feeling his way to the desk, his eyes protected by shooter's shades. Instead of his usually impeccable polyester, George Francisco was tieless, his collar was open, he had on a ratty tan windbreaker and torn blue jeans.

"I'll go see if I can find the number for Milkaholics Anonymous," Diaz cracked as he and Dobbs chuckled and returned to their work.

"George?" Sikes said. "Is that you?"

Francisco eased himself into his chair, folded his arms as though he were having a chill, and nodded. "I'm sorry I'm late, Matt. It's been one of those mornings." He shook his head. "No. It hasn't been one of those mornings. It has been this morning: Hell in a hibachi; the gridiron grind; everything down the great mother of all toilets."

"Having a rough day, George?"

Francisco removed his sunglasses and glared across the desk at his partner. "Your sarcasm is not appreciated, Matt."

"Look, George, ease off. Okay? What's wrong with you?"

"Nothing."

"Nothing," Sikes repeated. He took his feet from his desk and placed the keyboard on top of a stack of files. "George, you look like you're coming off a three-week bender."

"Bender?"

"Drunk, binge, bust, tear, milkman's holiday."

George slowly shook his head. "You're referring to an overindulgence of some sort with a drug. No, it's nothing like that. Susan thinks I might have a touch of *nia*."

"Knee-what?"

"*Nia*. I suppose the closest human equivalent would be influenza."

"Flu? You got space flu?"

"Just flu, although it might be something more serious. Susan wants me to see a doctor. Perhaps I will. I'll have to do something soon. Things are getting quite bizarre. Strange dreams, short temper, dizzy, forgetful." He glanced down at the weapon in his shoulder holster, closed his eyes for a grateful second, and looked again at his partner. "Quite forgetful."

"It happens to everybody, George. Don't sweat it."

"I don't sweat. Newcomers don't, you know."

"Just an expression."

George put his sunglasses back on and waved his

hand to dismiss the subject. "Have you heard any more about that shooting over in Hollenbeck?"

"Just what was on the news. The blue screws are down tight."

"Blue screws?"

"Police security. As far as the East L.A. cops are concerned, nobody knows *nada*. It stinks like the feds are into it, spin doctors and garbage handlers raining from the sky. Somebody sizable must be worried that he screwed up big-time. I'll bet anything it's because of who the shooter is. Sounds like the office routine finally got to Warden Rand. Maybe the guy who appointed him is trying to make himself invisible. It looks like the artillery the shooter used came from a sporting goods store in Van Nuys."

"Is there some significance in that?"

"Probably not. Van Nuys is on the way to Boyle Heights from China Lake. Anyway, Hollenbeck and Van Nuys both are sitting on what they have. Feds are in it up to their paper shredders."

"What could've caused the gunman to do such a thing?"

"The warden?" Matt's face grew very troubled. "Isn't that a slice of weird? I don't even get a hint. Maybe he just freaked." The man's protective layer of sarcasm moved between him and his feelings. "This morning he ran out of Fruit Loops, his wife left hair in the sink, he found a bottle of Scope in the mailbox, then bingo, he's popping weasel-jerky gourmands at Bucky's."

"He wasn't married." George lifted his dark glasses and rubbed his eyes. "I sort of knew him."

"The shooter?"

"Yes. All of the Newcomers who entered law enforcement when I did knew him. In a manner of speaking, he was our mentor. Tom Rand was one of the reasons I entered the police academy."

Matt Sikes thought for a moment, then shrugged. "People wig out sometimes, George. Newcomers too. It happens."

"There has to be more of an answer than that, Matt. Tom Rand was the most balanced human I've ever met. There has to be another reason."

"Maybe, ol' buddy, but we're not going to find it. It's not our case. Just poking around on my own, I got my knuckles smacked. When I tell you nobody over in Hollenbeck wants us, believe me—"

"Francisco! Sikes!" screamed Captain Grazer. "Don't you bastards ever check your zap pad? Francisco has an 'urgent' flag, and the damned thing won't stop beeping my terminal until one of you jerks acknowledges it! So someone push a damned button already! Today!"

Sikes looked up to see the captain disappearing into his office. "And they say PMS is a women's issue."

"Perhaps his wife's pregnancy is wearing thin."

"Yeah. I hear she's eating the planet." Matt leaned across his desk and said to George, "I've been trying to call up my menu for half an hour. What'd you do to the computer, partner?"

"Nothing." George reached out, punched on his unit, entered the code for the main menu, and in a moment it appeared. A red warning flag was flashing in the upper left corner of the screen. "There's nothing wrong with my terminal, Matt."

"Great," said Sikes. "That means there is absolutely no hope at all. It'll take maintenance a week to fix this."

"Allow me." George stood, walked around the

desk, and picked up Matt's keyboard. Flipping it over, he dropped it upon the desk a few times. When he again picked up the keyboard, the desk was filthy. "I didn't do anything to your terminal, Matt. You did."

With the eraser of a pencil, George pushed among the items that had fallen out of the keyboard. "Here we have a paper clip, two staples, a piece of pencil lead, a great deal of chocolate-chip cookie crumbs, some fingernail clippings, and I believe that small strip of desiccated animal flesh is a piece of pepperoni." He reset the unit, entered the code, and the main menu leaped upon the screen.

"Francisco!" Captain Grazer screamed. "Sometime this damned millennium!"

"Got it, Captain," George answered as he entered his code on Matt's keyboard. The screen blanked, and came back with his zap pad.

*** *** ***

DET. SGT. GEORGE FRANCISCO, NO. 27113;
OFFICER WILLIAM E. DUNCAN, NO. 10882.
ESCAPED PRISONER/PRISONER RELEASE WARNING
MAANKA DAK, NO. 77142, AND SING FANGAN, NO. 77147, INMATES AT THE CHINA LAKE FEDERAL MAXIMUM SECURITY FACILITY, ESCAPED FROM CUSTODY LAST EVENING. THEIR WHEREABOUTS ARE UNKNOWN. DAK AND FANGAN ARE CONSIDERED ARMED AND EXTREMELY DANGEROUS.

*** *** ***

"Old collar, George?"

Francisco frowned as he studied the screen. "Yes." He nodded. "Yes. Very old."

"Who's Duncan?"

"Bill Duncan. He was my T.O."

"Your training officer? Come to think on it, I never heard you mention him."

"He's not exactly one of my favorite idle conversation topics." George rubbed his eyes and shook his head. When he lowered his hand, he looked at his partner. "It was when I was still a probationer riding black-and-whites in Slagtown. I think we were paired up to discourage me and piss off Duncan. Bill Duncan hated me, hated Slagtown, and just about anyone with spots instead of hair."

"Prejudiced?"

"Not just against Newcomers. If your age, sex, shade, or physical configuration varied one iota from Bill Duncan's, he'd puke his venom at you. I'm not even certain he'd be able to tolerate an identical twin."

"Sort of a democratic bigot, huh, George?"

Francisco shrugged and looked down at his desktop. "I wasn't terribly fond of him either. He stank."

"I know humans smell a little different, but—"

"Matt, he stank because he smoked those evil damned cigars all the time and soaked himself in an after-shave lotion that reminded me of fermented underwear. I think he put it on double strength because he knew it made me ill."

"Gosh, George, I didn't think you had it in you to hate anybody."

Francisco's eyebrows went up. "Hate?" He frowned as a thought played behind his eyes to be replaced by a headache. George nodded toward his computer. "Will they run this flag on the beat screens in the black-and-whites?"

"Your old T.O. still in the rollers?"

"Yes. It's important, Matt. Will they notify Duncan right away?"

"If they don't catch him at home, they'll catch him at roll call. How come you're being flagged? Did this Dak and Fangan do an I'm-gonna-git-you-sucka on you and Duncan?"

George frowned as he scratched his neck beneath his right ear. "It was somewhat more than a threat." George walked back to his chair and dropped into it.

"So, what was it?"

"It was a bust in cooperation with the FBI regarding a string of bank robberies here in L.A. There was a mix-up about which bank we were to cover, the feds were on the other side of the city, and Duncan and I were left slightly understaffed. They shot it out with us. Maanka's biological brother, Sita Dak, was killed."

Sikes scratched the back of his neck as he nodded toward his partner. "You?"

"Yes. It was my gun that fired the fatal bullet." After a reflective moment, George said, "I knew them all from the ship, Matt. Maanka Dak and Sing Fangan believe they must perform the *vikah ta* to satisfy an oath they took long ago, before we came to Earth."

"What's that?"

"*Vikah ta.* Your word 'vendetta' seems rather close to capturing its intent. It means 'thorough revenge,' and it requires slaying, not only the object of the vengeance, but anyone related to the object of vengeance by family, employment, or any other kind of association. Anyone who thinks kindly of the object of revenge."

"That could be one helluva lot of people, George. Are they that wacko?"

"You're right. That could be a large number of persons, Matt. Family," he glanced up at Matt, "close friends, anyone who has any affection for the object." He punched up the file for Maanka Dak on his screen. "That includes you."

"Oh, swell. Terrific."

"Matt, are you certain they'll notify Duncan about this escape right away?"

"What do you care? He hates your guts, doesn't he?"

"Dak and Fangan don't know that. I doubt if they'll ask him before they shoot. Besides, he was my T.O. Whatever he thought of me, he taught me a great deal."

"Man, what kind of a ninja half-witted idiot would take an oath like that?"

George leveled his gaze at his partner and smiled. "I took the same vow myself, Matt. It was an oath for a different time, a different place. I had a different name then, it was on another planet, under much different conditions. The planet has changed, conditions have changed, and we've changed." Maanka Dak's image peered at George from the screen. "At least some of us have changed." He studied the screen until his eyes seemed to glaze, then he glanced up at Sikes. "Do you have friends at the morgue?"

"Among the living, I have a canoe maker who owes me a favor or two. Why?"

"I just thought of something. I want to be there for Warden Rand's autopsy."

Sikes snorted out a laugh. "You kidding? With the security they got clamped down on Rand's shootout, the cutters'll be lucky if *they* get in."

"Dak and Fangan were at China Lake. Maybe they had some connection to what happened to Warden Rand."

"Neither one of 'em are our cases, bro. We're still buried in the Thunderbolt Poet. Grazer's really on our tails too. We have about a hundred candy stores left, out of our share to cover, with those writing samples on the candy wrappers."

George frowned, shook his head slightly and held out his hands. "I don't understand, Matt. The candy stores are a dead end. Why don't we just pick up the perp?"

Sikes's eyebrows went up. "Why don't we just pick up the perp?"

"Yes."

Matt Sikes threw his hands up in the air and rolled his eyes. "You mean other than being short a name, an address, a reliable physical description, and a warrant? I can't think of a single reason."

Francisco's frown grew deeper. "She lives at 126 South Chicago."

"She?"

George nodded. "Yes. A woman. Tenctonese." George squinted and looked at a spot in space. "René Day. I don't recall a physical description."

"Recall?" Sikes shook his head and stared wide-eyed at his partner. "Are you putting me on?"

"Putting you on? You mean joking." Francisco shook his head.

"Yeah, are you joking?"

"I am not putting you on, Matt. I was simply inquiring why we haven't arrested her."

"Man, you better see a doctor, and soon. The task force's had a dozen officers and a platoon of poets sorting through mountains of the most dull damned poetry on the planet, trying to piece together some hint concerning the perp, and out of thin air George Francisco finds a name and address? Man, where've you been for the past few months?"

"I don't understand, Matt."

Sikes slumped back in his chair. "Okay, how do you know the Thunderbolt Poet is a Newcomer, that she is a she, that her name is René Day, and that she lives on South Chicago? One twenty-six South Chicago."

George frowned and looked toward the ceiling as though he were trying to piece together the pieces of realistic evidence to justify some kind of knowledge that is obvious on its face. "The handwriting samples she's left on those candy wrappers, 'Blade of Victory,' 'Climb This Mountain,' and so on. They're all signed with the lightning bolt emerging from a rain cloud."

"Rain cloud." Sikes nodded and raised his hands. "Right. Okay, I get it. Rain cloud; rainy day; René Day. But by the same evidence, her name could be Stormy Withers, Wet Butler, or something else."

George snickered and reached his fingers behind his shades to rub his eyes. "Wet Butler," he repeated. "That's pretty good."

"Frankly, my dear——"

"I know," George said, holding up his hands. "I know."

"Well?"

"Rainy Day. René Day." George's eyebrows went up as he shook his head. "The gag immigration name. I hadn't thought of that. It's really very clever of you, Matt."

"What?"

"The rain cloud. Coming up with René Day from that."

Matt drummed his fingers on his chair's armrest for

a moment and then pointed at George. "So, if you didn't figure the name like that, how did you guess it?"

"Oh, I didn't guess it." He looked at Matt. "What made me think of her name was that I saw it on a property theft report she filled out two years ago. There was a copy attached to a television set down in the property room. I saw it a few weeks ago when I was checking out the evidence for the Parker trial."

"You saw it on a TV set down in the property room?"

"That's right."

"You mean you spent your time down there examining theft reports on the off chance that the perp might have filled one out some time in the past?"

"No. That would've been foolish. I just happened to glance at it when I was picking up the Parker evidence. The handwriting on the report matched the samples found on the candy wrappers. That's all."

"That's all," Matt repeated dully.

"Yes. Her name and address were on the report."

After a beat, Sikes said, "You aren't kidding, are you, George?"

"Why would I be making jokes? Of course I'm not kidding. I just don't want to waste our valuable time hitting candy stores."

"Then I don't get it. Why didn't you say something before now?"

George shrugged and held out his hands. "The connection didn't occur to me until now, although how I could have missed something so obvious is quite beyond me. It was right there all the time. I suppose I've had too many things on my mind."

"Okay, George, back to Rainy Day. How do you know she's a Newcomer?"

"You mean besides the neighborhood in which she lives and the stupid joke name she was given?" George frowned, slightly surprised at the anger in his words. He took a deep breath, let it out, picked up a copy of the Thunderbolt's writing and handed it to Matt. "Look at the way those t's are crossed. See that little chevron at the ends of the crosses?"

"Yeah. What about them?"

"Only someone used to sine writing does that. I do it myself."

As he stared at the writing sample, Matt made a grabbing motion with his free hand. "Gimmie."

George held out another of the Thunderbolt's notes, and Matt shook his head.

"No. Something of yours."

George handed Matt his pocket notebook. Sikes flipped through a few pages, then dropped it on his desk and began going through his desk drawers. "Where is that damned card? The one Albert gave me on Celine's birthday." Matt paused as he located the object of his search and pulled out the blue and silver greeting card he had received three months before. He grunted, pulled out a magnifying glass from his drawer and held it over the card. "I'll be damned. There it is, as big as bald and twice as ugly."

George sat forward and clasped his hands together. "So, do we go do the autopsy?"

"Just a second." Sikes stared at the handwriting sample for a long time. He shook his head, picked up his handset, punched in a number, and tucked the handset between his neck and shoulder. "We'll see, George. If it turns out you're not on some weird kind of drug, and if the property room still has that TV, and if the handwriting checks out, and if Rainy Day is still at 126 South Chicago—" He looked down and said into the phone, "Yeah, I'll hold. No music pl—" He looked into his handset, his upper lip curled in disgust. "I thought disco was dead."

"Matt, do we do the autopsy?" George insisted.

Matt held up a hand, palm facing his partner. "As I was saying, George, if the TV is in the property room, and the handwriting comparison is enough for a warrant—"

A light began flashing on George's telephone. "One moment, Matt." He picked up the handset. "Officer Francisco. Oh, hello, Susan. There wasn't any need to check up on me. Matt's making arrangements for me to see a doctor right now." George smirked at Sikes, then his face became quite serious. "Are you certain?" He shook his head. "No, I don't understand. He hasn't said anything to me." He nodded, his brow wrinkled in concern. "Yes, I agree. We should talk to him tonight."

Sikes turned back to his phone. "Yeah, Kim? This is Matt Sikes. How are things?" He nodded. "Taxes, pollution, crime, rap, it's the same all over. I want a favor—"

George hung up his phone, and Matt blushed as he shook his head. "No. Not that kind of favor. Yes, I'm still seeing Cathy. Tell me, can you get me and my partner standing room when your bunch burgers the warden? It's real important." He held out his hand. "Your boss's got a big puzzle down there. My *goomba* thinks he might have a couple of pieces. How 'bout it? Can you be bought?" He nodded again, picked up a pencil, and began jotting down a list. "Ribs at Petro's, fries, plenty of ketchup, chocolate shake, two cherry rolls, and two large decaf diet Jolts. We'll be there for showtime, and thanks." He hung up and raised his eyebrows at Francisco. "We're in, and you pay for Kim's cholesterol attack."

"Good. What time?"

"We have time enough to bop on down to the property room, the judge's chambers, and South Chicago with special weapons to nab, and book the Thunderbolt before we go to the canoe factory. We need to get our own stuff done first, George. Okay?"

"When is the autopsy?"

"Late. The curtain goes up at around three this afternoon." Matt noticed the concerned look on his partner's face. "What is it? What'd Susan have to say?"

George frowned at his partner. "It's one of Buck's instructors at college. He called Susan at her office. Buck hasn't been to any of his classes in three weeks."

Sikes sat up and leaned forward in his chair. "Do you think it's connected to this *vikah ta* thing?"

"No. Dak and Fangan only escaped from prison last night." George frowned. "You're right about one thing, though. Buck's vulnerable. Emily. Vessna. Susan. My entire family is vulnerable. Susan and the children should be placed under protection until Dak and Fangan have been apprehended. Perhaps Susan could even take the children on a trip for a few days."

"After the chief's review committee made noodles out of Grazer's budget proposal last week, the captain isn't going to spring for any round-the-clock just on a I'm-gonna-git-you-sucka flag." Sikes stood and looked over at his partner. Francisco was looking back, his brow furrowed with confusion.

"George? What's the matter?"

"You're green, Matt. Bright green."

Sikes looked at his hands and found them their usual shade. "No, I'm not."

"I know," George answered as he reached for his phone, still frowning. "I better call Susan and have her gather up Emily and Vessna while I try to track down Buck. When I get the time, perhaps a doctor. I'm not altogether certain I'm completely fit."

CHAPTER 6

THE SHIP, THE *vikah ta,* and the pain ministers were a dimly remembered dream from a remote past. As Susan pulled her old Mazda wagon out of the ad agency's lot to pick up her two daughters, she remembered the *Ahvin Yin,* Those Who Resist, and the name no one dared even whisper: Maanka Dak.

As the great ship had pulled away from Itri Vi, they brought with them two things. The Overseers took with them the technology for the implanted neural controllers. The slaves kept the *Ahvin Yin.*

There was little that could be done about the oppression of the Overseers. As the Overseers were trained to oppress, the slaves were bred to serve in a state of complete passivity. There were flawed Overseers; men and women of compassion; men and women of obsessive cruelty. There were, as well, flawed slaves. Passivity was not their nature. It was, instead, a tactic; a mechanism of survival. They were the ones the Overseers attempted to control and punish with the neural implants. They were the ones who, in turn, retaliated through the *vikah ta.*

As Susan swung north and increased the vehicle's speed, she wondered if she had the capacity to resist. She could fight, of course. There were many kinds of work for which the slaves had been designed, including war. She did not know, however, if she had the capacity to fight authority. She knew George had it. He had the freedom flaw. He had been one of those in the *Ahvin Yin.*

And Maanka Dak. In the self-imposed darkness that was Susan's memory of the time before the crash, Maanka Dak stood out like some terrifying totem of retribution. Maanka had killed for the *Ahvin Yin,* and Overseers were the targets; Overseers marked for the *vikah ta.*

When judgement was passed and the *vikah ta* ordered against an Overseer, it was almost as though the order alone could kill. Other Overseers would avoid being seen with the target, or having anything to do with the target or the target's family or friends. The *vikah ta* killed not only the target, but any kind memory of the target. She had never met Maanka Dak, yet she remembered being more frightened of Maanka than she was of the Overseers.

She had seen some of the results of his work after he had killed an Overseer, his friends, associates, and family. In a span of one *iras,* a little more than an Earth week, Maanka had executed twenty-two men, women, and children. Her husband had quit the *Ahvin Yin* after that, but he had never mentioned it until the phone call that morning to gather up Vessna and Emily. Now he might be a target himself. It was an old threat and possibly nothing would come of it, but just to be on the safe side, grab the children, run for the hills, and pray that Buck turned up somewhere before the *vikah ta* found him.

The tan stucco walls and red tile roofs of Emily's school loomed ahead, and Susan squealed to a stop in a no parking zone in front of the administration office. A guard came walking toward her but held up his hand and waved when he saw who it was.

"I won't be long," Susan called as she got out of the car and slammed the door. "I have to get Emily. It's an emergency."

"No problem," the guard said. "Hope it's nothing serious."

"Me too," Susan muttered as she waved again, then ran into the main building past several students and a startled custodian. In the neon glare of the school office, she smacked her open palm on the counter and demanded, "Emily Francisco! Where is she?"

A secretary jumped up from her grade posting and looked over the tops of her reading glasses. "Mrs. Francisco?"

"Yes. My daughter Emily. I need her right now. It's very important."

"I can't leave the office right now, but in a few minutes I can send someone for her." The secretary reached to a bank of form files and pulled out a lime-green sheet of paper. "While you're waiting, if you could please fill out this parental absence request—"

"I need Emily *now!*" Susan demanded, her voice deep and menacing. "Where is she?"

"Mrs. Francisco, I really need you to fill out—"

Susan took the form, balled it up, and threw it

across the office. "Later! Once I've seen Emily, I'll be happy to fill out a hundred forms. But first I have to see my daughter! It's an emergency! Where is she?"

"Please, Mrs. Francisco. Your voice—"

Susan yelled out, "Where is she? Where's my daughter?"

The door to the principal's office opened, revealing a balding man heavy with scowl. "What in the hell is going on out here, Cloris?"

"Mr. Marquez, I have to see my daughter! It's an emergency! Where's my daughter? I have to see her!"

"Mrs. Francisco? Emily?" The principal faced his secretary. "What's the matter, Cloris? What's happened to Emily?"

The secretary's face flushed scarlet. "Nothing! Nothing has happened to Emily. It's just that Mrs. Francisco needs to fill out the proper request form—"

"For Christ's sake, Cloris!" Mr. Marquez exploded. "Where's her daughter? Don't you know?"

"Well, of course I know where she is, Mr. Marquez. She's in Bill Rafferty's room this period. It's just—"

The principal held up his hand and faced Susan. "I'm really very sorry, Mrs. Francisco. I'll take care of this. Your daughter's in room 312. Use the faculty elevator at the—"

Susan bolted from the office, ignored the elevator, and climbed the stairs to the third floor. In a moment she was at room 312. She looked in the open doorway, saw a young man at the chalkboard, his arm raised, his hand holding a white stub of chalk. "Mr. Rafferty?

He lowered his arm, turned his head, and looked over the tops of his glasses at Susan. "And you?"

"I'm sorry. I'm Emily Francisco's mother." She gave the large classroom a quick scan, searching desperately for Emily's gaudy hairpiece. "I don't see her." She looked at the teacher, her eyes frightened. "I don't see her. Where is she?"

"Emily didn't make it to my class today. I had to report her absent."

"That's impossible."

Bill Rafferty shrugged, held out his hands, and arched his eyebrows. "Nevertheless. Is it something important?"

"It's an emergency." She faced the class and looked over the faces of the students. "Her last class. Was she there?" she asked everyone. "Did any of you see her last period?" Three or four students nodded and held up their hands.

Another student, a pretty human girl, held up her hand and said, "I bet I know where Emily is." There was a distinctly catty tone to the girl's voice.

Mr. Rafferty held his head back and looked at the girl through his glasses. "Go ahead, Barbara. Where do you think she is?"

"She's in the back study room of the library—"

"I know where it is," Susan said, and ran from the room. She slid to a stop in front of the fire stairs, pushed open the door, and clattered down to the first floor.

There were Kyra and Pida, the children of Torumeh, the Overseer who administered pain. Pain for education; pain for punishment; pain for the amusement of Torumeh. Torumeh deserved to die. All of the slaves cheered silently in their hearts when the Ahvin Yin *executed Torumeh. But Kyra and Pida, they were such beautiful children, too young to have had their compassion killed. She had seen them after they had been killed by a tracked mechanical loader. The vehicle, still carrying a heavy load of scrap metal, had been left parked on top of the children's crushed bodies. The* vikah ta *spared no one with a kind memory of the target of the revenge.*

Susan slid to a stop through the library's open door and looked around for the librarian. No one, however, was in the room or at the stacks she could see. She walked a few paces past the door and heard a thin, reedy voice coming from another door at the back. "This will see the end of you, girl, and the end of that monster you love." She heard her daughter scream.

"Emily!" Susan shrieked as she ran toward the back into the darkened study room. Emily was on the floor, her eyes closed, her face and chest smeared with red. The handle of some wooden weapon protruded from her chest. "Emily!"

A dark-clad figure stepped out of the shadows, and Susan instinctively picked up a *Webster's Unabridged Dictionary* and smashed it into the person's face. She lifted the heavy book again and was stopped by a shriek.

"Mother! Mother! Stop it! You'll hurt him!"

Susan turned and saw Emily standing, the weapon still protruding from her chest. Mr. Rafferty, the librarian, and several students came to a halt at the door. The figure on the floor struggled to its feet, its hand held to its bleeding nose. "Rick?" Emily said, taking his arm. "Are you all right?"

"Yeah, right," he said as he pulled his arm free.

"Okay," Mr. Rafferty said to the students at the door, "the show's over. If there isn't a place you should be right now, I can find a spot for you in study hall."

As the crowd thinned, Susan could hear the girl named Barbara giggle and say, "I said she was down here with Ricky."

Susan looked at the boy with the bloody nose. "Ricky Martin?"

"Yeah," the boy said. "You must be the mother of Dracula's daughter." The librarian went over and held a wad of tissues beneath Ricky's nose.

Susan could feel her eyes change color from embarrassment. "The school play. Vampires. You're in it."

"Yeah."

"He plays Dr. Van Helsing, the vampire killer," the librarian said.

"And Emily cut her class to help you with your lines."

The boy removed the tissues, turned to a fresh piece, and held it to his nose. It was clear that he was going to have two black eyes as a result of his introduction to Emily's mother. Susan looked at Emily. Her eyes were filled with tears. "Oh, Mom. How could you?"

"I'm sorry, darling. It's just that . . . You see, there's an emergency that . . . Darling, I'm really terribly sorry." She turned to the boy. "Ricky, I'm very sorry about this. I really am. There's an emergency, and I thought—"

"It's all right, Mrs. Francisco," the boy said as he wiped his nose with a gentle touch. It looked as though his nose was broken, as well.

"I really am so sorry." She reached out her hand to touch the boy, and he took a step back to keep away from her.

"It's okay, lady. I understand. I really do. I got a buddy. His mom's got a drug problem too." He waved a fistful of bloody tissues and said, "It's been a lump talking to you, but I got to go see the nurse now. Bye." He turned to Emily. "Be sure to call me in a couple of hundred years." With the librarian leading him, the boy gave Susan a wide berth and left the study room.

"Mother," Emily said through her tears, "how could you? He'll never want to speak to me again. Why did you do it?"

"Well, dear," her mother answered, taking a deep breath and rubbing her eyes, "it seemed like a good idea at the time."

CHAPTER 7

BUCK STARED INTO the tiny pool, attempting to sort his thoughts, as a gentle breeze moved a dead leaf across the water. Some thoughts, however, would not sort. He sighed and allowed his gaze to drift upward. The garden of the *Rama Vo* was surrounded by high brick walls, which were cracked, pitted, and scorched. Inside the walls were flagstone paths lined by ornamental trees, flowers, and mineral specimens. At the door of the building, a *Hila* emerged and regarded the day. Although not frail, the Elder was incredibly ancient, at least to Buck's eyes. Buck picked up his rucksack and put his right arm through the shoulder strap as he turned to face Aman Iri.

Buck Francisco had never seen many elders. Few of them existed. Before the crash, the Overseers used to dispose of most of those who passed physical prime. The Tenctonese were genetically designed to live for

140 Earth years, but maintaining hundred-year-old slaves was simply not efficient, save for the few dedicated to mental tasks. Before the crash, the "old ones" were simply taken away somewhere and never seen again. Those who would dare to mention the subject presumed that the remains of the old ones were recycled. Before the crash, it was not a crime by the law of the ship. Buck glanced at the *Hila* as he approached.

Aman Iri wore nothing that indicated his authority, wisdom, or the esteem in which he was held by others. In fact he wore human slouch: jeans, joggers, T-shirt, and a ragged, straw cowboy hat. Buck looked down at his own "mad monk robes" and felt foolish. The spiritual goals he sought seemed to demand some outward sign of his aspirations. It was why soldiers, priests, and lawyers wore their particular uniforms and medals.

Yet the *Hila,* one who had attained the serenity and wisdom of an Elder, felt no need to make any outward sign of anything. He was who he was. No perception, judgment, or opinion of another had any bearing on Aman Iri's existence, meaning, worth, or future. Hence, what was the point of medals, uniforms, printed buttons, bumper stickers, and other such attempts to manipulate the feelings or opinions of others? Buck's mind knew the lesson by heart. His hearts, however, still felt that, in part, what others thought of him made him what he was. He did not feel very successful as a student of the *Rama Vo.*

"Good morning, *Hila.*"

The Elder regarded Buck's expression with kind amusement. "A generous sentiment, Buck, although I see that such a morning has yet to find you."

"I guess I still have a problem or two, *Hila.*"

"Have you told your parents yet about your attendance at the *Rama Vo?*"

"No. I mentioned something about it to my father a few months ago, but he wasn't really listening. It's real important to him that I complete a human university."

"When are you going to tell him?"

"Believe me, Aman Iri, today wasn't the right time. Mom and Dad were late, and Dad's gone super weird, blowing up, picking bizarre colors to wear, forgetting to set his alarm. Mom says his *nemeh* glands are puffed. She thinks he's got *nia.*"

"Oh? How old is your father?"

"In Earth years, almost sixty."

"He's closing his third *fav,* then. It's quite early, but conditions on Earth are considerably different."

"Early for what, *Hila?* Do you know what's happening to my dad?"

"I could be wrong, but it appears to be life. Feel joy for him, not concern. If he does not have a *Hila* of his own, it would be good if your father could talk to someone here at the *vo.*" He raised his eyebrows. "When the time is right, of course. Now, how did your meditation on acceptance go?"

"Nowhere. Those things I talked about yesterday, they still bother me. I know they shouldn't, but they do. It's not just what's happening to Newcomers. The humans have nothing left to teach me. I've been to their schools, listened to their professors and political leaders. I've seen kids in school beat up because they're black or yellow. Cruelty by some done to others simply because they're white or red. And now that the slags are here, everybody has someone they can hate. A black kid at the student union called me 'space nigger.' He didn't get physical, but he acted as

67

though he wanted to. I never saw him before, and he hated me enough to try and hurt me. How can I put all this aside? How can I forget the names, the looks, the beatings? Especially the names. Even from before, how can I forget the things the Overseers did to us? The things they're still trying to do to us? And they're running around free. What about the Thunderbolt Poet carving up Newcomers just to write a little poem? What about the slaughter just this morning over on Soto? Where is the fairness in all this? Where is the justice? Where is the sanity? How am I supposed to put all this aside and meditate? I just don't get it."

The Elder's eyes studied Buck for a moment. When Aman Iri had come to his conclusion, he turned, went to his flower bed, squatted, and picked two plants from it. Still squatting there, the *Hila* held the plants up for Buck to see. "What are these?"

"Plants. A flower and a weed."

"Which one is the flower? Which one is the weed?"

Buck suspected a trick answer would be necessary to answer a trick question. The first lesson Buck had learned at the *Rama Vo,* however, had been not to compete with the *Hila* by attempting to foil his riddles. It had been to learn about himself by answering the questions as honestly as he could.

"The plant with the blue blossom is the flower, *Hila.* The dark green one with the tiny leaves is the weed."

"Why?"

Buck frowned, shrugged, and held out his hands. "They just are. That's how they're classified."

Aman Iri shook the plants at the youth. "Take them. Did you bring the things I asked you to bring?"

"Yes."

Buck took the two plants. The Elder stood and faced the youth. "Show me.

Buck reached into the zip pocket of his rucksack and pulled out four small printed cards. Holding them out to the *Hila,* he said, "At the paint store they had hundreds of these chips in all different shades."

"These are the ones you need." Aman Iri took the four paint chips and placed them in a row on his open palm. He picked up one of the chips and held it out to Buck. "This is yellow?"

"Sure. Yes."

Aman nodded, shook the chip and said, "Here. Take it."

Buck took the yellow paint-color sample and frowned as the *Hila* held up the black chip. "This is black?"

"Yes."

"Take it." The exercise was repeated for the red chip and the white chip. When Buck had all four chips, Aman explained, "I wanted to make certain we were in agreement." The *Hila* thought for a moment and smiled. Turning from Buck, he went down one of the paths, bent over, and returned holding something in his right fist. He stopped in front of Buck and handed him a small green stone with a glassy luster. "Take this, as well."

Buck took the small stone and watched as the *Hila* folded his arms and stared into the depths of the tiny pool. "Buck, today your study is on the city streets. The subjects are words, slavery, freedom, and the beings who live on this planet. You are on a quest for truths. We live by truths and we die trying to live by fictions. Are you ready?"

"Sure."

"You have seen our modest collections of minerals, leaves, insects, and so on, as well as similar collections in museums, at the high school you attended, and at the university?"

"Yes."

"What is the primary purpose of such collections?"

Buck thought for a moment and then said, "They're teaching instruments."

"And the system of instruction?"

"They provide examples—objective referents—for the terms we use. That's so you can show someone what quartz is like, rather than just use other words to describe it."

"Yes, in part." The *Hila* nodded and held a hand out toward the building that housed the *vo.* "One of our collections here, Buck, is woefully incomplete. What I want you to do is to bring us the specimens to complete one of our most important collections."

"Okay. Sure."

Aman Iri tapped the paint-color samples with a bony finger. "Now that we are in agreement as to terms, I want you to go forth and find me one of each." He pointed at the black chip. "A black man." His finger moved to the next chip. "A red man." His finger moved to the next chip. "A white man." His finger moved to the remaining chip. "And a yellow man. To induce them to come here, you have my permission to offer up to ten thousand dollars apiece. The *Rama Vo* will be pleased to pay much more than that to see genuine specimens of white, red, yellow, or black men in its collection." Buck slumped in disgust. "Is there a problem?" the *Hila* asked.

"I don't intend any disrespect, but isn't this a little childish?"

"Childish?"

"Well, of course I know that whites aren't really white and blacks aren't really black."

"As you know hot isn't really hot and light isn't really light."

"It's not the same thing, *Hila.*"

"Go out and search for them, Buck: a white man, a black man, a red man, and a yellow man. I want you to keep looking for them as though your life and freedom depended on finding them, for indeed they do."

"I already know I won't find them."

"You have already found them, Buck. That is why you referred to the boy who called you 'space nigger' as black. That is why you call men and women by color names that have no relation to their respective colors. You have already found them. Your task is to keep looking for them until they are lost forever."

The Elder went to the solid gate set into the garden wall and pulled it open, revealing the pedestrians on the street outside the *vo*. "Out there, child. Do you see any blacks? Do you see any whites?"

The youth looked down at the paint chips and back at the people on the street. A black man who was not really black was winding down the awning in front of his small grocery store. A white man who was not really white was talking to him. *"Hila,* black is just a way of saying Afro-American."

"And Afro-American is just a way of saying what, Buck?"

"It means those Americans whose ancestors came from Africa."

A tiny smile tugged at the corners of Aman Iri's mouth. "With the exception of Libyan Americans and Egyptian Americans?" The *Hila* shook his head. "According to the science of this planet, Buck, every human you see out there has his or her biological

71

origins in Africa, including those called 'white,' 'yellow,' and 'red.' All human Americans, then, are Afro-Americans. All Afro-Americans are black, hence black is white. Is that what you mean?"

Buck glowered at the Elder. "I'm not sure what I mean."

"Truth is at last stalking you, my child." Aman nodded toward the street. "Now, do you see any blacks out there? Do you see any whites?"

"You've got to call them *something.*"

"Them," snorted the Hila. "That is the collection you must build. Find me the objective referents for 'them.' There is no *them,* unless you too are part of *them,* in which case the term means nothing." He lifted his arm and pointed toward the street. "Buck, do you see a black man out there?"

"I guess I don't."

"When your hearts agree with your head, you may come back to the *vo* and explain to me about the flower and the weed."

Buck looked at the rapidly wilting plants in his hand. "Explain what?"

The Elder smiled. "When you have the answer to that question, Buck, you may return."

Buck tossed the green mineral specimen into the air and caught it again. "What about this rock?"

"That's some waste from a copper smelting process. Pretty, isn't it? It's called slag. You don't have to find a slag, you see. You already have some. However, if you should find someone who resembles that specimen, you be certain to bring him along for your collection." He placed his hand on Buck's shoulder.

"Remember, child, it's not the words used by others that enslave your mind. Your chains are forged by the words you choose, and the powers you assign them."

CHAPTER 8

SING FANGAN PUSHED the legs of the body into the motel room's closet, stood, and placed his hand on the sliding door's handle as he regarded the corpse. The body in the closet was a Newcomer carrying the immigration joke name of Brick Wahl. When Maanka Dak had heard the name, he'd said, "For that alone he forfeited his right to exist. He had no respect for himself or for what he was."

But, Sing thought, the late Mr. Wahl was a sales representative for a worldwide industrial construction firm. Perhaps the name Brick Wahl broke the ice with new customers. Perhaps it amused him. Perhaps the late Mr. Wahl didn't take himself as seriously as did Maanka Dak. Sing Fangan looked down at the pale Tenctonese blood staining the fingers of his right hand.

Unconsciously he wiped his hand on his trousers. It really didn't matter about the name. Wahl hadn't died because of his failure to change his name to something acceptable to Tenctonese purists. By the time Maanka had heard the fellow's name, Brick Wahl was already a corpse. The only reason he was a corpse was because he was one of the few patrons at the Holiday Inn with a modem-equipped, laptop mega-computer compatible with Maanka's system.

Sing shook his head at the lack of choices marking the turns of his possible futures. Years ago their former brother of the *Ahvin Yin,* the Newcomer police officer Francisco, had arrested them and had killed Sita Dak, Maanka's brother. Francisco deserved to die. Perhaps those who loved the traitor condemned themselves by their own feelings. That was the oath of the *vikah ta.* They deserved to die, as well. The human officer, Duncan, also had to suffer the *vikah ta.* Warden Rand was part of the authority the *Ahvin Yin* had sworn themselves to destroy. He deserved to die. The late Mr. Wahl, however, just happened to be in the wrong place at the wrong time with the right piece of equipment.

The *Ahvin Yin* had been formed to fight against death. Now death seemed to be nothing more than another tool to serve the obsession of Maanka Dak. The conflicts within Sing Fangan had become a sharp, steady pain behind his eyes.

"Our brother's star has risen, Sing."

Sing Fangan took one last look at the body, pulled the door shut, and went to the table where Maanka was sitting before Brick Wahl's computer. "I didn't credit Nicto with that much respect for himself," Maanka said as he tapped his finger against the screen. "He changed his name from Sam Francisco to George. That's why it took so long for me to track him down. He's a sergeant now. A homicide detective. I've managed to locate his wife and children. He has a new partner, another daughter, and has become a property owner."

"When do we finish the *vikah ta?*" Sing asked.

"Are you in a hurry?"

"If we strike quickly, Maanka, we can accomplish our goal and make good our escape. The longer we stay here, the more we increase our chances of being captured."

"You heard what I said, Sing. Francisco has a new partner. He also has a new child. That means a *binnaum*. In addition, there are the three close associates Francisco would have invited for the presentation of the *binnaum*. His children's friends at school and in his neighborhood—I will have them all, Sing. I will leave no one alive who possesses a memory of this traitor, or of this traitor's family, friends, or associates. The game is just beginning." Maanka paused long enough to look up at Sing. "This is not for you, is it?"

"I am with you," Sing protested. "Let us kill Francisco. He's a traitor and deserves death. His family too." He hesitated for a moment, then said, "Maanka, we are no longer surrounded by the *Ahvin Yin*. It is just the two of us. Kill him and his family, this we can do. But we cannot eliminate everyone who has a memory of him. Before we could accomplish all of those killings, we would be captured again."

"As I said, Sing, this game is not for you, is it?"

Before Sing could answer, he saw Maanka's hands move in a blur as they threw the two heart picks. No one could have moved quickly enough to avoid them. Sing only had enough time to remember Maanka fashioning the ancient Tenctonese throwing spikes from two screwdrivers. As Sing's hearts stopped,

Maanka stood and pushed him to make certain that Sing would not fall into the computer.

After dumping Sing's body in the closet on top of Brick Wahl, Maanka Dak pulled the door shut. Giving the vestibule a quick check, he opened the door to the hallway, put out the Do Not Disturb sign, and allowed the door to lock behind him. "I will have him, Sing. Nicto swore to the *Ahvin Yin*. He betrayed us, and slew our brother. I will have him; I will have him and the memory of him. *Ahvin Yin. Rekwi ot osia*. Death to authority!"

"Death! Death! Death to authority! Death to the Niyez!"

They stood in the shadows of the thorn-covered likaeshia trees, the triple moons of Itri Vi high and red in the night sky. The initiates stood in a row facing the hooded cell leaders. The faces of the leaders were covered.

The Niyez, the masters of Itri Vi and holders of a slave contract, had made the meetings necessary. They regarded the genetically designed slaves as purchased rather than leased from their creators. And whether as house servants or deep level miners, the Niyez didn't know how to take care of their belongings. Even a few of the Overseers protested the treatment of the slaves. For their pains, the Overseers were either put to death or were themselves implanted by the pain ministers. After all, to the Niyez, they too were property.

There was only one defense. There had to be rebels among the slaves: secret fighters, shadow assassins, who could provide the retribution that would get the attention of the Niyez and modify their behavior. Thus the *Ahvin Yin*.

"Nicto," said the leader of his cell, "how came you before this assembly?"

"The Niyez have taken, tortured, and killed my friends, my father and mother, even my *binnaum.*"

"The *Ahvin Yin* cannot bring them back, Nicto."

"Perhaps the *Ahvin Yin* can discourage the Niyez from killing my wife and children."

The hooded cell leader took three steps and stood before Nicto as he handed him a single-bladed knife. "They say we are bred to be passive; that we have the will neither to disobey nor to resist. When a leader marks a Niyez for the *Ahvin Yin,* will you be able to kill? Can you bless your brothers with authority's death?"

There was muffled screaming, the sounds of a struggle. The leader stood aside and watched as a bound Niyez male was dragged before Nicto and tossed at his feet. The Niyez, with dark black hair and long yellow teeth, was clad in the iridescent robes of a pain minister of the plantationers. This one was Mro Sheviat, the one who had personally tortured and killed Nicto's parents.

Nicto bent over Mro, pulled back the Niyez's head by his hair, and pulled the edge of the finely honed blade across the Niyezian's throat. As he watched the life of the creature pump out onto the red soil, Nicto recited the prayer of revenge, the plea of the *vikah ta,* "Him and the memory of him."

"And how shall you die, Nicto?"

"In this manner, should I betray the *Ahvin Yin.*"

The cell leaders removed their hoods and Nicto was welcomed by his brothers of the Ahvin Yin: *Maanka Dak, Sita Dak, and Sing Fangan.*

In time the controllers voided the agreement with the Niyez and removed all of the contract slaves from Itri

Vi. Despite the horror of Itri Vi, the Overseers brought back with them the Niyezian neural transmitter technology. Soon the Tenctonese slave ship had its own pain ministers. The slaves brought back with them new additions to old sorrows, the Ahvin Yin *and the* vikah ta.

CHAPTER 9

HIS NAME WAS Checha Contreras. "You should've seen this neighborhood before the *escoria* moved in."

As Sikes talked on the radio, Francisco stood beside the car listening as the man waved toward the one-story pale yellow frame dwelling that was his home. He wore ragged jeans and a faded red tank top. A web tattoo covering the upper right quadrant of his body marked him as a former member of Los Araños, a long defunct East L.A. youth organization specializing in cocaine, protection, and ritual assassination, until they were run out of town by a Newcomer gang called Nightshade.

Three Newcomer youths sporting hot pink gang jackets emblazoned in turquoise with the name Chrysanthemums swung by, grab-assing and snickering. One of them threw a wine bottle that shattered on the pavement next to the car.

"Escoria!" the old man shouted. *"Mira!* Look at that," the old man continued. "Punks!"

"What do you care?" Sikes asked as he emerged from the car. "That's a police car they threw it at."

"Your car ain't marked, man."

Sikes shook his head. "What's your point?"

"It *might've* been *my* car, the lousy slag punks. Pink nylon. Whatever happened to black leather? They can make the fuzz, cut up old ladies, and bust windows, but what kind of name is Chrysanthemums?"

Sikes pointed at the car and said to George, "The captain sent Diaz over to help Susan gather up the kids."

"Thanks, Matt. That makes me feel better."

"Tiger lilies," growled the old man. "Marigolds, mums, baby's breath, f'crissakes—*pah!* This neighborhood's gone to terminal shit!"

"Perhaps you could tell us if the lady across the street is in?" George said.

"Look down there," the old man commanded Sikes, ignoring Francisco's question. "Look. See that thing the rubberheads call a church?"

Sikes turned his head to look in the indicated direction. His view, however, was blocked by a parking sign with the regulatory sentiment punctuated with seven rusty bullet holes. "Church?"

"Just what I say! That's no church! First Celinist Temple of Jesus? What kinda stupid name izzat? In there used to be a real church. It was the First Hebrew Christian Synagogue. What's it now? Slags for Jesus. What's the goddamn space freaks know about Jesus?" He glared at George, spat on the ground, and looked at Sikes. "I know it ain't your fault. Goddamn fuckin' slags're everywhere."

Matt Sikes apologized to George with a quick

glance and nodded toward the pink house across the street. "What about the woman across the street?"

"That's no woman, man. Big-headed, bald, spot-covered, alien, slag bitch. Don't call her no woman to me, man." He pointed across the street. "She and her whole family nested in there maybe four, five years ago. The slagman, he hauled a sack for the post office. Him and the bitch had two kids. Smart little slag bastards, like all of 'em. Sunny was the little girl. Stupid slag names they hung on 'em. The boy's name was Bat and the old man was Russ."

"I don't get it," Sikes said.

"Russ Day? Rusty? Get it?"

Sikes nodded. "Yeah. Okay."

"Her name's Rainy Day. The slag bitch."

"Yeah. So what happened to the family? The robbery report shows her living alone."

"By the time they ripped her off, man, she was alone."

George faced the pink house and asked, "What happened?"

Contreras curled his lips into a sneer that vanished as Matt stabbed the old man in the chest with his fingers. "You heard my partner, dog drool. What happened to her family?"

The old man backed off, rubbing his chest, a hurt expression on his face. "Easy man." He nodded toward the pink house. "You remember that anglo that slipped a cog three years ago over at the main post office? Shot up the place 'cause the slags was gettin' all the jobs? Myers. His name was Myers."

Matt frowned as he nodded. "Yeah. Albert Myers. He killed nine men and women—"

"They was all rubberheads, man," Contreras interrupted. He pointed at the pink house. "Old Rusty was one of the first. A week after that, the girl, Sunny, was hit by an anglo gang, the Hawks. It was a drive-by slag shoot like the kids do. They cut her spine in two. I heard it took her over a month to die. After that the boy, Bat, got mixed up in a slag gang, the Choya. You boys took care of him."

"What do you mean?" George whispered.

"He got blown away one night by a cop who mistook him for some other slag wanted for sticking up a mom and pop." The old man shrugged and held out his hands. "So, when the Hawks ripped off the slag bitch two years ago, she was alone. I heard the anglos raped her too. Slags're strong, and they had to thump her first a few times with a crowbar." He snickered and shook his head. "Rainy Day."

George grabbed two handfuls of Checha's tank top, along with some chest hair and skin, and hoisted him off the ground. "You have a funny name too, sir," George said. "Checha Contreras. Your name means 'hairy child with an attitude.' An immigration official with a sick sense of humor named René Day. What's your excuse, dirtbag?"

"Hey, *man!*" Contreras squeaked at Sikes. "Call off your partner. He's got me by the nipples!"

Matt's eyebrows went up, then he looked sheepish and put his hands in his pockets. "Hey, man, you said the S word. In fact, you said it a whole bunch of times. As much as I hate to see my partner wreck his career by yanking off your nipples, I can't think of any way to stop him. Maybe if you apologized?

"You kidding, man?" George squeezed, and Checha Contreras screamed, "Okayokayokayokay*okay!* I'm sorry, I'm sorry, I'm s-o-r-r-y!"

"Is Mrs. Day in her home?" George asked.

"Yes! No! I mean, I think so, man! I think so! I don't know! I ain't seen her in days. Let go!"

George lowered the man to the street and frowned as he opened his hands. Contreras whined like an injured puppy, backed away and stumbled off, holding his abused nipples. "George, are you all right?" Matt asked. "If internal affairs got a peek at that performance, you'd be looking for one of those jobs toting sacks at the post office."

Francisco turned and leveled his gaze at the pink house. "Our backup's overdue."

As if in a daze, George began walking across the street toward the pink house. Sikes reached into the car and grabbed the mike. "Hold on, George. You can't go in there alone. Let me check on the backup."

Matt's voice seemed very far away. Reality had an extra bend in it. George placed one foot in front of the other as though he were an automation powered by a singular, most desperate pain.

It was all so clear: the rain cloud with the thunderbolt, the cryptic messages on her notes, the victims. All names have meanings, even if the meanings are forgotten. The messages from René Day contained the etymologies of the victims' Tenctonese names, some from ancient languages no longer spoken, some from even older tongues no longer recorded or remembered, save through the names.

Reality had done a job on René Day. As a result, something precious within her had shattered. The pieces assembled themselves at random, harshly, and had bonded together, making her into a new creature that had declared war on a word.

Everything she had suffered could be traced to a word, a label—*slag*—and how it poisoned the minds of those who spoke it and heard it. Some of "them" were more "slag" than others: bigger heads, sillier names, more degrading occupations. She killed them, and in so doing, killed their names, denying the word "slag," the laughter and shame upon which it fed.

Morris Katz had died, and the meaning of his real name, Blade of Victory, was left behind to replace it. Advance the Mountain, Death Holds Sorrow Naught, Reach the Sun, Cry the People, Flowers of Blue, Green Stars Weep No More. Apparent fragments of poetry, they were instead the misunderstood hopes and dreams every parent has for every child in some ideal Never-Never Land. "My child is not a fool, an article of ridicule, the butt of threadbare humor. My child is Blade of Victory, Reach the Sun, Climb this Mountain."

Thus spake the Universal Mother, Parent of All, the Hearts of God. For a brief moment René Day had became all of these: a goddess avenging the honor a people could not grant themselves. And now there was no purpose to the search warrant, no point in calling for backup. As he reached the peeling white front door, George called to his partner, "Matt. Cancel the backup."

As George placed his hand on the doorknob, Matt Sikes bellowed, "No!"

Francisco turned the knob and the door swung in, allowing the familiar smell of decay to fill his nostrils. He stepped in and met nothing he didn't expect. The tiny living room was brightly lit from its many windows. The walls were papered with pages from the Los Angeles area telephone directory. Thousands of the names had been highlighted with a fluorescent green marker. Dozens of the marked names had been circled in pink, the Tenctonese color of death.

Behind George, Sikes somersaulted through the door and came to a stop kneeling, his back facing the wall to the right of the door, his weapon out, his eyes running a quick scan of the room. "Jesus, George, what in the hell do you think you're doing?" After a pause, Matt's nose wrinkled as his eyebrows went up. "What in God's name?"

"Against the back wall, Matt. On the table. It's René Day."

There was a cheap dinner table there, the burned-out shells of pink Tenctonese mourning candles at either end of a pink-draped corpse. George stood over the body and looked down upon the monster he and Matt had pursued for so long. René Day had been dead for more than a week, her throat slit by her own hand. Pinned to the mourning cloth was the last of her no longer cryptic notes. "Garden of Joy," George said. "A beautiful name. Saria Vo. It means Garden of Joy."

Sikes got to his feet, holstered his weapon and frowned at his partner. "The notes are names?"

"Yes. It all became clear for me out there with the help of Hairy Child with an Attitude. The notes she left were nothing more than the real meanings of the victims' Tenctonese names."

"What about the stand-up comic; the human?"

"Cain Fields?" George smiled sadly. "I'm afraid his onetime stage name was silly enough to get him killed. It marked him as a slag. My guess is that in the dark it didn't make any difference to Saria Vo, which is ironic. Remember the note she left there?"

"Yeah. 'Gentle Gray One.'"

"That was his real name: Kevin Lloyd. It means Gentle Gray One." George looked at Matt. "When we first became partners, do you remember you wouldn't allow me to use my immigration name?"

"Yeah."

"Do you remember why?"

"Sure, George. I wasn't about to have you running around the hood introducing yourself as Sam Francisco."

"Why?"

Matt shrugged and looked very uncomfortable. "I don't know. The joke name embarrassed me. I'm a cop, not part of a clown act. You didn't seem like you could be embarrassed for yourself, and I didn't want to be part of a joke. Cops is serious business."

"Serious business," George repeated, a wistful look on his face. "Bill Duncan used to say that." George faced the corpse of René Day as the wistful expression evaporated. "The joke name embarrassed me. That's why I eventually changed it. The name René Day embarrassed Saria Vo, as well."

"How come you knew she'd be dead, George?"

"Dead?"

"Yes! Dead!" Matt exploded. "You come waltzing in here like a damned probationer on Valium: no backup, no cover, no plan, nothing worked out with your partner. You didn't even have your piece out. You knew she'd be dead, right? Tell me you knew she was dead, George."

"I suppose I did. It was obvious."

"Obvious? Obvious? How about making it obvious to me, buddy, partner, friend, light of my life?"

Oblivious to Matt's concerned anger, George looked down upon Saria Vo's calm features. "Five days after Albert Myers killed her husband, her daughter was slain. Thirty-two days after that, her son was gunned down by a police officer. Fifteen days after that, plus a year, she was attacked, raped, and robbed. The deaths of all the victims fit in that cycle of four numbers. Something would set her off—probably a racial incident—and she would kill, following it with another killing five days later, a third at thirty-two days after that, and a fourth after an additional fifteen days. Then she would go dormant until the next incident triggered her. The last victim, Green Stars Weep No More, was the third in the Thunderbolt's last cycle. He died more than twenty days ago. There should've been another death five days ago. The Thunderbolt's almost a week overdue. She made herself the last death of this cycle. As I said: obvious."

Sikes shook his head. "Forty-four victims, and you have all their dates of death memorized? Not only that, you worked out this pattern just in your head so that when the Hairy Child out there shot off his mouth, suddenly you know all and see all within the next five minutes?"

Francisco frowned and rubbed his chin as he stared through the open door to the street. "That was rather clever of me, wasn't it?" He shook his head and looked at his partner as the sirens and tire squeals of the backup units filled the street. The sounds seemed to drive raging pains through George's head. "Not nearly clever enough, perhaps." George looked at Matt. "I should call Susan again. Then we go to the autopsy."

CHAPTER 10

BUCK SAT AT a table in a dark corner of the university student union, his eyes picking out the features, shades, manners, postures, and modes of dress exhibited by the students there. His sharp hearing picked out the word choices, grammars, pronunciations, and emphases. Life is the experiment taking place before our eyes, the *Hila* had said that first day at the *vo*. Buck was suspecting that what he had originally wanted from the *vo*—some sense of cultural and racial identity and pride—was exactly what Aman Iri was determined to extract from him.

"Isn't it true," he had asked the Hila, *"that there is a difference between racial pride and racism?"*

"It is true, Buck." Aman Iri had pushed his raggedy straw cowboy hat back on his head and gathered his words. When he was ready, he said, *"Racism is the result of the destruction caused by a horrible machine. The machine is the concept—the idea—of races*

88

*among the race of men and women. The machine does
its destruction powered by the fuel of racial pride: the
fiction that one may draw personal worth from the
accomplishments of others, even imaginary divisions
among the race of men and women. Everyone who
furnishes his or her mind with the idea of races,
everyone who has so-called 'racial pride,' is a racist,
most of them doing their destructions from the noblest
of motives, foremost of which is the end of racism."*

It gave a whole new meaning to "who's who." Buck
looked to another table, around which several students were standing and talking to four who were
seated. One of the students who was standing was
Randy Cook. "Observe the specimen in life's experiment," Buck muttered to himself.

Specimen Randy dressed "black," walked "smart,"
and spoke jive like he was laying it on with a trowel.
Randy called himself "Afro-American," and most of
the persons in the huge dining room would, if asked,
refer to Randy as either black, Afro-American, or
something more inflammatory. Yet his skin was lighter than many of the "whites" in the room. It was
certainly lighter than Todd Kimball's skin.

Todd also dressed "black," walked "smart," and
spoke fluent jive. After all, it was not only politically
correct, it was cool, two more terms that needed a
meaning check. In addition to being correct and cool,
Todd's skin was rather dark. Yet Todd would probably
refer to himself as white or Caucasian, while most of
those in the student union would use terms of a more
incendiary ilk.

Approaching a table carrying a tray were two engi-
neering students: Ravi Kothari and Tammy Kuro.
Ravi was from India and Tammy was from L.A.
Tammy's ancestors, however, had come from Japan.

Recalling his library notes, Buck suspected that it must be very confusing to have origins in India or Japan. In Los Angeles, Ravi was "white" and Tammy was "Asian" or "Oriental." In South Africa, however, Ravi was "colored" and Tammy was "honorary white." The old "honorary white" status of the Japanese in South Africa was due to the fact that at one time the South African whites needed business relations with the Japanese, and the Japanese weren't about to put up with the restrictions placed upon blacks, or coloreds, in South Africa. Thus they became honorary whites, which gave rise to an even more bizarre concept: economic race.

The more Buck poked at the concept of races among the race of men and women, the sillier the idea became. He looked down at the pile of paint chips on the table before him. He had put in his morning at the library fruitlessly trying to find referents for the racial labels used by humans and Tenctonese alike. There really were black cats and white cats, but there were no black men, no white men. The existence of real black cats and real white cats was not sufficient reason for science to attempt to divide up cats into black and white cat races, yet imaginary black humans and imaginary white humans had been all the reason necessary to come up with black and white human races. What, then, were the real colors?

After leaving the library, Buck had gone to the paint store and had selected one sample each of every color. He sorted through the samples until he found one that came very close to matching Randy Cook's actual color. According to the paint sample, Randy was not black, he was mocha cream. Todd Kimball was not white, he was cocoa. Ravi Kothari was mocha cream, as well, and Tammy Kuro was pale orchid. He sorted among the chips until he came close to his own color, and read the name: peach mimosa. Thus spake Marden Paints, Inc.

It sounded bad, strong, empowering, to make a fist and shout "Black power!" or "White power!" In certain breasts the sounds struck fear; in others, joy; in still others, pride. What would Randy Cook get for a reaction should he raise his fist and shout, "Mocha cream power!" Then Todd would shake his fist and scream back, "Cocoa power!" What would they get?

Puzzled looks? Giggles?

Buck had an almost irresistible urge to stand, raise his fist, and shout "Peach mimosa power!" He tossed the chip on the table and let his gaze wander. Colors filled the room: rose, gardenia, Tahitian blush, pebble, misty dawn, caramel, desert sunset, sugar 'n' spice, coffee lite, rawhide, sand, tutti-frutti. He pulled out his original four chips. He had found many colors, but he had yet to find a black, red, yellow, or white man, woman, or child.

"Buck!"

He turned his head and looked up to see Theo White, his best friend at the university, waving at him. Theo was a White, but he wasn't white. He was black, but he wasn't black either. Buck picked up the appropriate chip and read the names of the shades. Theo was somewhere between devil's food and chocolate mousse.

"Buck, where've you been? Professor Lee's been trying to track you down for days. He wants to put your name in for that language scholarship, but he can't do it unless you sign the application. Gainer's been looking for you too. You have three papers due, man, and can academic dismissal be far behind?" Theo frowned at Buck, glanced at the paint samples, and looked back at his friend. "You haven't heard a thing I've said. Where've you been?" He pulled out a chair facing Buck and dropped into it. "Buck, my man. What is it? We're friends, and friends talk. Talk to me, friend."

Still looking at his paint chips, Buck said, "Theo, I've been asking myself a lot of questions."

"Like what?"

"Like, is there a difference between my friend and my black friend." He looked up at Theo.

Theo White frowned, leaned back in his chair and shrugged. "Is this a trick question?"

"I'm not certain. Aren't all questions trick questions, depending on who asks and who tries to answer?"

"What was the question again? The difference? Is there any difference between my friend and my black friend?"

"That's right."

Theo thought upon the question for a long time. He shrugged, raised his eyebrows and held out his hands. "Okay, I say no. There is no difference."

"If there is no difference," Buck continued, "will my friend still be my friend if I refuse to call him black? And what happens if I refuse to pretend to understand what he's talking about should he call himself black, because I don't?"

Theo's eyebrows went up as he leaned his elbows on the edge of the table. "I can see you haven't been wasting your day." He pointed at the paint chips. "What's all this?"

Buck picked up the original four paint chips. "Theo, for the last three weeks I've been under instruction at a special kind of school called a *Rama Vo*. A *Hila* there, one of the Elders, gave me an assignment." Buck snorted out a laugh. "Actually, he threw me out of the *vo* until I can do two things. First I must look for and find one of each: a black man, a white man, a red man, and a yellow man." He pushed out the four paint samples.

"Man, that is a red red."

"That's a black black too, Theo. I am expected to fail in this assignment, of course. I must attempt it, nonetheless, and in so doing have revealed to me the mystery of the flower and the weed. Once I can report the mystery solved, I may return to the *vo.*"

"Flower and weed? This is why you haven't been to any classes for three weeks?"

Buck nodded slowly. "Yes."

Theo picked up the yellow paint chip. "I don't get it. What're you learning in that place?"

"I don't know. Maybe I'm unlearning. I think I'm learning that I don't think. I simply react to bad programming." He looked at Theo and smiled sadly. "Labels in my head have me and everyone on earth living by and in fictions. What I'm talking about, I guess, is that I don't know what I'm talking about."

"Thanks for clearing that up, Buck."

"Any time."

"You know, I have a cousin who was hit by lightning who talks just like you."

Buck snorted out a laugh, slumped back in his chair and looked again at the faces in the room. "What do you call 'them' if there is no 'them'? And if there is no 'them,' what are 'they'? What are we? What are you? What am I?" He faced Theo and pointed at the yellow chip in his hand. "Have you ever seen a yellow man?"

Theo tossed the chip into the center of the table. "Sure," he answered. "Homer Simpson. You know, Bart Simpson's old man?"

Buck laughed. "Yeah. And for a white man, how about the Pillsbury doughboy?"

Theo held up a hand. "What about Woody Woodpecker for a red man?"

"He's a bird. Besides, he's not red. He's just got red hair."

"Red hair, Buck? On a woodpecker?"

"Okay, red feathers. He's still a bird."

Theo leaned forward, folded his arms, and leaned his elbows on the edge of the table. "Okay, what about Spider-Man?"

"That's only a suit, like the Flash."

Theo shrugged and leaned back in his chair. "Okay, what about a black man?"

"How about Daffy Duck? If you'd go for Woody Woodpecker, Theo, you have to go for Daffy Duck for a black."

"Actually I was thinking of Marvin the Martian from the Bugs Bunny cartoons. He's black and he wants to blow up Earth." After a mutual stare, they both burst out laughing. "So, now that you've got them, you can go back to the *vo.*"

"The trouble is, none of them are real, Theo. They're animated fantasies. They don't exist. Neither do red men, white men, yellow men, and black men, but I already knew that. What's the *Hila* trying to teach me?" He grimaced as he looked down at the paint chips. "I knew they didn't exist, but I treated them as though they did exist. I used the words. Everyone uses the words. Everyone knows that they don't exist, yet treats them as though they do exist. Maybe I still do."

"We're not still talking about Daffy Duck, are we?"

Buck lifted his gaze until he was looking at the faces in the room. "Theo, have you ever seen one of those

optical illusion patterns where the steps seem to be
going up, then they're going down, then up again?"

"Yeah."

Buck held out his hands, indicating the other students in the union. "That's what's happening to my
head right now. One second I see blacks, whites,
Orientals, and so on, and the next all I see are humans
and Tenctonese, and the next all I see are students,
persons. Then I hear someone make a crack and
suddenly the place is filled with blacks and whites
again." Buck looked at Theo. "Are you a black man?"

Theo took a breath, used it to puff out his cheeks,
then let it rush out in a sigh. "Man, I only cut class to
come in here for a cup of coffee and to cram for my
organic quiz next period."

"Sorry."

"Buck, this school you're going to, how come you
just disappeared? You didn't say anything to me or
Roger or Tammy. I know you didn't say anything to
any of your instructors. I've checked."

"It's okay, Theo. I didn't tell my family either.
Guess I'm feeling pretty guilty about it. I suppose I
didn't tell anyone about it because I didn't want to be
talked out of it. The *Hila* wants me to tell my father."

"Why don't you?"

"Theo, my father is like just about every other
Tenctonese parent his age. Fit in, adapt, copy, do
anything to join up and become an invisible part of
things. Human kids my age go to high school; then I
should go to high school too, even though I'd finished
every course my school had to offer by the time I was
fifteen. You don't know what a fight I had getting my
parents to allow me to go to college, even though I'm
paying my own way, and even though there are
numbers of human kids under the age of eighteen in

college. The *Rama Vo* would really get him. It's run by a bunch of old Tenctonese who don't fit into anything anywhere and don't even care to try. They are who they are, and they find that just fine. On top of that, the *vo* isn't accredited and they don't award a diploma or have a football team."

Theo shrugged and held out his hands. "You still look like you feel guilty."

"My dad, he's going through some kind of weird physical thing. Aman Iri, the *Hila,* he thinks he can help my dad."

Theo simply sat there, his lips pursed, his eyebrows arched.

"Okay, okay. I'll tell him. I don't expect I'll figure out the flower and the weed thing any time soon, anyway."

There was a different tone to the room, a hush replaced by anxious words and glances. Two students rushed from the union, quickly followed by a third and a fourth. "Hey," Theo shouted to a passing female student. "What's going on?"

"A student over in Professor Gainer's two o'clock. Someone shot him just a few minutes ago. Killed him dead. There's an army of cops over at the Learning Center. Somebody said that one of the police officers was killed too."

"Jesus," Theo said, his face blanketed with shock.

"They were both just rubberheads. The student in Gainer's class—" The girl stopped in the middle of her comment when she noticed Buck sitting there, staring at her. Her cheeks flushed and she muttered "Sorry" as she held her books to her breast and rushed away.

Theo stared after her for a moment, then shook his head. "If your *Hila* wants to add a genuine asshole to his black and white collection, I know where he can find a slightly bent specimen. Sorry, man."

"Who're you apologizing for?"

"I don't know. The human race, maybe." Theo eyes widened as he checked his watch. "Gainer's two o'clock? That's *our* class!" He reached across the corner of the table and grabbed Buck's arm. "Did you hear me? The dead kid? That had to be Roger! You and he were the only two Tencts in the class." Theo frowned and looked down at the table, seeing nothing. "Man!"

"What is it?"

Theo raised his gaze until his frown was centered on Buck. "Last week Roger moved from the back of the room and took your old place. You hadn't been to class for weeks. He had to be sitting in your seat when——"

"It can't be Roger," Buck said, his words almost a prayer. "Theo, maybe some other Newcomer was monitoring the class. That has to be it." Buck shot to his feet. "We better get over there and see if we can find out what happened. Oh, hell."

"What?"

"I should call my mother too. If she hears this on the news before I reach her, she'll freak."

As Theo raced from the union, Buck began to gather up his paint chips, but stopped when he felt a strange itching sensation between his shoulders. He turned around slowly, examining the faces in the room. Threats seemed to lurk in every expression, every shadow, every corner. It was the ultimate "them," and he was a very small, lonely "us." He glanced down, grabbed the original four paint color samples, and ran from the building.

CHAPTER 11

"I'M DETECTIVE MARK DIAZ. I'm here to see Susan Francisco."

Rita Jessup looked up to see a LAPD badge dangling in front of her. Above the badge was a human face wearing a kind smile, thick black moustache, sunglasses, and a gray suit. "I'm sorry, but Mrs. Francisco had to leave this morning," Rita answered. "Is this about the escape of those two convicts from China Lake?"

"I'm sorry. I'm not at liberty to say," he said as he replaced the badge inside his coat pocket. "We've tried her home, but she isn't there. Do you know where she went? It's really very important."

"She hasn't been in since this morning, not since that call from her husband. She went to pick up her children from school. She couldn't locate her son, Buck."

"He's been located, and we know she's picked up

her two daughters. Since we couldn't find her at home, we thought she might've come back here."

"No, she hasn't. I certainly hope nothing's happened. We're all so fond of the Franciscos here."

"Oh?" Detective Diaz looked up and surveyed the faces in the room. There were seven persons there besides the receptionist: two humans—one male, the other female—and five Newcomers, all female. Although they were at desks and drafting tables, they were all looking at him. There was apprehension, expectation, in their eyes. The corners of Mark Diaz's mouth went down slightly.

"All of you?"

Rita frowned as she saw a tear slip down the detective's cheek from behind his sunglasses. "Are you all right?" She stood, pulled a tissue from a box in her drawer and held it out toward the policeman. "What is it?"

"All of you," Mark Diaz repeated as he removed his sunglasses, revealing his left eyelid crusted with dried blood.

"Should I call 911?" She turned and looked at the others in the room. "Should I call someone?"

"Him," said the detective as he pulled the automatic from his shoulder holster. "Him, and the memory of him." He aimed the weapon at Rita's face, pulled the trigger, sent a round between her eyebrows, blowing off the back of her head. Blood, hair, and bone fragments spattered the two sitting directly behind her. One began screaming, the others were struck silent. Swinging the weapon toward the others in the room, Diaz blasted the two humans and one of the Newcomers as a door in the back opened, revealing a Newcomer wearing a tan suit. Behind him was a human. With two quick shots he drilled the foreheads of both before he turned his weapon back on the production crew, executing the remaining two employees.

"Him and the memory of him," he repeated as he stood in a growing pool of blood and replaced the empty clip in his automatic. "Him and the memory of him."

Detective Mark Diaz then cycled a fresh round into the chamber, cocked the piece, and thrust the weapon's muzzle into his own mouth. He pulled the trigger, and long after he was dead, his trigger finger kept flexing.

CHAPTER 12

THE TWO STAFF pathologists on the autopsy team were human, with a Tenctonese intern observing. The room was surprisingly warm, lending an extra pungency to every odor, real or imagined. Matt Sikes looked down upon the mutilated body of his partner's mentor, Tom Rand. The warden had been taken down hard.

Given their first split second of opportunity, the SWAT team had riddled the gunman. There were over twenty entrance and exit wounds, some places so chewed by misshapen lead flying through tissue that the damage from individual rounds couldn't be determined. The shooters had done everything by the book, too. No head shots, no John Wayne shooting the gun out of the hand, no hit him in the leg and bring him down crap. All of the hits had been in the torso, mostly in the upper left quadrant. Tom Rand's heart wasn't traumatized, it just wasn't there.

George stood silently at the head of the corpse, looking down at the dead man's face. He studied it, seemingly unmindful of the minor dramas being played out around him. It was almost as though his entire concentration was devoted to communicating with his dead mentor.

The FBI agent, an altogether too serious-looking Tenctonese named Paul Iniko, faced Charlie Truman. "I believe there was an understanding that attendance here was to be limited to the staff and the official representatives of the concerned jurisdictions." He nodded toward a slender human with too-big glasses and prematurely balding hair. "Collins here is from the Bureau of Prisons. I represent the Federal Bureau of Investigation." He flipped his hand at a plain-clothes officer and two uniformed officers. "Ratik, Myers, and Browning represent Hollenbeck Division and the L.A. SWATs." He nodded toward Sikes and Francisco. "And them?"

"Tourists," Kim Nishida answered. "I invited 'em."

"For what purpose?"

Kim opened her huge bag of edibles and peered inside. "To peek, to poke," she answered, "to boldly go where no one with a sack of ribs has gone before."

Agent Iniko held out his hands, revealing the Overseer's mark tattooed around his left wrist. "What is their authority?" he demanded.

"I sell the tickets to this theater, sonny," Charlie said to the agent. "If you want to keep your ticket, maybe you better knock off ragging the rest of the audience." He nodded at the Tenctonese intern, and the intern punched on the recorder.

Collins, the official representative from the Bureau of Prisons, and Browning of the city SWATs, staggered out soon after the body had been uncovered. Although he didn't look ill, the agent from the FBI's field office left soon after. Sikes grimaced at the two canoe makers as the pair continued their performance. They handled their own queasy stomachs by being ghouls and drawing what entertainment they could from grossing out visitors. While hulking Charlie Truman gormed in one of the wounds with a probe, petite Kim Nishida mugged for the TV camera, gnawed on a barbecued rib, and talked into the microphone suspended from the ceiling above the slab. Officer Ratik lasted until Kim began sucking the barbecue sauce from her fingers.

Charlie took a scalpel and ripped open the tatters of Rand's abdomen with an eleven-inch incision that reminded Matt of unzipping a torn gym bag. Kim continued to eat and report as she bent over the remains. The deceased was so long (slurp), so heavy (munch, munch), so old (smack), and simply full to his eyes with lead, scrambled guts, and goo. With a bang Kim tossed a cleaned rib into a waste can, and Myers, the remaining Hollenbeck officer, stumbled off toward the rest room.

"Don't you two ever get tired of this act?" Sikes asked as he struggled to hold down his own lunch.

Kim tossed a ketchup-coated fry toward Charlie, who caught it with his mouth, ate it, and swallowed, leaving a smear of red on his upper lip. "What act?" he asked.

"Where's the X-ray series on the head?" George asked.

Charlie Truman looked up from the incision and faced Francisco. "Are you joshing?"

"No. Where is it?" George faced the observing intern and asked again in Tenctonese, receiving only a shrug in response. "There must be a head series. If one wasn't made, it needs to be made."

Truman held his bloodstained hands out above the corpse. "Man, could you possibly be in some doubt as to the cause of death here?"

"Hmmm," Dr. Nishida muttered as she reached for another rib and wiggled her eyebrows Groucho style at the TV camera, "this is the worst case of suicide I ever saw."

"Of course, I'm sure the shooting had something to do with it," George said, growing anger clipping his syllables.

"At least," Kim Nishida said around a greasy mouthful of pork.

"Look at him, Francisco," Charlie said. "There're two places on this carcass the SWATs didn't burger: the head and the feet. You might not believe this, but we didn't do an X-ray series on the feet either."

"We need at least a side shot of the head," George insisted.

Kim tossed another rib bone into the waste can. "Detective, maybe you figure he had a stroke? Or are all of those bullet-hole-looking things just a bad case of acne?"

"He doesn't need pimple cream," Charlie chimed in. "He needs spackling plaster."

"Maybe it was an allergic reaction," Kim suggested. "A sensitivity to heavy metal."

The morgue vaudeville act of Truman and Nishida failed to get either a laugh or a rise out of Francisco, who continued to study Tom Rand's face. Matt stood next to George. "What is it, partner?"

George reached to a dispenser, took a rubber glove from it, and turned back to the body of Tom Rand as he pulled on the glove. "Look at this." He glowered at the Tenctonese intern. "Doctor? Would you look at this, please, Doctor . . . ?"

"Rivers," the Newcomer completed as he looked down at Tom Rand's head.

"Rivers," George repeated dully, his eyes changing color from red to black.

"Cool off, George, okay?" Matt cautioned.

George turned the head of the corpse toward Matt and placed a finger on the body's left eyelid. "Look at this mark. Here, just above the eyelid."

Leaning forward, Matt saw a reddish-black pit partly hidden by the warden's bushy eyebrow. "What's that? It looks like a cut or a burn."

Charlie Truman frowned and squinted at the mark. "It's a burn. A deep one, too." He looked up at Francisco. "What do you know about it?"

George looked at Dr. Rivers, his eyes an even deeper black. "What does it suggest to you, Doctor?"

"Of course it suggests something to me. But this is a human," the intern protested. "It's unlikely that a mark there on a human would be anything more than a coincidence."

"Even though his death is connected to Maanka Dak and Sing Fangan, *binnaumrokh*?"

The intern's eyes changed color as well: from blue to red and from red to black. *"Triahna!"* demanded the intern.

"I will not apologize!" George pointed with his thumb at the corpse. "How did he die, Doctor? Rivers? Dr. Rivers? What's your whole name? Red Rivers? Sandy Rivers? Muddy Rivers? Cruddy Rivers?"

"Arthur Rivers, actually."

"Lighten up, George," Matt ordered as he shook his partner's arm.

George Francisco closed his eyes, took a deep breath, and let it escape slowly from his lungs. He let his gaze take in everyone in the room, stopping on Matt Sikes. "I apologize. I haven't been quite myself lately." He looked at Arthur Rivers. "I'm sorry, Doctor. I do apologize. This has been one of those days."

"Are your *nemeh* glands swollen?"

"Forget about my damned *nemeh* glands!" He pointed toward the mark on Tom Rand's eyelid and asked the intern in Tenctonese, *"N'teegas tees visri na x-lo, yidyih il es'sa neh tew chai k'Maanka Dak?"*

After a moment's consideration, Arthur Rivers answered, *"Kwen.* Yes, I agree."

"What gives, George?" Matt demanded.

"Nothing. Dr. Rivers has agreed to the need for a head series."

"Sikes!" someone shouted from the door.

"What?"

"Telephone. Urgent."

"Timing is everything." Matt turned, went through the swinging doors, and followed the pointing finger on the wall to the telephone. Picking up the receiver, he tucked it between his chin and shoulder and began searching his pockets for some chewing gum. "Sikes here."

"Sikes, this is Grazer."

"What's up, Cap?"

"Diaz. He's dead."

Matt took the receiver in hand, stared at it for a second, and held it to his other ear. "What? Mark? Dead? What in the hell are you talking about, Cap?"

"Diaz bought it. We sent him to track down Susan Francisco and the kids after we learned that Maanka Dak killed Sing Fangan along with a Newcomer construction rep named Brick Wahl at a motel in North Hollywood. Matt, Mr. Wahl had a very sophisticated computer in his room. The boys on the scene called in a button thumper, and she says Maanka Dak definitely accessed the police computer and could have accessed just about any other system he wanted, including the school system or any of the universities. That'd give him everything from Buck's class schedule to George's pension account number."

"What happened to Diaz?"

There was a long silence on the captain's end of the line. When he finally answered, his voice was very rough. "We don't know what happened to him. It looks like he killed almost everyone in Susan's office, seven or eight people, and then killed himself. One of the office workers there managed to describe the nightmare before she passed out. Susan and the kids weren't there."

"Jesus H. Christ, Cap! What . . . how? Are they sure it was Diaz?"

"It was Diaz, all right. Matt, you knew him better than I did. Did he do any drugs? Was he on any medications or under psychiatric care? You know, something not authorized by the department shrinks?"

"Hell, no!" Matt closed his eyes and shook his head. "I don't know. I don't think so. Hell." Matt rubbed his eyes and took a ragged breath. "Has anyone told Felicia?"

"Dobbs is on his way now. He took it hard, Matt. Real hard. Thank God at least Diaz didn't have any kids." There was a puzzled silence, then Grazer asked, "What're you two doing at the canoe factory?"

Matt automatically opened his mouth to lie, but stopped before he spoke. Game time was over.

"George thinks Warden Rand didn't just freak. He thinks the McBeaver Massacre's connected to Maanka Dak's escape. My guess is that Mark Diaz just confirmed that."

"Dak? You think Maanka Dak is connected somehow to what Diaz did?"

"Cap, I'll bet you a month of overtime and my outfielder's glove that Mark Diaz has a small wound of some kind above his left eyelid."

"What's that mean?"

"I'm not sure. George knows what's going on, though. I'd bet my life on it. If Diaz has that wound above his left eyelid, you clear it with Hollenbeck Division to put us on the case, okay?"

"I'll see what—"

"And Cap, be sure they take an X-ray of Diaz's head. Got it?"

"Sikes!" someone yelled from the end of the hall.

"What?"

"Your partner. He just collapsed."

"What's going on? Sikes? What happened?" Grazer demanded, but there was no one on the other end of the line.

In a nearby room, Agent Paul Iniko was slumped in a chair, his gaze fixed to the video monitor. As Sikes and the Tenctonese intern wheeled Francisco from the autopsy room, Truman and Nishida rolled the portable X ray into place on Tom Rand's body. Iniko stood and went to the telephone. He punched in a number, waited a moment, and then said, "This is Iniko." A click and a buzz.

"Iniko?" a man answered.

"That's right."

"Are they doing a head series?"

Iniko turned his head and glanced at the monitor. "They're getting ready to do it right now."

The voice at the other end of the phone was silent for a moment. "Will they know what they have once they find it?"

"I think they already know what they're looking for. One of the interns, a Tenctonese, appears to have had experience with the neural controllers. It was a police officer, though, who demanded the head series."

"A police officer?"

"LAPD. His name's Francisco; a homicide detective. I made a few calls and checked him out. He was the officer who took down Maanka Dak and Sing Fangan. He knew them from the ship. As I said, they know what they're looking for."

"There's nothing to do, then, except erase. Hang in there with Collins, Rittenhouse, and Lipscomb and see what you can do. Whatever happens, keep us out of it."

"What about Maanka Dak?"

"We're taking care of it."

The muscles in Paul Iniko's cheeks flexed. "Taking care of it?"

"We're handling it, Iniko. That's all I can say."

"There are a lot of dead men and women out here, and the police are short on information. I just overheard a phone conversation and there's been another mass killing. It was a police officer implanted by Dak."

"You know what your orders are, Iniko." There was silence at the other end of the line, then the sound of the connection being cut.

Paul Iniko hung up his receiver, and with his hand

still on it, glanced at the tattoo that surrounded his wrist. He turned his head and looked at the video screen. Truman and Nishida were positioning the portable X-ray for another exposure. Paul Iniko returned to the chair, dropped into it, and resumed studying the monitor.

CHAPTER 13

NICTO WATCHED AS his friend, Vullos, sat and stared out at nothingness, his eyes deep green and unblinking. The vibration of the ship's engines provided an almost soothing hum, tempting Nicto to believe that Vullos was not in pain.

But his eyes were green. More deeply green that Nicto had ever before seen on a Tenctonese man, woman, or child. The neural implant, the tiny robot the Overseers had placed in Vullos's brain, was telling Nicto's friend certain things. First, it told Vullos to sit calmly and do nothing. Second, it told him to feel pain, towers and oceans of unimaginable pain.

There was no sign anything was going on. There was no screaming, no thrashing about, no struggling, no pleading, no need for manacles or muscular arms to restrain him. Vullos did all the work himself, in motionless silence. The only sign that he was in pain was

*the color of his eyes. The pain program had allowed
that sign in order to be certain that the proper degree of
suffering was being obtained.*

*It continued until Vullos's eyes began to cry
blood. . . .*

The images of three Newcomers holding cans of Dr
Pepper swam in a sea of hot colors as George fought
his way back to consciousness. When he could again
focus his eyes, he saw that he was looking at the front
of a vending machine. Next to the canned beverage
dispenser was a machine containing candy bars, dry
roasted insects, flavored popcorn, and dolphin chow-
der.

He was stretched out on a couch with plastic-
covered cushions. George allowed his head to turn to
one side and saw that he was in the morgue's staff
lounge. Seated in a chair before him was Matt Sikes.
His partner was leaning with his elbows on his knees,
his hands rubbing the back of his neck. "Matt?"

Sikes sat bolt upright and shouted, "Doc, he's
back!" The door to the lounge opened and Dr. Rivers
pushed his way in as Sikes placed his hand on
George's arm. "Glad to see you again, buddy."

"What happened?"

"What they tell me, while I was on the horn with
Grazer, you did a swan dive right in the middle of the
autopsy."

"I didn't land in anything gross, did I?"

"Don't be fussy, Detective," Dr. Rivers said.
"You're alive and well, and that's what counts."

"Who had me brought in here, Matt?"

"I did."

"Why?"

"Call me crazy, George, but I thought it would freak you out a whole lot less if you woke up here rather than on a slab in the ghoul room with Kim and Charlie sucking on their fingers and smacking their lips."

"I see. Yes." George nodded. "Thank you, Matt." He looked past his partner at Dr. Rivers. "Doctor? I am so sorry for my behavior in there. I can't imagine what's going on with me."

"Perhaps I can help clear things up for you." The intern pulled up a chair, sat down facing Francisco, and opened a file folder in his hand. "Detective, I have some good news and some bad news."

"No, not good-news bad-news jokes," George protested as he pushed himself up to a sitting position.

A puzzled expression settled upon Dr. Rivers's face as he looked at Sikes. "The tests are completed and I have both good news and bad news for your partner. What I don't have is all day to deliver it. You might recall I did these tests as a favor. It's not like either of you or anyone else is paying for the extra work."

"Okay, okay, Doc. You're a saint," said Sikes. "What's the bad news?"

Rivers turned and looked at George, a note of true compassion entering his voice. "You are going through *riana,* Detective Francisco. Your child-conception-and-bearing years are over. I'm sorry."

"Impossible!" George protested. "I'm much too young. In Earth time I'd have to be in my eighties or nineties before having to be concerned about *riana.* I'm not even sixty. I'm much too young."

"Nonetheless. I did both blood and saliva tests, Detective." He held out the file folder. "The findings on both tests were positive."

George shook his head. "Impossible. Absolutely impossible. You must've mixed up my results with someone else's tests."

"With someone else's tests? If I'd done that, Detective Francisco, the only thing these results would've shown is that you're dead." Rivers held out a hand as the sarcasm in his voice sharpened. "If you cast your mind back, you'll recall the general condition of most of our patients here at Graveside Memorial. Mmmm?"

Matt turned and faced Dr. Rivers. "Are you saying that George is going through some kind of Tenctonese menopause?"

"That's one way of putting it. At least he is doing so in a biological sense. There are other changes, mental changes, with which I have little experience."

George shook his head and fixed Dr. Rivers with another red-eyed look. "No! You cannot possibly be certain of this. You don't even work with the living."

Arthur Rivers returned George's look with a steady gaze devoid of emotion. "Back on the ship, one of my tasks was to perform these very tests to identify those slaves past child-bearing years so that the Overseers could cull them out. My own existence and the lives of thousands depended upon me never being wrong. About this, Detective Francisco, I am never wrong. You are undergoing *riana,* and all that is left to consider is whether you accept it and get the help you need. Do you know a *Hila?"* He glanced at Sikes. "An Elder," he explained.

"What's he need an Elder for?" Matt asked.

"Simple, really. Elders have been through it, have studied it, and are now living on the other side. They are an important resource for those undergoing *riana."*

George stared blankly at the floor as he slowly shook his head. "None personally." He thought of Uncle Moodri and the few other Elders he had known. He frowned as old memories filled blank frames. On the ship those who went through *riana* were always taken away. Almost all of them simply disappeared. *Riana,* then you die.

Sikes shrugged and held out his hands. "Doc, if it was part of your job to identify those going through the change, how come you don't know anything about the mental changes, and what happens after? And Elders? You must know dozens or hundreds. How about an address?"

"Riana, then you die," Dr. Rivers repeated. "The only ones who lived long enough to become Elders were those who had a necessary mental skill that was in short supply. We are speaking here of very few individuals. There were those and Overseers, of course. That's why there's such resistance on your partner's part about accepting the biological facts. When my time comes, I'm certain my instinctive reaction will be the same."

Matt looked from Dr. Rivers down at George, then back at the intern. "You said you had good news."

"Yes, I did." Rivers faced George. "The good news, Detective, is that the changing is almost over. The symptoms you've been experiencing thus far, nightmares, forgetfulness, audio and visual hallucinations, increased mental clarity, mood swings, light-headedness, fainting, that's just about finished. There may be other symptoms beyond those, but I never came in contact with anyone undergoing late stage *riana*. By the time any of my subjects reached late stage, they were either dead or had been taken away."

Dr. Rivers closed the file and got to his feet. "If you

don't know a *Hila,* I suppose you can put a notice in the newspapers. According to the immigration records, there should be close to a hundred or more of them scattered among the population. As far as the actual changes go, it doesn't matter whether you seek the advice of an Overseer or former slave. Physiologically and mentally, *riana* is the same for either, and either kind of *Hila* can give you the information you need."

"An Overseer?" George said. "Impossible."

"Everyone has the capacity to change, Detective. Even the Overseers. In any event, you need a *Hila.*"

George frowned as he thought. "There was something my son said to me a few weeks ago; an idle comment concerning some kind of school he might want to look into. He said something about Elders." He looked up at Arthur Rivers. "Are you certain there can be no mistake?"

"I'm certain," he answered as he smiled sheepishly. "Just as certain as I was that the mark above the left eye on Thomas Rand meant nothing. We took the head series you suggested and found a very crude neural transmitter implanted in the parietal lobe of the left hemisphere. A very crude instrument must've been used. There were several bone splinters in the brain tissue along the insertion path." The doctor turned his head toward Matt. "Captain Grazer called a few minutes ago. He said to tell you that you were right about Detective Diaz's eye. There was a puncture wound—"

"Diaz?" George looked at his partner. "What about Mark?"

Matt glanced at the intern and gently cocked his head toward the door. "Then, I'll be going now," Dr. Rivers said.

Looking away from the intern's departure, Sikes leaned back in his chair, rubbed his eyes, and let his hand fall into his lap. "He's dead, George. Mark Diaz is dead."

"Dead? How?"

"First, George, understand that Susan and the two girls are okay."

George sat bolt upright. "Susan?"

"I said they're okay. Look, George, they found Sing Fangan dead in a motel along with one of the motel customers. It looks like Maanka Dak killed both of them. The customer had a computer, and it looks like Dak's gotten hold of every bit of information possible about you, your family, and everyone who ever worked with you or knew you. Because of that, Grazer sent Diaz over to Susan's office to help her round up the kids and find a safe place. He didn't know you'd already called her."

"But what happened?"

Sikes bit at the skin on the inside of his lower lip. "Somehow, between the station and Susan's office, Maanka Dak caught up with Diaz and jammed one of those controllers into his brain. Mark showed up at Susan's office and pulled a McBeaver's freakout. He killed or wounded everyone there. Then he killed himself."

"Celine's mercy," whispered George. He swayed as he got to his feet. "Susan and the children. Where are they?"

"They're okay, George. The captain has them in a safe house under enough security to fill out a couple of pro football teams—"

"But if Dak accessed the police computer—"

"Grazer's thought of that. The safe house is recorded nowhere. It appears in no records, official or otherwise. The officers have special instructions, and there's a complete communications blackout. Everything is controlled out of a command center that's swept for bugs every fifteen minutes, and Grazer is sitting on top of it personally. There is no way Dak is going to find Susan and your kids before we find him."

"I must speak with Susan and Emily. I need to—"

"Use some of your new smarts, George. If you, or anyone else, called the safe house, suddenly there's a big fat electrical trail to Susan, Emily, and Vessna. Is that what you want?"

"No. Of course not. I wasn't thinking."

"You can't call her anyway, George. The safe house doesn't have a phone. No phone, no record of a phone. The house doesn't even appear on any tax records."

"What about Buck?"

"We haven't been able to track him down yet. There was a double killing at his campus." Matt held up his hands. "It wasn't Buck. A campus security guard got it and one of Buck's classmates, a Newcomer named Roger Dillon. It looks like the victim was sitting in Buck's place when he was smoked by the campus cop. The accounts are pretty confused, but it sounds like the campus cop offed himself after killing the student. They're checking now to see if the cop has a controller stuck in his brain."

"We already know how that investigation is going to turn out." George frowned and looked up at Matt. "It's been weeks since Buck's been to classes."

"That's something that wasn't on any computer, partner. Several of the students there said they saw Buck at the scene, though."

"There?"

"Hold it, George. After the shooting, he rabbited.

Anyway, it might not be Buck. All the witnesses were humans, and they all—"

"They all look alike."

"Yeah. Grazer's got an APB out on Buck, and all that can be done to find him is being done."

"We have to find him, Matt. The *vikah ta* cannot be completed if any of my children are left alive." His eyes widened. "Albert!"

"Albert?" Matt repeated.

"Yes, Albert. You know, Albert in maintenance? Our friend? The *binnaum* to my children?"

"Yeah, of course. Look, no sweat, George. Albert's been stashed too."

"You're sure?"

"I'm sure. You don't look very relieved, George."

"Buck. I'm still worried about Buck."

Matt shrugged and held out his hands. "Well, George, as insensitive as it sounds, Buck might be off the hook if Dak still doesn't know he juked the wrong kid." Sikes pointed at George. "As far as you're concerned, the captain wants me to take you to the safe house to join Susan, Emily, and Vessna. As soon as we track down Buck—"

"No. I'm going to stay at my own home. That's where Buck will look for me."

Matt smacked himself in the head. "Now why didn't I think of that? Come to think about it, why didn't Maanka Dak think of that? Do you think that little thing might just occur to Maanka Dak? Possible, George?"

George Francisco stood and began stumbling toward the door. "Susan and the girls are safe. Buck is out there. He needs me to be at home."

"Look, George, Buck's a smart kid. He wouldn't've taken off if he hadn't put two and two together. He

119

knows going home will just put him right in the middle of a target."

"Buck needs me to be at home," George repeated. "We'll arrange with the captain for security on the way." He leveled his gaze at his partner. "Matt, I'm the best piece of bait the department has right now. If we deny Maanka Dak access to me, he'll only shift his focus on the men and women who know me and my family. That's dozens, hundreds, of potential victims. I'm going home and that's all there is to it."

Sikes followed his partner out the door of the staff lounge, waving his arms in the air. "Great! Terrific! It sure sounds like a plan to me. You think we ought to spray paint a 'Follow Me' sign in Tenctonese on the car just in case we've read it all wrong and Dak is really as stupid as you are? How about that, George? Should we take out an ad? Does that sound like a program to you?" Matt paused in the hallway outside the lounge and looked toward the double doors leading to the burger palace. Mark Diaz would be in there soon. Matt shut his mouth and ignored the tears on his cheeks as he thrust his hands into his pockets and stormed toward the parking lot.

CHAPTER 14

"THREE-A-FOURTEEN, DUNCAN AND KAVIT," called out the watch commander. Lieutenant Yuker looked up from his clipboard and surveyed the academy-fresh Newcomer officers sitting at the tables for mid-afternoon watch roll call. The clock above his head said that it was three-forty in the afternoon. "Is that how you pronounce that?"

"You pronounce it 'Duncan,' like a doughnut," growled a rough voice from the old-timer tables at the back. A brief wave of laughter crossed the room.

"I was asking your new probie," said the watch officer.

"Kah-veeth, sir," said Ruma Kavit, trying to keep her voice strong.

"Okay, Kah-veeth," said the lieutenant. "You two roll in Fourteen. That'th Bill Duncan'th perthonal mobile polithe univerthity."

More laughter, and as Ruma turned toward old-timer's row to see a hard-eyed cop with steel-gray hair and a thorough pot gut nod back, she heard another Newcomer probie, one of her former classmates named Louis Louis, mutter, "Better you than me."

As the watch commander continued reading off the black-and-white assignments, Ruma Kavit turned to her right. In a low voice she asked, "What do you mean by that?"

Louis muttered, "Duncan's a slagraker. Heard about him from some of the others in the locker room. He got transferred to University Division because of an incident." Ruma's former classmate raised his eyebrows and sadly shook his head. "Watch your back. I think he hates women cops more than he does Newcomers."

Ruma glanced once more at Bill Duncan. He had four service stripes on his sleeve, which meant he already had in his twenty. The veteran officer was talking to another old-timer, his eyes still on Ruma. His mouth was laughing but his eyes were narrowed and cold. She returned her gaze to the watch commander. Unless she made her own boundaries clear to the slagraker, the watch would be hell. She wasn't physically afraid of Duncan. If it came down to it, she could probably take him. Duncan was not only human, he was in his fifties, overweight, and was a smoker. But Ruma wanted to succeed as a police officer, and that meant being accepted. She also wanted to stay alive, and that meant being able to trust your partner.

The watch commander went into the crimes, and the officers at the tables turned to fresh pages to take notes. The lieutenant looked up and said, "Before we wade through who's who, the Black Slayer is still looking for a few good men. Same as yesterday, even though it looks like he's only after blacks, the boy gets confused now and then. So, don't separate, wait for your backups. The slayer gets his man alone, so stay cozy and don't be alone." The officers laughed, and the watch commander turned to a red slip of paper.

"Duncan."

"Yo."

"Duncan, we got a I'm-gonna-git-you-sucka flag on you. A couple of Tencts, Maanka Dak and Sing Fangan, escaped from China Lake last night. Nobody has a clue where they are, but when they went over the wall, they had the warden with them. That's the same guy who emptied a sporting goods store in Van Nuys and juked all those customers at the Bucky McBeaver's this morning. So keep a sharp eye. For the rest of you, there're mug shots of Dak and Fangan on your boards. Next . . ."

Later in the small parking lot, Ruma Kavit walked alongside Duncan as the veteran talked around the chewed stub of a cigar, ticking off the law: "Okay, Kavit, I drive. You handle the radio and you do the paperwork."

In a clipped voice, Ruma asked, "Do I ride the clipboard because I'm a Newcomer, or because I'm a woman?" She stopped, turned her head, and looked up at Duncan.

"Spunky, huh?" Bill Duncan's eyes never changed as he plucked the cigar from his mouth and used it to point at Ruma. "I hate Newcomers, Kavit. I don't like how they look, how they sound, how they smell, and I especially hate their stupid names. I don't like tits on cops neither. I hate 'em all, Kavit: Newcomers, women, blacks, Asians, hippies, intellectuals, Italians, nerds, Native Americans, Republicans, jocks, Mexicans, college graduates, Libertarians, green Irish,

Jews, cornpone southerners, opera buffs, rich kids, Yankee flatheads, and snot-nosed assholes from Virginia give me an extra super pain right between the cheeks. I hate 'em all and I've run 'em all through *my* car and made damned good cops out of 'em. Every goddamned one of 'em handled the radio and did the books while I drove, because every goddamned one of 'em was a slick-sleeved fuzzy-shirted probationer who couldn't find his, her, or its own ass without a mirror, both hands, and a goddamned pack of bleedhounds." He jammed the cigar back into his mouth.

"Now, listen up with those supersharp ear folds, Kavit. Cops is serious business. I'm gonna teach you cops and you're gonna learn cops. Rule number one is to come home alive. Rule number two is never forget rule number one. You're gonna watch out for my fat ass like it was your own, and when you know the streets, scams, places, and players as good as me, I'll still be driving and not doing the books because by then you'll've figured out how to ask for a new partner and I'll be stuck teaching cops to some other piece of punk-bald space crud fresh from the academy. Now, was there anything else your assertiveness counselor wanted you to say to me?"

"Yes." Ruma Kavit folded her arms across her chest. "Are you on drugs?"

Duncan's eyebrows went up a notch. "Drugs?"

"If you aren't, you ought to be."

Despite himself, the veteran grinned, then pulled out his baton and pointed toward the black-and-white. "Let's roll, space bunny."

They put their hats and flashlights in the backseat and thrust their batons between the seat cushions, leaving the handles sticking out for easy access.

"Three-A-Fourteen, night watch, clear," Ruma said into the mike as Duncan pulled out onto Jefferson. Ruma hung up the mike, put the new hot sheet on her clipboard, and flipped down the sun visor against the glare of the afternoon sun. "Duncan, tell me about the flag. Dak and Fangan."

"Nothin' much to tell."

She turned her head to the left. "They wouldn't flag you if it was nothing."

Duncan shrugged. "Nothin' to worry about, unless you take that *vikah ta* stuff serious. You know anything about *vikah ta?*"

"When I was a child, back on the ship, there was a family that all died violent deaths. The older children said it was *vikah ta*. How do you know about it?"

"Years ago, back when that first crop of Newcomers graduated the academy, I had a probie named Francisco. His second week out with me as his T.O. and we stumble into a shit storm. It was a federal fubar operation and the FBI was everywhere except where they were supposed to be. So we had three Newcomers who're making off with the contents of a Wells Fargo car, no backup; zip. Francisco knew the perps from the ship and tried to talk 'em, but they came back with lead. I got dropped, Dak and Fangan were wounded, and the third one, Dak's brother, was killed. We took 'em in, they swore the *vikah ta* on us, and that was about it."

"Did you do any of the shooting?"

Duncan shook his head. "Couldn't. I got a slug through my wrist before I could get off a shot. Francisco took 'em all down. Let me tell you, that boy could shoot. Top of his class, you know."

"That Francisco? Samuel Francisco?"

A slightly pained look flitted across Duncan's face. "Yeah, but he changed his name to George. Why? You hear about him?"

"Sure. He was the first Newcomer to make detective. You were his T.O.?"

"That's right."

Ruma smiled and looked back at the street. "You're a fraud, Officer Duncan."

"What?"

"You're a fraud, a fake, the original three-dollar bill. You're a complete failure as a racist, sexist monster. You sound as though you're proud of Francisco, filthy rubberheaded slag that he is."

Duncan cocked his head to one side and held up a hand, dropping it back to the steering wheel. "Well, hell, he saved my life. For someone who's really desperate, that's worth something. Maybe I am a little proud of him. But don't kid yourself, Kavit. I am one of the big haters of the universe. Maybe I'm proud of a slag cop, but I wouldn't let my daughter marry one, if I had a daughter and believed in marriage." He moved the cigar from one side of his mouth to the other as he gave Ruma Kavit a long, vertical leer. "I might marry one myself, though. For a bald space-freak cop with tits, you're not bad. A wig on you and a couple shots of Right Guard for me and we could get it on."

"You better stop smoking that stuff, Duncan. It's burning a hole in your reality pan. A dead skunk couldn't kill the stink of that after-shave." She nodded toward her T.O. and asked, "Did you ever tell Francisco you were proud of him?"

"What? Francisco? Hell, no!" Duncan's eyebrows were arched in shock at the suggestion. "I wanted him to learn cops, not kiss me." He pulled the black-and-white over to the curb and stopped. Pointing with his cigar toward a news and smoke shop, he asked, "Got a brand?"

"What? Tobacco?" Ruma's eyebrows went up. "You really want a probie who stutters so bad she can't make a radio call?"

"Sorry. I forgot. How 'bout some otter noses or maggot muffins? They got all kinds of rubberhead snacks."

"Eye of newt, toe of frog?"

Duncan laughed and nodded. "Okay, okay. Serious, though. They have Tenct snacks."

"I have to watch my waistline, but thanks."

"I don't worry about my waistline."

"I noticed."

"Okay. Keep an ear open for the radio."

Duncan took his hat and baton, opened the door, walked around the car, and crossed the sidewalk into the smoke shop. Ruma listened to the radio calls and shook her head at her inability to pick out the call signs. It seemed like so much gibberish. She looked at the 3-A-14 she had scribbled at the top of her note pad and allowed herself a tiny feeling of victory. She had a lot to learn, but Bill Duncan had a lot to teach. In his own way, the slag-hating terror of the University Division was treating her like a cop; not an equal, but a student worthy of being taught. There would be, should she choose, even a free cigar or bag of otter noses now and then. It was going to be all right.

"Three-A-Fourteen, Three-A-Fourteen, see the man—"

"Duncan!" she yelled out the window as she scribbled down the Western Avenue address. "Duncan! We have a call! Duncan!" When there was no response from the smoke shop's open door, she reached over and blew the horn. She debated touching off the siren, but there was a directive restricting the gratuitous use of sirens for anything other than moving through traffic at speeds higher than the posted limit. She rogered the call, stepped out onto the sidewalk, and ran the eight steps to the door of the smoke shop. "Duncan? Duncan! We have a call."

She stepped into the shop, the rich aromatic tobaccos making the air thick and close. Duncan was standing before the counter at the far end of the narrow shop, his back toward the door. "Hey, Duncan!" she shouted.

Bill Duncan turned, pulled his weapon, took aim, and fired three rounds in rapid succession at Kavit. The first shot whizzed past her head, while the second went through the fleshy part of her left upper arm. As she leaped behind a display shelf filled with porcelain figurines, the third shot went through the open door and hit the black-and-white's windshield, shattering it.

By the time she had her weapon out, a fourth shot exploded one of the porcelain figurines, dusting her dark blue shirt with white powder. "Duncan, what in the hell is wrong with you?" she shouted. A fifth shot went through the shelf and struck her in the front of her left thigh, making her cry out. She returned fire, rolled to her right, came to a kneeling position and fired again. The gun dropped from Bill Duncan's hand as he teetered in place, then fell facedown on the green-tiled floor.

Ruma slumped to her right side as the pain in her left leg forced her to cry out. She placed her weapon on the floor and reached to place her hand over the wound to stop the bleeding.

"Are you all right?" asked a male voice from the open door.

"Check my partner," she gasped as she closed her eyes. There wasn't much she could do about anything right then. Someone else would have to take care of things. But what in the hell had gotten into Duncan?

"I'm afraid you've killed him, Officer Kavit." The man pronounced the name correctly. Ruma opened her eyes to narrow slits and saw that the good citizen was a Tenctonese male in his early sixties. She was about to explain the curious-looking circumstances when she saw something silver flash in front of her eyes.

"It really was terribly inconvenient of you to kill Officer Duncan. He figured rather prominently in my plans. Now you'll have to take his place."

"Take his place?" She frowned, unable to comprehend what the man was saying. Dimly, awareness fought its way through her pain. "Dak." She reached for her weapon, but it was no longer next to her on the floor. "Maanka Dak." He removed her handcuffs from her belt and cuffed her hands none too gently behind her back.

Dak pulled her down and cradled Ruma Kavit's head on his lap, steadying it, and said, "Now this is going to be a little uncomfortable." First she felt a pin prick above her left eyelid, then her entire being exploded in electric shocks. Then nothing.

CHAPTER 15

LATER THAT NIGHT Cathy Frankel stretched out in the strange bed and looked past the back of Matt Sikes's head at the hotel room's alarm clock. The yellow numbers showed the time to be just after ten at night. She listened carefully and could hear Matt's breathing between the roars of the planes going in and out of LAX. He wasn't asleep. Her left hand reached out and her fingers traced down his spine to his tailbone.

"That doesn't work the same on humans as it does on Newcomers," Matt grumped.

"I wasn't doing it for you, honey bumps. I was doing it for me."

"Honey bumps?"

"Yes. It's a term of endearment." She leaned over, molded the arc of her body against his, pressed her naked breasts against his back, and nibbled at his ear.

Matt shook his head, rolling it on his pillow. "Not

for me it isn't. Not honey bumps, sweetums, pookie, pumpkin, thunder thighs, or huggy bear."

Cathy froze, sat up, and held the covers to her breast. "Look Matt, if you're worried about George, why don't you call him?"

"Who said I'm worried about George?"

"In about fourteen hundred different ways, you did. Give him a call. Once you find out that he's all right, you'll be able to relax."

Matt pounded his pillows, sat up with his back against them, and ground the heels of his palms into his eyes. "I can't call him. There's a communications blackout. Maanka Dak's computer mania has everybody spooked."

"What's the point of the blackout, Matt? It's no secret where George's home is."

Matt lowered his hands. "It's still a secret where we are: you and me. It's a secret, unless Dak put a bug in a cop's head outside the door or down at the command center."

"Is that really likely?"

"The computer geeks Grazer called in seem to think that Maanka Dak is capable of anything down to and including walking through walls. They say he wiped his records from the police, Justice Department, and federal court computers and from the computer at China Lake. Not just the working files, but all of the backups too. How could he do that with just a lousy little portable?"

"I don't know." Cathy pulled her knees up and wrapped her arms around them as she frowned at the question.

"All we have on the bastard right now are a few notes found in the back of Warden Rand's desk and whatever the individuals who knew the clown can remember about him. Most of them are cons and they're not real cooperative. The electronics and computer instructors at China Lake's vocational rehab unit are sure impressed with Dak. There's also a Dr. Carrie Norcross, a neurosurgeon. There was some correspondence with her concerning Dak on Rand's desk. Grazer's trying to track her down. She seems to think Maanka Dak is some kind of technomedical genius."

"He is."

Matt turned his head and frowned at Cathy. "You knew him? Back on the ship?"

"Not well, but I knew him. He was a technician in the ship's biological maintenance unit."

"Where you were assigned?"

"Yes, but my assignment was in a different area, caring for children. Dak was assigned to surgery and later to pain administration."

"Pain administration?"

She nodded and stared into the dark. "After our slave transport unit was removed from Planet Itri Vi, Maanka Dak was one of several technicians assigned the task of programming and implanting the neural control modules the Overseers received from the Niyez."

"What about his buddy, Sing Fangan?"

"He was another, and Maanka's brother Sita too. The remaining technicians were killed in the crash."

"Go ahead. You were saying about Dak."

"Maanka Dak was as hated as any Overseer. The modules were used to control those men and women who couldn't be controlled chemically. They were also used for punishment. Indescribable punishment.

What's the worst pain you ever had, Matt? When you were shot in that arrest attempt last year?"

Sikes instinctively placed the palm of his hand on his right side, above his hip. He shrugged and then shook his head. "That hurt. It hurt a lot. To tell you the truth, though, that didn't hurt half as much as an abscessed tooth I once had. I was a week into the wilderness and there wasn't a thing I could do about it for days. That really brought me to my knees—or to the dentist, which is about the same. Why?"

"The frightening thing, Matt, is that it wasn't your abscessed tooth that was doing the hurting."

"It sure seemed like it was hurting."

"Matt, if I have complete control of your mind, I have complete control of your pain. Pain is not in your side or in your teeth. Pain is in the brain. You see, with a neural controller implanted in your brain, an experienced operator could give you the pain of that abscessed tooth, or the pain of thirty-two abscessed teeth, or a thousand abscessed teeth, if he wanted."

"Okay, I get the picture."

"I always wondered why the *Ahvin Yin* didn't execute Maanka Dak until I found out he was the organization's leader."

"What better cover for a resistance leader than being part of the problem?"

Cathy reached out her hand and placed it upon Matt's shoulder. "Look, you could call the command center and ask them to call George, couldn't you? That wouldn't give Dak anything he could use to find us."

Matt frowned, thought upon it, and frowned again. "Damned Maanka Dak has me spooked too." He gave a grudging nod. "Okay. That sounds good. I mean, he can't be everywhere, can he? He's only got two ears and there must be fifty lines going into the command center." He reached to the telephone, picked up the handset, and punched in a number. Cathy slid down in between the covers and listened as a slight panicky feeling teased at the back of her mind.

Although she hadn't known Dak well, she remembered him very well. Brilliant, yes, but cold, emotionless, devoid of compassion. At least, that was what everyone had thought. He was almost under the control of one of his own implants, with all feeling pegged to the dead side. Cathy hadn't known him well because no one had known him well.

"What the devil?" Matt said as he looked at the handset, then he nodded. "Hello? Hey! Yeah, hello. Good. Lost you for a second. Yeah. Look, this is Sikes. Detective Sergeant Matt Sikes. I want to talk to Captain Grazer, Lieutenant Yamato, or whoever's running the command center. That's right: track-a-Dak." He glanced at Cathy and covered the mouthpiece. "I got 'em."

Cathy nodded absentmindedly as she allowed the panicky feeling to fill her. As Matt talked, the feeling within her grew until it was overwhelming. At the center of her panic was the look in Maanka Dak's eyes.

It had always bothered her, that look. Every slave on the ship had a look, but the look was different. Usually it was a dull, beaten look; a visible sign of passive resignation. If not that dullness, the look was one of fear. Yet Maanka Dak never had either look. He always appeared as though nothing could touch him. It wasn't that he was in control. It was just that nothing could touch him. The hammer would come down, as it always had come down, and men and women would be crushed. The look in Maanka's eyes said, however, that Maanka Dak was not going to be one of them. It was not a desperate boast or an article of faith; it was a known of the universe. His look back then had frightened her. The memory of that look still frightened her.

Matt punched off the phone and placed it on the nightstand. "I talked to Bradley. He's running the command post tonight." He turned and faced Cathy. "George's okay. The whole block is blue with officers, uniforms and plainclothes both. Bradley says nothing larger than a flea can get through. Susan, Emily, and Vessna are hidden away too."

"What about Buck? Have they located him?"

"Not yet. All of the officers on George's house are on the lookout for him, though."

Cathy studied Matt's eyes. As he turned away, she asked, "What is it?"

"Nothing."

"A big something, your nothing."

He turned back and shrugged as he faced her. "I mean it might be nothing. Bradley told me an officer named Bill Duncan was killed late this afternoon in a shop on Jefferson. The owner of the shop was killed too. Duncan used to be George's training officer."

"Is there a connection to Maanka Dak?"

Matt nodded. "When George tangled with Dak and killed his brother, he was with Duncan."

"There's more, Matt. I can see it in your face."

Sikes scratched the back of his neck and bit at the skin of his lower lip. "Duncan had a tiny wound above his left eye, just like Mark Diaz and Warden Rand."

"But you said he's dead."

Matt nodded. "Yeah. There's another thing too. Duncan's probationer, a Newcomer named Kavit, is missing. They went out together and no one's been able to track her down. I figure it's a good bet that Maanka Dak has her and she has one of those gadgets stuck in her head." He looked into Cathy's eyes. "All those cops around George's house; she wouldn't exactly stand out in a crowd like that." He swung his feet to the floor, reached for his clothes and began putting them on.

"You're not going to George's."

"Bad guess."

Cathy tugged on his arm. "The task force knows about this missing officer, doesn't it? They'll be on guard for her."

"Who is they? What about the other officers, Cath? All that bastard has to do is get someone alone for a minute and he has himself another gun. Any of the officers guarding George could be next. Hell, for all I know, Bradley down at the command center has a plug in his head." He shook his head as he stood and pulled on his jeans. "I can't trust anybody. George is my partner; my friend. To the task force, George is just a slab of bait."

He picked up his joggers, walked to the window and peeked through the blinds as he pulled on his foot gear. "Look at 'em. Our own cops already have the yawns. I should be able to get by them without much trouble."

"Matt?"

"What?"

"Did you hear what you just said?"

"Yes." He pulled on his shirt and looked through the blinds once more. A palm tree, its fronds motionless in the dead-still air, stood out blackly against the motel's floodlighted pink stucco exterior. A figure was poorly concealed by the shaggy trunk. Sikes shook his head as the shadowy figure lit up a cigarette and loosed a cloud of tobacco smoke. "It's like going after Professor Moriarty with the Keystone Kops."

Cathy rose from the bed, walked around it and stood in the dark behind Matt. "Don't go. Please. I'm afraid."

He tucked in his shirt, checked and holstered his weapon, and pulled on his jacket. "I'll get word to you as soon as I can. Don't let anyone in." He turned, put his arms around her, and whispered into her ear fold, "It'd take someone a lot braver than me to sit here and just wait. I gotta go."

He kissed her, escaped from her arms, and opened the door. After a quick check outside, he slipped silently into the night.

Cathy pulled on her robe, sat on the edge of the bed and stared at the dark until the monsters that lurked there grew too real. She switched on the light and, picking up the remote control, turned on the room's television and switched channels to the sci-fi network to see what was on. Matt had introduced her to the old science fiction movies, and she had been fascinated, when not amused. On the screen was yet another running of the immortal copper-bottomed pot and pan with the pistol-grip-handle commercial. Once more the battle between the aluminum pot and the stainless steel pot was reenacted. Once more the aluminum pot crumpled in defeat.

When the commercial ended, it took all of half a second for her to recognize the film that was running. She punched off the remote and threw it on her nightstand. She didn't feel up to another viewing of *Invasion of the Body Snatchers*. She looked toward the window and placed Matt in the hands of Celine and Andarko.

CHAPTER 16

THE NIGHT AIR was thick and clammy as dark clouds rolled in from the Pacific, blotting out the moon. The street was silent, save only the barking of a dog and the distant wail of an ambulance siren. More than one of the officers guarding the Francisco home commented about the irony of sweating and shivering at the same time.

Few of the officers had the slightest doubt as to his or her ability to defeat Maanka Dak. To some of the human officers, Dak was just a Newcomer. To all of the officers, he was just a convict: a loser; another crowbar crazy bent on revenge. Dak was a "them." In any contest between "us" and "them," of course, the thems had to lose. It was only fair, just, God's will, and the right thing for reality to do.

The ends of the street were blocked, and officers on foot were hiding in the shrubbery, pretending to be lovers, bikers, joggers, skaters, skate boarders. Supposedly there wasn't a blade of grass that could move without at least three officers noticing.

Despite that, there were many things the officers weren't noticing. Six houses away toward the east, a burglar was disgusted at the state of the economy as he crept out the back of a darkened house and put an eight-year-old VCR into the trunk of his car. Two houses away a shadowy figure crawled into a ruptured storm drain and cursed as he ran into a spiny weed and jabbed himself in the eye. Across the street and two houses away in the opposite direction, Officer Ruma Kavit sat motionless, leaning against the rough bark of a palm, looking through the leaves and branches of a rhododendron bush at the two black-and-whites in the center of the residential street. The cars were close to each other, and the officers inside were talking directly, thereby avoiding their radios. Their efforts were so pathetic, she would've laughed or wept, always providing, of course, that Maanka Dak would run the programs that would allow her tear ducts to flow, her laughter to come.

The pain from the wound in her left arm had spread over her entire shoulder and neck, while the pain from the wound in her left thigh seemed to have focused on the small of her back, despite the swelling that stretched tight the skin covering her thigh. She could feel the pain but could not cry out. Her captor had stopped the bleeding with his handheld remote control prior to bringing her along to the Radio Shack he had broken into. Even her severed veins and arteries seemed to obey Maanka Dak. He willed the bleeding to stop, he entered the proper program, pushed the proper buttons, and the bleeding stopped. The pain skyrocketed because the blood rushing to the wounds had no place else to go, but the bleeding had stopped. Ruma knew that Maanka Dak could stop the pain, as well, but had chosen not to do so.

She tried to move her mind from her pain. It was an art the Tenctonese developed early on the ship. Pick up the mind, detach its connection to the pain, and plug it into something else. Ruma tried to focus on Dak's plan.

What was it?

What role had Bill Duncan been assigned?

What use had the old cop been to Maanka Dak?

How had she spoiled the plan by gunning down Bill Duncan?

Dak had taken very little from the electronics store. Most of what he needed was already sewn into his coat. Despite her pain and fear, Ruma had been astonished at the hundreds of tiny loops and pockets that had been hand sewn onto the coat's lining. There were tiny tools, miniature printed circuit boards, and row after row of short, gleaming silver threads next to delicate needle-tipped instruments. There were hundreds, perhaps thousands, of the short silver threads.

"Look at your brother and sister officers, Ruma Kavit," Maanka whispered into her ear fold. "Look at all the blind, stupid creatures. I tell you I can move through them as though I were as invisible as the wind. You believe me too. I can tell. You've seen me do it." He smirked as he nodded his head once.

"Yes, Officer Kavit. It's like having a war of wits with a boxful of banana slugs."

He picked up his controller and attached a lead from it to a connector set just behind his right ear. He pressed a button, and suddenly Ruma felt an alien presence inside her, invading, surrounding her sense of self. He was in her mind. He was everywhere.

Rape was only a body thing. It didn't invade the

self, the soul, unless allowed. Maanka had gone beyond that. He had invaded her self, had become her self, had taken and violated it all. There was no screaming; no sound; no way to flail against the pain; no way to bellow out her rage. Silence here was the ultimate torture.

"Look at them," she felt her own lips say as she pulled her weapon, cocked it, and aimed at the officer in the passenger seat of the nearest black-and-white.

"I can kill them all. And see how I have improved your aim? There is no shaking, no wavering, no twitching, no blurring of focus. With me to help you, my dear, you could shoot a perfect score every time. Indeed, I—we—can kill them all. But they really kill themselves, don't they? A fool who walks in front of a speeding car kills himself more certainly than any junkie seeking nothingness in an overdose."

Dak fell silent as he studied the dark windows of the Francisco home. "He's in there, looking out, waiting for his son. I knew he'd stay home waiting for his son. He's a magnet of care, drawing those who care for him out of hiding. They are so predictable. Duncan, Sikes, Diaz, Francisco, Grazer, Bradley. Cops. Predictable. They are biological machines following the orders of biological computers. Push the correct buttons, enter the appropriate program, and the machine does just what the operator wants. I've studied all of them in detail for years. I know them—knew them. Studied their programs. Designed new programs for them." There was a chink in the smug calm of Maanka Dak's presence.

"Diaz, of course, died in the line of duty," she felt her lips say as her forehead wrinkled in a frown. "In other words, he died the way I planned for him to die. You, on the other hand, Ruma Kavit, killed Officer

Duncan much too soon. That *was* inconvenient. You are the one I didn't know, Ruma Kavit. But now I know you—all of you."

Everything within Ruma Kavit that was still Ruma Kavit writhed in revulsion at what was within her brain. It was a thousand maggots, a reptilian thing coiled behind her eyes, a foul thing equal to anything driven from the depths of some human hell. It stank, it crawled, it carried with it the filth of a million festering sewers. It glistened with vomit, excrement, and drool.

She lowered the hammer on her weapon, brought it down, and replaced it in her holster. Shade by gentle shade she felt the presence withdraw from her mind. "You listen to my idle chatter, Ruma, and you think I am some sort of deranged serial killer. That's not true, you know. I am neither deranged nor a serial killer." He pointed with his controller at the police officers on the street, jogging by, hidden in the shrubbery across the street.

"I am not going to kill them all. Look at them. Most of those banana slugs in blue don't even know Francisco, my dear. Hence, there would be no point in killing them. There would be no point in killing everyone. That would be murder. I am not a murderer. The *vikah ta,* you see, is on Francisco; my brother Nicto; the traitor who took up authority's bloody cause against me and executed my brother, Sita. Soon, now, you will gain me my access to Nicto. Then my treacherous brother of the *Ahvin Yin* will die. Perhaps you will die, as well, but you are part of the same authority. Anyone who stands against the *vikah ta* becomes its target. This we swore lifetimes ago on Itri Vi." Dak's voice was almost a growl, then he fell silent, his eyes studying the telephone headset and flashing circuit box on the water-starved grass.

Itri Vi; it was a name from her childhood, a badly remembered nightmare. An older sister died there in a manner Ruma's parents had always refused to discuss. So many pains in a life. So many more pains trying not to feel them.

The heat from Ruma's wounds filled her, blotting out the mutterings of the madman at her side. The madman, however, was still inside her head, watching her thoughts. The pain from her wounds eased. It eased more, and Ruma could feel herself want to cry in gratitude at the relief.

Dak's fingers traced circles about her right ear fold.

"Ruma, my dear, do you have any idea how long it's been since I've made love to a woman?" He pushed a button, and Ruma felt her head turn toward Maanka Dak as her lips were forced back in a seductive smile. Something within her tore, flooding her universe with pure, evil hatred. She watched as the hatred ate her alive, and no longer cared.

"Ah, you feel the same as I do. How convenient." He began unbuckling her gun belt as he continued. "There were two human convicts at China Lake who served adequately as my sexual partners until they became homicidal. It's a pity the effect the neural controllers have on humans. In any event, there have been no women, human or otherwise, for far too long."

He put his lips close to her ear fold, his breath moist and foul. "Dare we to make love here?" he whispered. "Here, on the grass, in the midst of all this oppressive authority? Dare we?"

He grinned and leaned forward. "I'm guessing that

we do." He reached out, put on the telephone headset and adjusted it. "You won't mind if I watch the phone, will you, my dear? I'm expecting an important call. Wasn't it thoughtful of Captain Grazer and the authorities to route all calls to and from the principals through one command center? It's enough to renew an old cynic's faith in human nature."

He cackled beneath his breath as he unbuttoned Ruma's trousers and pulled out the tail of her uniform shirt. Inserting his hand beneath her shirt, he ran his fingers up her spine. She could feel her mind shatter as she felt herself forced to become sexually aroused. As her soul twisted in agony, she longed for the blessed, blotting occupation of the pain of her wounds.

"Now, Ruma, we wouldn't want to be too mechanical about this," Dak said, then laughed quietly and his fingers began to probe between her legs.

There was a cry that no one could see, a scream that no one could hear. Ruma Kavit whirled down a smoking blackness, deep within the infinity of herself, where no one, nothing, could ever touch her again. There she was alone. There she could hide. She wrapped her mental arms about herself and became very very still. Outside of her there was motion, sound, Maanka Dak talking into the headset with a strange voice, but it was over there: not connected; nothing to do with her.

CHAPTER 17

"IN A FEW MOMENTS *viewers will see this amazing home video taken by Ruby Begonia, a customer at the Bucky McBeaver's on Soto, scene of the massacre earlier today . . .*"

George stood in his darkened living room, at the window next to the telephone table, and searched the shadows of his small front yard for his son Buck as Amanda Reckonwith and the sounds of the "Slagtown Beat News" came from the kitchen television set. He didn't concern himself about seeing the Begonia tape about to be shown. It was the kind of thing the media would play and replay in ghoulish delight, over and over again, morning, afternoon, evening, and all night long, endlessly and forever, until the next horror came along.

George kept the set in the living room dark for two purposes. First, it made him less of a target from outside. Second, it allowed him to keep his eyes adjusted to the dark so that he could see outside. Buck was still out there, scared, lost, not knowing who to trust. Where once his thinking processes were jammed with feathers, George could now see his son's options very clearly.

Once he had seen his dead classmate sitting in his seat and had gotten a glimpse of the campus security cop who had done the job, Buck wouldn't have needed a detective to figure out his life was in danger.

Buck would have called his mother's office, first thing. There, he would've either gotten nothing or the news that Buck's old baseball coach, Detective Mark Diaz, had killed everyone at his mother's office, including himself. Would he have tried to get in touch with his father? The command center had reported no calls. Would he come home? If he was smart, he wouldn't. Buck was smart, but he wasn't that kind of smart. More important than his own life would be the knowledge of what had happened to his parents and sisters.

Then why hadn't he called home? Twice George had checked the telephone company to make certain that everything was functioning. He would have done it more often except for fear of having the line busy if Buck finally did call. Captain Grazer down at the command center had assured him that Susan and the girls were safe. But George knew that such assurances meant little when the threat was someone who had walked out of a federal maximum-security facility by operating the warden like a Tonka Toy.

Buck was smart. Maanka Dak was beyond genius. His hate was beyond hate, his capabilities beyond comprehension. Survival on Itri Vi had required

146

nothing less. A familiar voice, the voice of Warden Tom Rand, came from the kitchen television set.

"Those three or four kids I could've hired . . . instead of working for me, they're out there on the streets, getting into trouble, mugging, taking down their despair with chemicals, killing to get more, lashing out in frustration and hate against the universe! I can't hire them! I can't screw with W-2 forms, withholding, child labor laws, liability insurance, worker's comp, (bleep) *bureaucrats, goddamned lawyers, idiot after idiot after idiot! No! I'm not all right! I don't know anyone who is all right—"*

"There are, between the gunman's lines, wheels within wheels," Amanda Reckonworth interrupted. *"Before he went berserk, Thomas Rand was the warden of one of the nation's newest federal prisons, in daily contact with the results of our welfare, economic, and law enforcement systems. Listen as he tells his victims his assessment of it all."*

Tom Rand's voice came through some kind of reverb unit, making it sound deep, thundering, the utterance of Judgment itself:

"—all a cesspool: courts, bureaucrats, politicians, lawyers. It's the wrong kind of people, their heads filled with the wrong kinds of ideas, killing the country by sucking it dry to implement unworkable solutions!"

"Madman or social critic?" Amanda Reckonwith demanded. *"We'll never know, because the only man who could have answered that question is . . ."*

The street beyond the white picket fence was well lit. An officer George didn't recognize jogged by, being ultracareful not to look at the Francisco house. To George, the bogus jogger looked as though he wasn't looking because he shouldn't look like he was looking.

147

He shouldn't look like he was trying not to look either, George mused. It didn't matter. Such games were as nothing to Maanka Dak. As Tom Rand's rage-crazed voice screamed from the television for everyone to kill a lawyer for Jesus, George no longer saw the jogger. He saw, instead, the pain ministers of Itri Vi. The horrors inflicted upon them by the beastly Niyez, the physical pain as well as the pain of hearts and soul.

Was it some odd coil of DNA, some part of the stuff of life that they had used to engineer a race of slaves, that had balked at the treatment of the Niyez? He remembered the look in the eyes of the Niyezian pain minister he had killed as part of the *vikah ta* in revenge for his dead parents; his initiation into the *Ahvin Yin*. The rightness of what he did, when he did it, had not been in the slightest doubt. When the creators had removed them from the control of the Niyez and they were back on the ship, however, the doubts began.

"—*a thing we haven't touched on yet is the Diaz slaughter on Wilshire,*" Amanda said. "*Here we have Mark Diaz, a Hispanic, a detective on the LAPD, who goes seemingly mad and kills almost the entire staff of an advertising agency. The average age of detectives in Los Angeles is thirty-seven, yet Detective Diaz was forty-nine. It is no secret that Newcomer officers, men and women of just a few years service, have been promoted over other officers. Add to this that most of the employees at the ad agency on Wilshire are Newcomers, and maybe we can see a glimmer of the real problem.*

"*Is the Wilshire Boulevard Massacre happening only scant hours after the killings on Soto only a coincidence? Or are our social chickens finally coming home to roost? Only time will tell.*"

George looked for the remote control for the kitchen set as Amanda Reckonwith injected a thick, dramatic pause. *"During the riots of the Sixties and the nineties,"* she continued at last, *"large portions of this city's population stood up and with vehemence argued for and justified vandalism, robbery, arson, assault, and murder, in the name of unfocused rage. Now, when portions of the city leveled in the Watts riots of the sixties and the Rodney King riots of the nineties have yet to recover, are we getting a preview here of yet the next horror?"*

"If you have anything to say about it, it is," George muttered disgustedly as he punched off the kitchen TV with the remote control. "One thing you have to admit: a city eating itself alive sells a lot of hemorrhoid ointment."

He thought about Amanda Reckonwith's phrase, "murder in the name of unfocused rage." Was murder ever justified? If it's justified, it's not murder, he answered himself. In the '92 riots, dozens were killed supposedly to protest a single instance of injustice. As time passed, the excuses, justifications, and rationalizations expanded and multiplied to fill the available talk-show time, because nothing less than more reasons could even hope to outweigh the horrors that were committed. Few called the murders murders, however.

"Who am I to judge?" George asked himself aloud. "I never called my own murder a murder." He thought about it, and felt ashamed when he realized that he had never called it anything. He had never mentioned it to anyone.

He had never told Susan about his initiation to the *Ahvin Yin* and what he had done to be accepted. There were many ways to cast his act in a different, more acceptable, light. Under the authority and the laws of the time and place, however, Nicto had done murder. Unlike most other peoples of the galaxy George knew of, humans played games with the rules of murder, sorting killings by motive, intent, context, and socio-economic standing of the killers and the deceased. On most other worlds, the established rules governed, murder was murder, and George Francisco was a murderer.

He looked down at his hand, seeing there the tiny scar that had made him brothers with a monster. On Itri Vi, after Nicto had slain the Niyezian pain minister, Maanka Dak had pierced Nicto's palm with the point of a knife and then cut his own palm. As the pale blood seeped out of the small wounds, Maanka Dak had said, "This blood we have shed together over the body of our slain enemy. Here, in the hated dust of this world, it mixes together and makes us brothers. *Lewca ot Ahvin Yin.* Welcome to Those Who Resist."

George felt annihilating sadness fill his hearts. At one time he had worshipped Maanka Dak. Even when they had been taken away from Itri Vi and relieved of the horror of the Niyez, he had said nothing as the *Ahvin Yin* continued exacting its retribution. After all, the *Ahvin Yin* itself was a law of sorts, a seat of authority. Even when Maanka Dak learned the technical skills of the Niyez and helped the Overseers administer the new pain, Nicto had said nothing. It was better to have a spy in the midst of the Overseers, he had thought. From his vantage point, in addition, Maanka could best direct the *vikah ta* when the outrages of an Overseer exceeded any kind of endurance.

But what had brought Maanka to the level of bank

150

robber, convict, torturer, and murderer on earth? Was it a taste for excitement? An addiction to death? Andarko's messenger of vengeance gone insane? Everyone who was sworn to the *Ahvin Yin* had done so to achieve a little piece of justice; to bring some small evening of the scales. Most wanted peace; a feeling of safety for themselves, their mates, and children. Long before Francisco and Duncan had shot it out with Maanka, Sita, and Sing, Maanka's purpose had become twisted.

All the authority the slaves had ever known had been cruel, demeaning, deadly, corrupt, and against life. From that, Maanka had taken the premise that all authority is evil, hence he and his followers should be and would be bound by no authority. It had begun in the desert quarantine camps. While Nicto and a few others listened to Warden Tom Rand talk to them about law and the opportunities in law enforcement, Maanka had led Sita Dak and Sing Fangan through the wire and into the dark world of the fugitive.

Could it have been that the evil authority that made Maanka's special genius and special hate so valuable on Itri Vi, and before the crash, had to be re-created to keep Maanka important in his own eyes? Unless he is fighting the powers of evil, perhaps Maanka has no value to himself?

"Don't be so understanding," George muttered to the shadows. "Mark Diaz is dead; Warden Rand, Bill Duncan, and all of those bystanders. The man is trying to kill you and your entire family. Don't be so understanding."

He reached out his hand to check the lock on the window, but before his fingers touched the lock, he lowered his hand and let it hang at his side. He had checked that lock and every other lock in the house a dozen times. There was no way that Maanka Dak could get through.

Logic said that any brand of security capable of protecting him from Maanka Dak would also make it impossible for Buck to get through. Still, he expected Buck to come through the front door, drop his books on the hall table, and toss his bomber jacket over the back of a chair as he began his inquiries about what was for dinner. George checked his watch and noted that it was just short of eleven.

Such ordinary things, George thought. Memories are such mundane anchors to such important matters. And memory was one of the things that now either deserted him or buried him, depending on his biological moods. George turned from the window and felt his way through the dark toward the kitchen.

Dr. Rivers had to be mistaken. It simply could not be *riana,* although the changing here on Earth was not the death sentence it had been before the crash. That was what George's reason said. His feelings, however, said that it could not be so. If it were, then it would be the end of everything. He paused before the television set, tempted to turn it on again just for the illusion of company.

A sound came from the basement. George froze and lifted his head. He held his breath as he strained every muscle to catch every sound. He could pick out the beating of his hearts, the footsteps of the jogging officer, the creaking in the southwest corner of the house as it continued cooling off from the day.

There was something more. From the direction of the basement. There was the sound of grit beneath a shoe sole as it was ground into a concrete floor. The

152

earlier sound had been one of Emily's old plastic toys being accidentally kicked. Emily had yet to clean up her toys in the basement. In addition, she probably hadn't gotten around to putting away the skillet she'd left on the front steps. George promised himself to scold her just as soon as he finished hugging her to pieces. "Always supposing I live that long," he whispered to himself as he moved his hand toward his revolver.

Another footstep grinding grit into the floor, then a creak as weight was placed on the bottom step leading to the kitchen. As he pulled his weapon and held it up, George looked at the kitchen door and saw that it was slightly ajar. He had left it that way when he had gone down into the cellar to make certain the outside door and the basement windows were locked.

An additional squeak, one that George recognized: third step from the bottom. He'd been threatening to screw down those squeaky steps since they'd moved into the house. He'd promised Susan, but it was always one thing or another—

George shut down his nervous mental chatter and listened. Whoever it was on the stairs was taking them very slowly, two at a time.

George's mind raced through the possibilities. Maanka Dak knew that he was armed and that he would be on his guard. Would he be fool enough to come up those steps himself? He was bold enough; crazy enough. George shook his head. He didn't believe Maanka was stupid enough. But then, George reminded himself, he hadn't been able to imagine Maanka being either sufficiently bold, stupid, or demented to do half the things he had already done.

Who would be coming up those steps? Maanka? If

so, armed with what? What was Maanka Dak's ultimate *vikah ta* fantasy against George? What sick little script had he picked at and polished all of those years he was locked up at China Lake?

Maanka's sense of revenge would certainly be served, George thought, if he could get one of those neural controllers into my brain. Perhaps Maanka would have some kind of tranquilizer gun or knockout gas. A concussion grenade. If it was a grenade, maybe he'd have enough time to grab it and toss it back through the basement door before it exploded.

There was another footstep on the stairs, and George paused as he thought of another possibility. What if, instead of Maanka Dak, the person coming up those stairs was one of Maanka's unfortunate robots? What if it was the missing probationer, Ruma Kavit, or another officer? One of the men or women who were guarding the house?

He felt he needed another response, something beside a gun. George looked toward the counter, and in the dim reflected light from the street, he made out the counter drawers. He reached out his hand and pulled open the drawer containing the carving knife. As quietly as he could, he felt among the kitchen utensils until his fingers touched the familiar rough bone handle of the carving knife. He wrapped his fingers around the handle, lifted, and something slid off the blade and into something else, making a clatter in the drawer. He froze in horror.

On television once George had seen a cartoon where a sneak thief accidentally made a noise, waking up the owner of the house. The cartoon thief then made a "Meow!" sound like a cat. He had the temptation to do the same. In the cartoon, however, the owner of the house did a double take in his sleep as he realized that he didn't own a cat.

George realized that his head was full of meaningless sludge and that it was almost impossible for him to concentrate, listen, or even focus his eyes.

There were no more sounds from the basement stairs. Withdrawing the knife from the drawer, George squatted, turned, held out the knife, and aimed his revolver at the door to the basement.

He could sense whoever it was on the stairs holding his breath—her breath—its breath. George noted that if the door opened, he would be in full view of the assailant. If he crept across the floor to get behind the door, however, the intruder would probably hear him moving, if the intruder were Tenctonese.

Where he was, squatting before the kitchen sink beneath the level of the counter, the shadow caused by a light from next door shining through the window provided good concealment, provided he didn't move. And providing the intruder didn't carry a light. George felt light-headed as realized he was holding his own breath. As slowly and as quietly as possible he began drawing air into his lungs. As he did so, the images before his eyes grew dimmer and dimmer until everything was a uniform shade of inky black. The door was gone. The kitchen was gone.

He held the knife in front of his eyes. He could make out nothing.

Quickly turning his head, he looked toward the window above the kitchen sink. The light from the neighbor's house was gone.

He was stone-black blind.

Riana, he thought. It is *riana,* after all. *Riana* and then you die.

A redness crowded the edges of the black filling his sight. A streak of bright yellow shattered the blackness as his ears heard the basement door fly open and slam against the wall.

Holding up the revolver, George jumped to his feet and fired as he threw the knife toward the door. A body slammed into his middle and things behind his eyes went all sparkly as the wind was knocked from him. He slammed into the cabinets and hit the floor. He fired again and could hear the picture tube on the television shatter and sprinkle the floor with glass.

"Dad!" he heard a voice scream into his ear. "Dad, stop shooting! It's me!"

"Buck? Buck?"

"Yes! It's me, Dad!" Buck's voice calmed down as he released his father and sat up. "Are you all right?"

"All right?" George repeated. He took several deep breaths and tried to pull himself up against the cabinets. "All right. That covers a lot of territory, Buck. No. I'm not all right. I almost killed my son, my head's full of fog, I think I busted a rib, and I can't see. I fear Muddy Rivers was right about the *riana.*"

"Muddy what?"

The flashes before George's eyes began again, forming quickly into psychedelic patterns and shades. "It's not important, son. You're here. That's what counts. Are you certain you're all right? I didn't hit you when I fired or threw the knife?"

"No problem, Dad. You missed me by millimeters. What about Mom, Emily, and Vessna?"

"They're safe, Buck. At least I think they're safe. I guess they're at least as safe as anyone can be from Maanka Dak. There's no way to get in touch with them without endangering them."

It all began to whirl about, the colors, the floor, the

walls, the feel of Buck's hands holding him up. Just before George went completely unconscious, he reminded himself, upon awakening, to ask Buck how in the hell he had gotten past all of the police officers, Maanka Dak, and the locks, and had gotten into the basement.

CHAPTER 18

"I WOULDN'T WORRY about anyone sneaking in through the basement, Dad. I can't see how anyone could be quiet and make his way through that mess of Emily's down there."

The darknesses in the living room seemed to swim before George's eyes as he rested on the couch. "How did you get in, Buck? I'm certain I locked everything down there from the inside. I must have checked it half a dozen times."

"A secret of my youth, Dad."

"What secret? What are you talking about?"

"I've had a secret passage into the house ever since the summer we moved in. Remember that time you caught me coming out of that concrete storm drain behind the house?"

"Yes. You said you'd been trapped in there."

"I lied, sort of."

"Sort of?"

"Well, Dad, I was caught, wasn't I? That's sort of like being trapped . . . isn't it?"

"I don't know, Buck. What do you think?"

"I think I lied."

"I think you're right." George half sat up, felt the room spinning, and eased himself back down on the couch. "How do you get from the drain into the basement?"

"About two-thirds of the way up there's a big hole in the concrete pipe. I figure it must've crumbled during an old earth tremor. Anyway, when I first found it, I got my flashlight and went back. The storm water going through the pipe carved out quite a little chamber in there between the huge rocks they used for fill. Anyway, it's right next to the basement. It took a lot of digging and a bit of work with a rock chisel, but I loosened four of the concrete blocks behind the furnace for a door. That way I could go in and out whenever I wanted."

George nodded and was about to demand a listing of the times in the past Buck had sneaked out of the house when something more important occurred to him. "Buck, does anyone else know about your secret passage? Any of your friends? Emily?"

"No. I never told anyone about it. I never told any of my friends." He was silent for a moment. "Emily might know, though. I never told her, but back then she used to follow me around like a puppy. She might've seen me go in or out or stumbled across it and figured it out for herself. Do you think she'd tell any of her friends?"

"I don't know. I don't even know if it's important." George tried his eyes again and was treated with a light show in kaleidoscopic patterns of oranges, reds, and golds. He closed his eyes and let his head relax on the couch's thick armrest. "Buck, I know you were frightened after that nightmare at the university, but why didn't you call me here at home?"

"I tried. Every time there was either no answer or I got a wrong number. Some police command center."

"That's right," George said. "They've routed all of the calls through a central board for tracing and screening purposes. I don't see why they wouldn't have sent your calls through, though. Some kind of computer foul-up."

"Dad, right after I found out about Roger Dillon getting killed by that campus cop, I tried to call Mom at her office. All I got hold of was someone who wouldn't tell me what was going on and kept pumping me for information about where I was. Then I heard on the news about Mark Diaz and what happened. I tried to call here a dozen times and got nothing."

George kept still and listened to the silence as Buck paused to take the fear from his voice. He wasn't very successful.

"Dad, I tried to call you and Matt, but no one could track either of you down. Then I remembered your old training officer, the hard-ass you hated so much after you graduated from the academy."

"Bill Duncan?"

"Yes. I tried to get hold of him."

George opened his eyes and studied the flaming red and turquoise silhouette of his son. The lights in the living room were off, yet the sight before him was electrified in brilliant colors. It was almost as though he could see heat through a computer-enhanced video setup. George rubbed his eyes and nodded. "That's when you found out that Bill Duncan was dead too. It must've been very frightening."

"He's dead, Dad, and not only that. Another cop

killed him. There are bodies littered all over L.A. today, and most of them were dusted out by law enforcement employees. Duncan, Mark Diaz, that campus cop at the university, and that warden who hosed down all the people at the McBeaver's on Soto. That's why I wasn't real keen about bringing my problem to my friend Mr. Policeman on the corner, if you get my meaning."

"I'm hip."

"I called the day care center and Emily's school and found out that Mom had picked up the girls, but both times I ran into someone who was short on answers and long on questions about me and my location. Who was I supposed to trust?"

"Not that voice on the telephone, that's for certain. You did very well, Buck, and we are very, very lucky. I'm as proud of you as I can be."

George opened his eyes and saw the red silhouette rest its head in its hands.

"I've never been so scared in my entire life, Dad."

"Including before the crash?"

"The Overseers ran some horrors, but we knew who the Overseers were. Damned right I was scared, but what they did on the ship was done by rules we all understood. I don't know what's going on here, who's doing it, why it's being done, and does anyone know the rules?"

"I'm not sure."

George saw the silhouette turn toward him.

"Dad, who was that voice on the telephone? Who is Maanka Dak, and what in Celine's name is happening?"

George closed his eyes and asked, "Do you remember the *Ahvin Yin?*"

"Sure. The resistance. The young children used to

worship them. Do you remember the game we used to play after we left planet Itri Vi?"

"Su nas otas. I remember. It was sort of like the hide-and-seek game children here play. As I recall it, though, *su nas otas* was more like hide, seek, and destroy."

"It was always the *Ahvin Yin* versus the Overseers, Dad." Buck paused for a moment, then continued, his voice strangely thoughtful. *"Su nas otas,"* he repeated. "Us and them. *Su nas otas."*

"What is it?"

The silhouette of Buck shook its head. "Something. Just something I'm supposed to think about." The figure turned its head to face George. "What was it about the *Ahvin Yin?"*

"Maanka Dak was the leader of the resistance. Years ago, during the course of an arrest, I killed Maanka's biological brother and wounded Maanka. He and his accomplice swore the *vikah ta* against me and the memory of me. That's what's going on out there right now. That's why all those persons are dead."

"I don't understand, Dad. The way I remember it, the *vikah ta* can't be sworn against someone unless the individual is a particularly cruel Overseer or a member of the *Ahvin Yin* who betrays the resistance."

George frowned as he realized how ashamed he was of the words he was about to say. "Buck, I became a member of the *Ahvin Yin* on planet Itri Vi."

"You, Dad?" The thrilled admiration in his son's voice did little to alter the shame he still felt. "Yes. For a time I became Maanka and Sita Dak's brother in the resistance." As he said the words, George felt the weight of centuries lift from his hearts. The red and turquoise faded to the dark shadows of the living room.

"I never had a clue. That makes you a hero. That—"

"No, Buck. That only makes me a parent who was frightened for his family."

There was a puzzled silence, then Buck said, "We always heard that the only way to get into the *Ahvin Yin* was to execute an enemy of the resistance."

"That's correct."

"You killed someone, Dad? I mean, not in a fight or defending yourself? You executed someone? An Overseer?"

"It was a Niyezian on Itri Vi," George answered in a whisper. The justifications for what he had done, his dead parents, the suffering of his family, the suffering of all of the slaves by the pain ministers, were dammed up in his chest, threatening to burst forth to try to excuse what he had done for the sake of his son's continued love. He remained silent for the same reason.

George felt Buck's hand on his shoulder, and he placed his own hand atop Buck's. "You know, your mother and I were planning on putting you on the griddle tonight about all the classes you've missed." His shoulders shrugged slightly. "As selfish as it sounds, and as sorry as I feel for Roger Dillon's parents, I'm grateful that you cut class today." He held his son's hand and squeezed it.

"Dad, I suppose you still want me to tell you where I've been for the past three weeks."

"If you want to tell me, I'm willing to listen."

Buck rose from the chair and walked until he stood in front of the living room's picture window. With his

Barry B. Longyear

back toward his father, he said, "Dad, for a long time I've been searching for something. I didn't know what it was. Belonging, meaning, some way of looking at myself, knowing what I saw, and feeling good about it. On the ship we were property: labor units designed, built, owned, and operated by persons we never saw. Purpose for us was to serve the purposes of others; purposes we never knew or understood." He held out his hands.

"But here on Earth, in America, we're told purpose is our own individual choice. What I want to do with my life is my own thing. That would be tough enough to deal with for a Newcomer, but on top of that is everybody else who thinks that my purpose is to serve either their purpose or the purpose of whatever fantasy it is they have about me."

He turned and faced his father. "That's exactly why I was to be placed on the griddle tonight. You and Mom have a purpose in mind for me, and I wasn't living up to your plan. Right?"

"Go on."

Buck returned his gaze to the shadows in the front yard. "There are others—perhaps everyone—with purposes for me to fulfill. The ones who call me 'slag' think I ought to change, become human, or get on a rocket and get the hell off the planet. At the very least, they want me to do less than I can do. They want me to get lower grades, perform less strongly at athletics, and earn less money than I'm capable of earning. *Su nas otas,* right? Us and them. If 'us' can keep 'them' down, it may not make 'us' any wealthier, but it will decrease the amount of envy 'us' has to carry. At least I can understand that."

"What don't you understand, Buck?"

Again he faced his father. "It's my fellow 'thems'

that want to keep me down—the Newcomers, slags, rubberheads—my own parents. That's what I don't understand."

George pushed himself up to a sitting position and placed his feet on the floor. "Buck, your mother and I only want the best for you."

"But who figures out what's best? Who knows what's best for anyone else? Dad, the things that were best back on the ship—fitting in, blending, not making any waves, doing what you're told—that was fine for a particular time and place. But we're here now." He waved his hand, dismissing his own digression.

"Dad, I was searching for something, a direction; perhaps I was even looking for some reason to be proud of what I am—proud of being Tenctonese. I heard about a special school in south-central L.A. run by a few Elders. It was said that they dealt in the kinds of questions and answers I was thinking about."

"Did you find what you were looking for, Buck?"

The young man burst out with a cynical laugh. "Well, no. Not exactly. The first thing I learned, Dad, was that the racial pride I was seeking was an intellectually dishonest attempt to create a false self-esteem from the real and fictional accomplishments of others. The 'thems,' I also learned, don't exist. I was thrown out of the school by my *Hila* until I can solve the mystery of the flower and the weed. While I'm working on that, I am supposed to find a black man, a white man, a red man, and a yellow man, none of whom exist." He folded his arms in disgust.

"What is the consistently identifiable referent for any of the racial 'us' and 'them' terms out there?" Buck asked. "A fellow named Berry wrote that races aren't real things that man's discovered. They're pigeonholes man has constructed. The problem is that most of humanity—and I include us in humanity—most of humanity doesn't fit the pigeonholes. We aren't talking about anything. I have found French vanillas, toasts, Devonshire creams, blush beiges, pebbles, king's pinks, and chiffons, but no red, no black, no yellow, no white. I guess the answer to your question, Dad, is: no. I haven't found what I'm looking for. The problem is that I don't even know if what I'm looking for even exists." He glanced back over his shoulder. "And now's when you're supposed to say 'I told you so' and nag me back to school."

"No, Buck. I'm not going to do that. You do what you need to do for you."

"But you'd rather I went back to the university."

"This morning the answer to that would've been yes. Now, though, I think there is something very important for you to learn at this school."

"Honest?"

George opened his eyes and was grateful to find his current reality properly colored and shaded. He placed his hands on his knees and struggled to a standing position. "Buck, what I'm going through right now gives an individual moments of insight. Perhaps they are even flashes of brilliance. I tracked down a wanted killer today because of it: the Thunderbolt."

"No kidding? I hadn't heard anything about it."

"I imagine it's been driven out of the news by all of the other things that've been happening today. In any event, I think I've solved your *Hila*'s mystery of the flower and the weed."

"You have? What is it?"

George stood at his son's side and placed his arm across Buck's shoulders. "It's something so simple, it's almost impossible to see. Buck, you're looking for a simple answer with a head tuned to complexities. The answer to the mystery of the flower and the weed is so simple it's invisible unless a particular window in your brain is open. The answer to the mystery is important, but it's nowhere near as important as opening that window. If I told you the answer, you would never learn what it is you need to learn through the search for that answer."

"You talk just like the Elder."

"I'd like to meet your *Hila.*"

"Aman Iri asked me some time ago to tell you about the *Rama Vo.* He seems to think he can help you too. I told him about how weird you were acting this morning, and he seemed to think it had something to do with a changing."

"Riana."

Buck's eyes went wide. *"Riana?* Are you dying? Dad—"

"No, son. I'm not dying. I'm becoming something different. A doctor with a bit of experience in *riana* suggested that I see a *Hila* about it. I—" Someone wearing a light-colored jacket ran across the front lawn beneath the window. "Did you see that?"

"See what, Dad?"

"Someone—something running past the window," he whispered.

"A man?"

"It looked like a man. It could've been a man. Let's get away from the window." George reached to his holster and found it empty. "My gun!"

Hellishly loud pounding came from the front door as the doorbell rang and a voice shouted. "George! Damn it all to hell, George, let me in!"

"It's Matt!" George fumbled with the locks and eye hooks on the door, trying to open them. "That idiot is out there in full view. Buck, turn on the hall light so I can see these damned locks."

The light came on, and squinting against the brightness, George flipped hooks and turned back the two dead bolts. As he turned to tell Buck to turn off the lights, he saw a smear of dried blood on Buck's left eyelid. Letting his gaze travel down the length of Buck's arm, he saw that his gun was in Buck's hand.

"Matt, watch out!" he screamed as he grabbed Buck's wrist, held up the gun, and slammed his son into the door of the hall closet. The front door burst open behind him.

"George?" Matt called.

"Turn off the light, Matt! Dak's got one of those damned things in Buck's head!"

"Dad, what're you talking about—" Buck began, then kneed his father in the stomach. "Get out of the way, Dad! Get down!"

George doubled over just as a shot exploded next to his head. He looked around and saw Matt aiming his automatic at Buck. Buck was sliding down the door, a bad gash along the right side of his head, a bullet hole in the closet door. Matt was taking aim again, between Buck's eyes, and George grabbed his partner's wrist and swung his aim wide. Matt fired twice, one round shattering the hall mirror, the second digging into the hardwood floor.

"Matt! Stop shooting! Matt!" He could see Matt's face: his eyes. He had no mark, no cut, no scab on his eyelid. It simply couldn't be. "Matt, stop it!"

Sikes kicked George's feet out from beneath him and aimed his weapon again as the back of George's head struck the floor. The universe filled with giant streamers of hot pink, electric blue, and Big Bird yellow. George knew he should roll, but he was so woozy he couldn't make up his mind which way he should go. He looked up and, in between the streamers, saw the muzzle of Matt's gun staring him in the face. In the next split second he heard a strange metallic clank, then Matt was lying facedown on top of him, out cold, his trigger finger automatically pumping round after round into the baseboard. In a matter of a few seconds the weapon was out of ammunition, but Matt's finger kept pulling the trigger.

George looked up through a haze of brightly colored geometric images to see Cathy Frankel standing there with the heavy iron skillet Emily had left on the front steps. "George, are you all right?" she asked.

He turned his head to the right. "Buck. Look at Buck. Is he alive?"

Cathy dropped the skillet, reached down, took Matt's handcuffs and cuffed Matt Sikes's hands behind him. As she did so, tears filled her eyes. She pulled Matt off George's legs then went and checked Buck. As she lifted first one eyelid, then the next, Buck moaned. "He's alive. We ought to get him to a hospital, though. That bullet put a nasty crease in his head. He might have a concussion."

"He saved my life. That bullet was mine."

"He's a good kid."

George got to his knees and bent over his son. "What about his eye? Look there. Maanka Dak stuck one of those things through his eyelid."

Cathy dried her tears with the heels of her hands and squatted next to Buck. She examined his eyelid and shook her head. "No. There's no penetration. He has a scratch on his eyelid. A little cut, that's all."

"Are you certain? After all, he managed to get in here, eluding all of the officers out there—"

"What officers? There are none. Your admirer, Maanka Dak, must have sent them all away." Cathy nodded her head toward Matt's now still form. "He's the one implanted with a neural controller." She grabbed the closet's doorknob and pulled herself to her feet. "You better call an ambulance while I pack him in ice. We have to lower his temperature to halt the implant's biofilament invasion."

"Will he live?"

"Matt said the only humans who've had these implants have turned homicidal and either killed themselves or were gunned down."

George picked up his gun from the floor, holstered it, and got to his feet. He looked from Buck to Matt and looked again at Matt's eyes. "He doesn't have a mark on his eyelid. How could he be implanted? Warden Rand, Mark Diaz, Bill Duncan—they all had wounds on their left eyelids."

"I'm not sure," Cathy answered, "but I know that the implants the Overseers used on the ship didn't always need to be inserted that way. When the controllers were implanted over the eye, it was usually for punishment purposes. Pain control. The long-term control implants were more sophisticated. It took a very specialized instrument. The controller would be inserted through a blood vessel." She opened Matt's collar and pulled it away from his neck. "The controllers on the ship were considerably smaller than the crude thing Matt described to me from the Rand autopsy." She pointed toward an almost invisible hematoma on Matt's neck beneath his ear.

"There." She frowned and pursed her lips. "That implant wasn't done with any tool whipped up in a China Lake prison workshop. Maanka Dak's gotten his hands on a *tivati urih*. The implantation instrument with which the Niyez supplied the Overseers before we left Itri Vi. We better call an ambulance."

"I don't think that would be a very good idea."

"Why?"

"I don't think we can trust whoever shows up."

Cathy stared at George for a moment, then frowned as she slowly shook her head. "No. As a matter of fact, we can't. George, the reason I came out here is because something funny happened when Matt made a call to Lieutenant Bradley at the command center. It bothered me, so I called the station from a neighbor's phone after Matt left and talked to the lieutenant outside the command center. The lieutenant had never talked to Matt. Routing communications through that command center made it real easy for Maanka Dak to intercept calls. If you called from your phone, I have no doubt that you'd reach Maanka's personal switchboard."

"Susan's got my car. Give me your keys."

Cathy reached into her jacket pocket and threw George the keys to her station wagon. "I'm parked a couple houses east. Be careful." She turned and walked off toward the kitchen.

George looked down at his son and his partner. "Where has being careful gotten us?"

"Dad? Dad?"

George squatted next to Buck and squeezed his son's shoulder. "I'm here."

"Are you all right?"

"I'm all right. Just take it easy. We're going to get you to help soon."

"Dad, it was Matt. Dak got Matt. Will he be all right?"

"I don't know, son. Just lie quietly for a bit. I have to get Cathy's car."

He stood, turned, and looked through his open front door, knowing that he was lighted from the back and ignoring it. He looked east and west, across the street and around his own house. All of the police officers, uniformed, disguised, on foot and riding, were gone. Maanka Dak had pressed the right buttons, said the right words, and everybody had called it a wrap. When the nightmare first started, Maanka's twisted talents had frightened him.

"Maanka!" he shouted into the night as his fear and concern for himself, his friends, and family mutated into rage. He stepped out onto the small landing. "Maanka Dak! Start running now, *vuloch!* I'm coming for you!"

As the sound of his voice was absorbed by the shadows, George heard a whimper, a woman crying. He drew his revolver and reached into the doorway. As he turned on the outside light he saw what had been making the noise. Near the sidewalk, coming from behind the neighbor's azalea, was a Tenctonese woman wearing only a police uniform shirt with the left sleeve hanging in ribbons. As she came fully into view, George could see the black wound in the front of her left thigh. Her eyes were sunken and haunted, the eyelid of her left eye crusted with dried blood.

Ruma Kavit, George thought. Bill Duncan's missing partner. That was how Maanka had gotten to Matt Sikes. Matt was hard-bitten, cynical, suspicious, and made that way from years of banging his head against crime and the brutality of criminals, cops, and civilians who no longer cared about the rights and wrongs of anything. But show him a hurt kitten, an injured child, or a weeping girl, and Matt Sikes would follow his stupid, predictable heart right into his own grave.

She carried her service revolver in her right hand.

Her arm was limp, the muzzle of the weapon pointed at the concrete path.

"Ruma Kavit?" George asked, aiming his weapon at her. He knew that Kavit served a double purpose. Besides luring Matt into a vulnerable position, she was Maanka's plan B, in case the implanted Matt Sikes didn't achieve the intended objectives. Dak's plan B called for either Ruma Kavit to kill George or for George to kill Officer Kavit, which would be almost as destructive. "Ruma Kavit?"

The woman nodded, her eyes glistening. "Yes."

"Drop the gun."

"I can't. I'm sorry, but I can't." She raised her arm, aimed her revolver at George, and fired at the same time George leaped back through the door. He dove for the floor as two rounds in quick succession chewed into the frame of the already shattered hall mirror. Rolling to his side, George saw that Ruma Kavit was on the front steps, the gun aiming at his face. Buck raised a hand and tried to get up.

"Stay down!" George bellowed as he rolled to the opposite side, a slug splintering the floor next to his head. As he rolled past the skillet, he grabbed it and held it in front of his face. Ruma fired a fourth time, and the lead striking the frying pan made a hellishly loud bonging sound. George heard a clicking sound, and he looked from behind the skillet.

She was standing there, her face in tears, her gun aimed at George, and she was pulling the trigger again and again, the hammer falling on spent shells. She swooned against the door, and George got up and caught her before she fell to the concrete. Picking her up in his arms, he turned and stepped into the house. Buck, his back up against the closet door, nodded at the frying pan still in George's left hand.

"Boy, Dad, I bet Emily's going to catch it for not putting away the skillet."

George looked dumbly at the pan, then up at Cathy. She was standing at the end of the short hall, a plastic bag full of ice cubes in her hands, staring at George. "Who is she? What happened?"

George looked down into Ruma Kavit's tortured face. "One of Maanka's victims; still alive." He looked from Cathy to Buck and Matt as he felt his knees buckle and the universe began melting, revealing the living hearts of stars.

"Let's get to Mount Andarko emergency. Cathy, you better drive."

Every part, every aspect, every direction, every mood had its twist, mark, and color. On the drive to the Tenctonese hospital, George witnessed and reacted to the entire range of everything his hallucinations had to offer. There were colors that he heard, sounds that he saw. Tastes had touches and touches had tastes. Everything in the universe had an odor, and each odor filled his nervous system with numbing electric shocks. Matt's head was on his lap, each of his eyes a tiny mouth crying, gasping for air.

"It'll be okay, partner. It'll be okay."

CHAPTER 19

THE MORNING LIGHT came through the window gray and dirty. Some part of George's awareness noted the light, the fact of morning. The barely audible beep of Matt's vital signs monitor showed his partner's heart barely beating. His respirations were down to six a minute and his temperature was down in the forties. None of the red danger lights were flashing. All but Matt's face was submerged in a refrigerated bath that was cold enough to make steam in the warm room. In another room, in an identical bath, Ruma Kavit's monitors showed her equally suspended between death and the activation temperature of the controller implanted in her brain.

Because of Dr. Rivers's experience with the implants, George had asked him to assist Cathy and the emergency room staff. Shortly after two in the morning the X rays showed the astonishing differences between the crude version of the implant in Ruma's brain and the almost microscopic sophistication of Matt's implant.

"That's a Niyezian implant," Cathy had said as she examined the negative. "Nothing at China Lake could produce something that delicate."

Dr. Rivers from the morgue had nodded, paused, and then slowly shook his head. "Where would he get a Niyezian implant, and where would he get the instrument to do the operation?"

"From the ship?" George had asked. "From the wreck of the ship?"

Cathy had thought for a moment. "Everything from the ship was emptied or cut out and sent to I don't know how many different government military and scientific facilities. Even the pieces of the ship itself are stored in a Smithsonian warehouse somewhere in Virginia."

"Virginia," George muttered now to his unconscious partner. There was something else. Something that Muddy Rivers had said.

The doctor had frowned and folded his arms across his chest. "What I can't get out of my head is how vehemently opposed that FBI agent was to you and Sikes attending the Rand autopsy. Why do you suppose that was?"

"Why?" George repeated to himself as his gaze moved up to Matt's vital signs monitor. Things seemed to connect for him, knots seemed to unravel.

What Maanka had placed deep within Matt's brain was something that a federal prisoner had no way of obtaining. "Unless," George said to the silence. He focused on a point in space and bore down on the thought. "Unless."

All of the records on Dak had been wiped. There was, however, that sheet of paper in Maanka's case file. Thank the powers of the universe that Matt Sikes hated computers and still relied upon scraps of scribbled paper in manila folders. Maanka Dak simply could not have gotten his hands on those controllers, "Unless," George repeated.

He looked around the room and found a wall phone next to the door. Taking his notebook from his pocket, he stood, walked to the phone, and dialed the number for the station's maintenance department. After five rings a voice answered, "Maintenance. This is Albert speaking."

"Albert, this is George."

"You're all right?" Relief flooded Albert's voice. "I was so worried, and no one'd tell me anything. All they'll tell me is to stay out of sight, don't stick my nose out of the station, and empty the wastebaskets. What about Susan and the children? What about Matt? What about that officer from University Division?"

"Ruma Kavit. She's critical. Matt too. Everyone else's as good as can be expected right now. Albert, I want you to do me a favor."

"Sure, George. Anything. What do you want me to do?"

"I want you to go upstairs, get Captain Grazer, and have him come to the phone."

A puzzled silence filled the moment. "Why don't you call him yourself, George? Captain Grazer's surrounded by phones up there."

"I don't have time to explain, Albert. There's something wrong with the captain's phones. Have him go down in the basement and use the phone you're holding in your hand right now. Tell him to bring the Maanka Dak case file from my desk. Got that?"

"It's not like the captain ever listens to me. I just sweep up around here. What if I can't get him to come, George? What if he just tells me to scram?"

"Threaten him, damn it! I don't care! Just get him to the phone and don't forget the file! Hurry!"

As he heard Albert running up the stairs, George felt ashamed at having yelled at his friend and *binnaum,* the being who completed the triad necessary to the conceptions of George's two daughters. The threat of Maanka Dak seemed to be staining everything in the universe with hate, anger, and suspicion. Dak left little remaining for love, compassion, understanding, or courtesy.

In a few moments there were the sounds of heavy footsteps and Captain Grazer's loud cursing. "What?" he bellowed into the phone. "Francisco? What in the hell is going on? Why did you have Albert pull a gun on me?"

"A gun?"

"A goddamned shotgun! He stole the damned thing from the arms room! He's got the muzzle stuck in my back right now!"

"Put Albert on, Cap."

There were a few words as Albert came on the line. "Yes, George?"

"Thanks Albert. You did great."

"Gosh, George. I was glad to do it."

"You can give the gun back to whoever you got it from, Albert, and I'm sorry I yelled at you."

"That's okay, George."

"Put the captain back on and don't forget to put the safety on the shotgun, okay?"

"I didn't load the gun, George. I don't know how."

"That's okay, Albert. Thanks again. Put the captain on."

Grazer's gruff voice returned. "Thanks for calling off your artillery, Francisco. So what's so goddamned urgent, and why am I standing here in the middle of mop city talking to you about it?"

"Maanka Dak is tapped into the command center network. More than that, his computer setup controls it. I'm not certain, but I have pretty good evidence that Maanka also does pretty good impressions of you, Lieutenant Bradley, and Lieutenant Yamato."

"What're you talking about? The command center lines're secure. Christ, we certainly paid enough for the computer setup and the daily leak sweeps."

George felt, growing within him, a grudging admiration for Maanka Dak's daring. What could Maanka have achieved had his aim not been crippled by hate? "Captain, I think you'll find that at least one of the electronic sweeps for system leaks was done by either Maanka Dak or Sing Fangan. In fact, considering when the Dak task force set up its command center, Maanka Dak himself could have installed the computer communications."

"That's impossible. Everyone who's ever come near the center is security cleared up the wazoo."

"Captain Grazer, all Maanka Dak needed to do was enter the LAPD computer and create a couple of phony files keyed to whatever name he used. We already know he entered the police computer and wiped his own files."

"I don't know, Francisco. We're using the most advanced computer technology in the world. Ultra secure. I don't see how a damned convict—"

"That's his legal, and perhaps social, status, Captain. It has nothing to do with his mental capabilities. Let me ask you something. Were you the one who canceled the police security on my house last night?"

"Canceled? What are you talking about? I've been getting regular reports from Lieutenant Blackwell's crew covering your place, and from Sergeant Lupo covering the motel where we stashed Sikes and his girlfriend." There was a brief, puzzled pause, then the captain's voice came back on the line. "How in the hell did you call the maintenance number without the call going through the command center?"

"I'm calling from Mount Andarko."

"The Newcomer hospital? What's wrong? How come nobody flagged the command center about you moving from your home?"

"As I said, Captain, Maanka Dak controls the command center. All security was pulled off my home hours ago. Check it out, but don't use any lines controlled by the command center. I'm here at the hospital with Cathy Frankel. We took my son, Matt Sikes, and Ruma Kavit here. We need some security here and fast."

"Ruma Kavit? You mean the missing probie?"

"Yes. I'll fill you in on what happened, at least as much as I know, when I see you again. Right now we need some handpicked security over here."

"I'll get right on it. What happened?"

"Buck was grazed when Matt Sikes tried to shoot me. Matt's been implanted, Captain. I think his best chance is here where some of the staff has had some experience with the neural controllers."

Grazer's voice was silent for a long time. When it came back, it was trembling. "I think it's just getting through to me what this Maanka Dak's done—what he can do. Jesus, I got to shut down that entire command center. We're running the entire search and investigation out of there."

"That might be a mistake, cap. Don't shut it down.

Keep running it business as usual. If Maanka doesn't know we're on to him, it might give us some kind of an edge. Maybe it'll keep him busy putting on a show for you while we sneak up on him."

"It sounds like you're taking that shuttle to Fantasyland."

"Maybe. If I had better suggestions, Cap, I'd let you have them."

Grazer let the air sigh from his lungs, and Francisco could hear the cellophane wrapper coming off another cigar. "Okay. We can keep the show going for a while. How's your boy?"

"He'll be all right. Matt and Ruma Kavit are the ones with problems. Kavit's been implanted, but the doctors here think that it can be removed from her brain without a lot of damage. After all, the technology was designed for Tenctonese neural systems. However, she's also been wounded twice. She was raped too."

"Raped?"

"Does that surprise you?"

"Surprise me?" The sound of Grazer spitting out his cigar came through the phone. "No, it doesn't surprise me. Nothing in this goddamned city surprises me anymore. I'll send a cop shrink over there along with the officers for when Kavit comes out of it. I'm going to have to set up another command center. Hell, it's going to take hours. All of the officers in the task force have been sent home, right?"

"Most likely."

"Damn. All their phones are routed through the command center, and we can't risk sending black-and-whites after them by radio. I'll have to send out cars from the station and drive to each house. Jesus, what a mess."

"Captain, do you have the case file on Dak with you?"

"Yeah. Machine Gun Albert there had me pick it up when he stuck that shotgun in my back. What am I looking for?"

"There was a copy of a letter in there. It was from a Dr. Norcross addressed to Maanka Dak's next parole hearing."

"Yeah. It's right here. Carrie Norcross, chief of neurosurgery at the Walter Reed Army Medical Center."

"Walter Reed?"

"That's right, George. The army medical center in Washington D of C. We've grilled some of the prisoners at China Lake, and we've heard everything from this Norcross having the hots for Maanka Dak to wanting to spring him so she could take him into her private practice, making big bucks through benevolent mind control. Why?"

"Cap, I want you to find out everything you can about Dr. Norcross, the official stuff, but particularly the nonofficial stuff. I want to know everything she's done with Dak, with the Bureau of Prisons, and any and everything else."

"What's the drift?"

"I'm not certain. Right now Matt has something stuck in his brain that cannot be stuck in his brain unless at some point Maanka Dak had a direct pipeline to some very powerful people who have broken some rather important laws. Also, I'm guessing that this Carrie Norcross is the only one who can get her hands on an instrument vital to saving Matt's life, if it can be saved at all."

The door to the room opened quietly and Buck

peered in. The right side of his head was bandaged and his right eye was swollen shut. "Dad?"

"One moment, son." George frowned and turned back to the phone. "Cap, later on I'll come in, tie in with the new command center, and get the information you gather on Norcross. About setting up the command center, Cap . . ."

"What about it?"

"Set up a portable X ray, and don't let anyone into the command center until they've had their heads cleared. I'll have Cathy bring over a couple of X rays to show you what to look for."

"That's a pretty good shot of radiation just to get in to work. We're going to get a few objections to that."

"Let them object. Send them home for the day. The alternative is putting Maanka Dak on the payroll."

After hanging up the phone, George went over to Matt's side and looked down at his partner. Buck entered the room and stood at his father's side. "Will Matt be all right?"

"I don't know. It doesn't look good at all. How come you aren't in bed? I thought the doctor wanted to keep you overnight for observation."

"I have a headache, Dad, but otherwise I'm fine. Just about the last thing I want to do right now is lie around in bed."

"Buck, you need rest. And the doctor wants—"

"Dad, what's easier to shoot: a moving target or a sitting duck? I don't figure I'm going to get much rest here with my family on the run and this Maanka Dak waiting for me to stay still so he can get a bead on me."

George glanced at his son, nodded, and placed his hand on Buck's shoulder. "I get your point. You can't go home, though."

"Dad, what're you going to do? You can't go to work. I can't go to the university. Are they going to stash us with Mom and the girls?"

"I don't know, Buck. If you were Maanka Dak, what would you be waiting for us to do?"

Buck thought for a second, then met his father's gaze. "If *vikah ta* was the only thing on my mind, I'd be waiting for us to lead the way to the rest of the family."

"Then maybe it's time for us to begin being unpredictable."

"How are we going to do that?"

"To begin, I think instead of having Cathy bring over those X rays, I'll take them myself and help Captain Grazer find out about this Carrie Norcross."

"The doctor who was working with Dak?"

"Yes. Too many things are pointing to a federal connection to this mess, and we need to know what it is." He placed a hand on Buck's shoulder. "First, though, how about some breakfast?"

"Okay. Then we go to the new command center?"

George shook his head and opened the door for Buck. "No. After we eat, we're going to visit the *Rama Vo*. I've been putting off who I am and where I am in life for far too long."

CHAPTER 20

"THIS IS A disaster," Collins muttered. The representative of the Bureau of Prisons wiped a hand over his balding head and stared glumly at the center of the small steel conference table.

"SNAFUBAR," Rittenhouse agreed glumly. He was an older suit from the National Security Agency. "I figure our only hope is to give the story to the tabloids so no one will believe it once it breaks." No one even forced a polite chuckle at the joke. It was too close to the kinds of answers they had been considering deep within the administrative walls of the China Lake facility.

Lipscomb sucked at a tooth, shook his head and said, "If you and Iniko had controlled this thing at the autopsy—"

"How?" Collins demanded. "Were we supposed to throw out those two showboat pathologists? Or that

Greek chorus from Hollenbeck Division? Hell, Ritt makes sense. Let's call the *National Turd Flinger* and tell all."

"This story is not going to break," Lipscomb said. "All we have here is a simple spin problem. Damage control; perception polishing."

FBI Agent Paul Iniko sat stone-faced in the Spartan conference room as Morton Lipscomb, the appointee of the Director of Central Intelligence, looked around the white-painted room for effect. The effect didn't appear to be what the well-groomed fellow from the CIA obviously wanted.

How does one put a good face on a couple of massacres? Especially when the disasters had been made possible by an ambitious scientist in bed with an ambitious intelligence community, both of them drooling over the possible applications of Niyezian neural control technology?

The possibilities were towering. For a suffering world, most kinds of mental illness could be simply programmed away. Many of those that were genetic in origin could be patched over by activating the full potential of other portions of the brain. Many physical ailments could be eliminated, as well. The power of the mind had never been in doubt. Control of that power had been the stumbling block, and neural transmitters modified not to turn humans into homicidal maniacs might be the answer. And the scientist would get the credit, the fame, the Nobel Prize, the adulation of a suffering earth.

The intelligence community was thrilled at the prospect of no longer having to explain to oversight committees why there were no agents of a particular type in a particular hot spot when, with a little shuffle at a diplomatic function, the intelligence chief of the aforementioned hot spot could become an instant, unsalaried, and totally reliable operative of the CIA.

So, why not supply Maanka Dak with everything he needed to reinvent neural controllers? Even better, have the scientist set up a top secret research station nearby with a batch of the controllers and some of the implantation instruments recovered from the ship. Dak needed the information, supplies, and instruments for his work, and after all, he had promised to be a good boy and work for the advancement of science, the security of the American way, and the betterment of all mankind. And everybody thought that everybody else was keeping watch on Maanka Dak, except Tom Rand. He knew watching Maanka Dak was his job. Curiously enough, however, Warden Rand was, for security reasons, the only one cut out of the loop.

So Maanka used his crude implant to bust out of China Lake. Then he obtained a computer that could do the things he required, and he tracked down the location of the secret research station and stole the implants and instruments. This gave him the ability to place any Tenctonese under permanent control and any human under temporary control, as long as he was willing to risk the consequences of that minor side effect of the subject becoming a homicidal maniac. Courageous researcher that he was, Dak appeared more than willing to take such risks.

Everyone had come to the operation with an agenda: power, career, fame, patriotism, getting one for the gipper. They all assumed, of course, that Maanka Dak had an agenda as well. Their mistake was assuming that Dak's agenda was freedom, rehabilitation, and the pursuit of happiness through service to his fellow beings, not to mention quite a few bucks. What no one understood, though, was that Maanka Dak's only agenda was *vikah ta*.

Now, nightmares and massacres later, the information was becoming known and understood outside of the loop, and there was nothing in place to quash it. Their only hope appeared to be that the truth revealed such depths of stupidity and cupidity in high places that no one would want to believe it. In an age forged from Watergate, 'Nam, Iran-Contra, the S&L and BCCI scandals, and institutionalized check kiting in the House of Representatives, such hopes were a vapor in Hell's mouth.

SNAFUBAR.

To Iniko, acronyms had always seemed a mindless human endeavor. They were on a level with puns and reciting baseball statistics. SNAFUBAR, however, was an identification of this operation made by the finger of the universal spirit itself. The truth will out, of course, everybody knows. The Washington spin doctor simply wants to make certain that once out, the truth lies like a bastard.

Collins, although he represented the Bureau of Prisons, was neither a criminologist nor penologist. Neither Rittenhouse from NSA nor Lipscomb from CIA were agents, cryptologists, or analysts. Instead, all three were professional public relations advisors; spin doctors; handlers; conniving, double-dealing, lying bastards.

Part of Paul Iniko's mind avoided asking himself what he was. He knew, and that knowledge was making his head ache. He looked up at Lipscomb with that same stone face and asked, "How exactly does one go about correcting the spin on a prison break and murder of a warden assisted by the federal government that has by last count resulted in over thirty deaths in two separate mass killings?"

Lipscomb flushed slightly, immediately grinned, and leaned back in his chair, his fingertips pressed together. "Now Agent Iniko. How helpful it is to have you wade in at the appropriate moment and smack us in our faces with your fucking guilt brush."

"I apologize. I hadn't intended on wrinkling your serenity."

"Look, pal, I feel bad about all the people—the Newcomers too—who were killed in that crazy mess at the fast food restaurant and that agency over on Wilshire. I'm sorry for them and I feel the pain of their families and loved—"

"You're not on camera, Mort," Rittenhouse interrupted. "Give the poor dead dog a rest."

Lipscomb's face went bright red. "I *do* care!" he protested. "I'm not some kind of super insensitive monster."

"Of course not," Collins said, "although you did manage to squash that story about those CIA supplied weapons the Stavropol Front used to kill all those civilians." He turned to Rittenhouse and raised his eyebrows. "How many deaths was it? Six, seven thou?"

"More like ten. How'd you find out about it? It's not like the Bureau of Prisons was in the loop."

"There are no secrets," Collins answered. "Especially inside the Beltway." He glanced at Lipscomb. "Now, Mort, you were about to tell us all about how you felt the pain of all those dead Ukrainians."

"As you well know, there was nothing we could've done about that, all right? Wallowing through the blood, corpuscle by corpuscle on prime time, wasn't going to bring them back, was it? Would bringing down the administration bring them back? No."

"But you felt their pain," Iniko added.

"I am not about to take this from a fucking goddamned Overseer, Jack! I heard what you bastards did on that ship! Torture, oppression, killing off the old, the diseased, the malcontents. But you're going to tell me you were one of the pilots, right? You were down there in navigation playing with your calculator, or below decks shoveling goddamned coal!" When he noticed the spittle flying from his mouth, Morton Lipscomb calmed himself through sheer willpower and lowered himself to his chair.

"No," Iniko answered. "I wasn't a pilot. The ship didn't have pilots. That would've provided too tempting an opportunity for someone to rebel and take the ship where it wasn't supposed to go."

"That doesn't invalidate the point," Lipscomb insisted.

"No, it doesn't."

"So what did you do, Iniko?" Lipscomb reached out and tapped the tattoo around Paul Iniko's left wrist. "Give us the skinny, boy. We want to know."

"I don't," Rittenhouse said. Turning to Lipscomb, the man from NSA said, "Chill out, Mort. We've all been and done things we don't want our grandkids to find out about. Easy does it. We've got big things to decide on here if we want to find our limos in the garage when we get back to old foggy."

"Go ahead," Lipscomb said to Iniko, ignoring Rittenhouse. "What did you do, man? What did you do, Overseer? What was your contribution to slavery and oppression?"

The conference room was dead silent, save the quiet

hiss of the air circulation system. Collins and Rittenhouse looked embarrassed, and Morton Lipscomb looked as though he could eat live boar, hair and all. Iniko looked down, and where his hands were clasped on the edge of the table, he saw the Overseer's mark surrounding his wrist. There, centered upon the back of his wrist, were the four letter dots that had marked him for what he was to be from the moment of his choosing. He could remember treasuring those marks, the fierce pride he had in being a *charkah*. Later came the shame; later came the pain.

"I did for the creators pretty much what I do now for the bureau," answered Paul. "I was a *charkah;* a watcher." He smiled thinly for the first time. "In other words, I was a police officer."

"Police officer?" Collins repeated. "I didn't think Newcomers needed cops; at least, not on the ship. Didn't they design and engineer you people to obey the rules?"

"Just like the American educational system," Rittenhouse said, "and with about as much success."

"Persons change," Paul Iniko said, "and rules change. Our rules changed a lot, especially after we left Itri Vi."

Rittenhouse snapped his fingers, pointed at Iniko and said, "That's why the local field office picked you. You know all about these neural transmitters."

Iniko shook his head. "No. I have no specialized knowledge concerning Niyezian neural control technology. I was a watcher, not one of the punishers. I fear the reason why I was picked to assist you three gentlemen is no more complicated than that the director dislikes the odor of feces on his fingers."

191

"Feces?" Lipscomb repeated.

"I think he's talking about you, Mort," Rittenhouse said.

Before the man from the CIA could explode again, Paul Iniko interrupted. "The director, I believe, wants nothing to do with what we're doing; in fact, he wants no official bureau recognition of even the existence of this problem. When all of this lands in a committee cesspool, the FBI simply knew nothing about it, Agent Iniko acted on his own. We can toss him to the dogs with no loss. He's an Overseer, you know. Then everyone goes home with clean-smelling fingers."

"Except you," Rittenhouse said.

"As I said, no loss." He nodded toward Rittenhouse and raised his eyebrows. "And thus the spin is adjusted."

Lipscomb shook his head. "Look, this is not going to wind up in front of any damned committee. Maanka Dak, as far as we know, only killed Fangan and that construction equipment salesman."

"Brick Wahl," said Iniko.

"What?"

"His name was Brick Wahl."

"That figures. Very well. As I was trying to say, a good case could be made that Sing Fangan killed Mr. Wahl. Enough of a case, at least, to muddy the media waters."

"What's your point?" Rittenhouse asked.

"The point is, maybe Maanka Dak is simply a fellow who made a daring escape from our nation's newest federal penitentiary. He even might have stopped the murderous rampage of his fellow escapee, which means by the time everything is sorted out, the—"

"By the time everything is sorted out," Iniko interjected, "Maanka Dak turns out to be some sort of bloody folk hero and the local cops nothing but a bunch of insensitive louts straight out of Nottingham, condemned by the media for gunning down Rubberhead Hood. And we'll have to make certain the sheriff's men gun down old Rubberhead, won't we? We don't want any embarrassing testimony coming out in any old nasty trial before King Richard, do we?"

"Iniko," said Lipscomb. "I think you're losing your grip."

"It's even more likely, Lipscomb, that I am about to lose my lunch."

"My, aren't we delicate for a graduate of Simon Legrees R Us? I didn't think you Overseers were terribly concerned with trivialities such as right and wrong."

"We had a very strict code of right and wrong. Much of it is not your code, and much is no longer mine. When it was mine, however, I abided by it. One thing we never did was to place murder aside simply to cover up a blunder." A mask seemed to fall upon Paul Iniko's face as his eyes focused on a point in space.

"Asshole," Lipscomb muttered.

"Gentlemen," Collins broke in, "we might get more done more quickly if Agent Iniko went somewhere else until we've decided what we're going to do."

Rittenhouse reached out a hand and placed it on Iniko's shoulder. "Look, Paul, maybe he's right. What we do is sort of like making sausage in the jungle. The results look, smell, and taste just great, but you don't want to take too close a look at the manufacture or pay much attention to the bacteria count. You especially don't want to swallow it whole. Know what I mean?"

"Sausage." Iniko looked around the table, smiled thinly, and nodded as he placed his hands on the edge of the table and stood up. "Yes, I think I know what you mean. You're right, of course. I'll leave you gentlemen to your sausage making."

Iniko walked briskly from the room, paused at the security post at the end of the hall, and went to the glassed-in gallery that looked out upon the China Lake facility's exercise yard. It was a huge space, grassed in and equipped with a running track, weight-lifting area, tennis and volleyball courts. A high wall surrounded it, but there was no barbed wire, no towers bristling with armed guards. Everywhere Paul Iniko had visited within the China Lake facility had shown him Thomas Rand's care for his prisoners. Not just prisoners, Tenctonese in general, humans in general, everyone in general. Thomas Rand cared. He didn't look at hair or lack of it, accent, color, past, or anything. He knew the flower and the weed for what they were. He had opened that window of his mind long before the Tenctonese came to earth.

At the quarantine camp when Rand had come to talk to his group about law enforcement, Iniko's group had been special, segregated from the rest for its own protection; Overseers. It had made no difference to Warden Rand. He believed that men, women, and children were creatures sacred to the universe, valuable segments of life who had earned the right to be cherished, nurtured, healed, and applauded. Overseers, even Vuurot Iniko, had spent their lives as the "chosen." Hence, the human who regarded them as special hadn't registered at the time. In the years that had passed, however, Iniko had come to realize what a very special human being Tom Rand had been.

The Overseers, by and large, had no interest in law

enforcement. There was a world of opportunity out there, and the newness of that fact had overwhelmed them. Iniko, however, had been interested. There were moments as a watcher that had captured him more strongly than any drug could have done. There were crimes on board the ship, mysteries, puzzles. Who did it? How was it done? How was it to be proven? Those were the things that had captivated the *charkah*.

Others processed the accused; others punished the convicted. He had been insulated from it all on the ship. It had kept the puzzle-solving function clean and fascinating. Tom Rand offered him those puzzles again, and Iniko had accepted.

None of the other Newcomers who had expressed interest in law enforcement were Overseers. The ones who had decided to try out for the few openings that had been made available through Warden Rand's intervention wanted nothing to do with an Overseer, reformed or otherwise. It was Tom Rand who had suggested the FBI and offered to make the arrangements. Iniko would have to go to college, law school, and the bureau academy in Quantico. A lot of work, yes, but he would become a part of the most technologically advanced law enforcement agency in the world. The bait had been irresistible.

Tom Rand would've made a fortune in sales, Iniko thought, because he believed the company lies with all his heart. Iniko sadly shook his head. Tom Rand had his naive areas, and his perception of the FBI had been one of them.

We need to show the media the FBI is affirmative-oriented.

Stick Iniko in front of the camera. A picture of one rubberhead is worth a thousand slags on the payroll.

TV ambush investigators are dropping on the San Francisco office to count colors, sexes, and preferences.

Send Iniko. Once they see the S.F. office has a rubberhead on the staff, they'll back off. Yeah, it's the same slag that was on the air in Washington, but it won't make any difference to the media. They all look alike, right? Be sure to change his tie, though.

For his first two years after graduating from the academy, Paul Iniko had spent most of his time assigned to public relations, with an occasional assignment elsewhere when it was necessary to show congressional types the bureau's token Tenctonese. He had taken on the name Paul at the suggestion of the bureau's own spin doctor.

"Believe you me," he had said, "if the crooks, drunks, and doddering old farts on that congressional committee can look at you and call you Paul or Harry, they'll listen to whatever you have to say. But if you come at them with some kind of Kunta Kinte, Darth Vader handle like Vuurot, all they're going to think is, 'This boy ain't tryin' to get along.' Try to get along, Kunta, and they won't chop off your damned foot."

Puzzles.

Where had all the puzzles gone?

The only assignments he had been given other than showing his bald head before a camera or a committee had involved two separate hostage incidents. Both hostage takers were eventually gunned down. In both cases, by the time Paul Iniko had been called in, there was nothing left to solve, nothing left for him to do, except watch. The man with the gun would have to be taken out, he is Tenctonese, and we needed a bald head among the shooters just to show that the execution wasn't racially motivated. Once the perp was perforated, it was back to public relations.

Down in the exercise yard there was a familiar face among the humans and Tencts. Iniko frowned as he tried to bring back the context of the ship, and place that face within it.

Jarak Ati.

Murder.

On the ship, Jarak Ati had slain another slave to obtain his position. Nothing complicated, it was strictly premeditated murder for gain. Early *riana,* Ati had called it when he eventually confessed. No remorse, no guilt, not even a fear of punishment. Jarak Ati had been a bad piece of engineering. He was part of the evidence that should've sent the creators back to their drawing screens. And here he was again, in prison, for the commission of some serious crime. One didn't get sent to China Lake for jaywalking. Jarak Ati was a criminal, plain and simple. There was no society that had yet been invented in which Jarak Ati would not be a criminal.

How many others from the ship like him, Iniko wondered, were criminals here on earth?

"Tom Rand didn't believe in criminals," he said out loud, the sound of his own voice startling him. He glanced around the gallery. Perhaps the guard on the surveillance monitors had gotten an earful, but Iniko was the only one on the gallery. He shifted his gaze to the exercise yard and the face of Jarak Ati.

Tom Rand didn't believe in criminals, and that was another of the warden's amazing areas of naiveté. There were criminals: beings destined through genetics, environment, or choice to run unrepentantly and habitually counter to any society's rights and wrongs.

During his long time as a *charkah,* he had known many. As he searched the faces in the exercise yard, Paul wondered how many others of his criminals were behind these and similar walls.

Jarak Ati, condemned to be tortured to death for the termination of biological property, had been turned loose by the human immigration officials immediately after the crash. The Overseers had convicted him, hence the conviction by definition had been unjust. Go forth Jarak Ati, among the peoples of Earth, breathe free, fly, and sin no more.

Except some persons were criminals, and if the society has crime, they will be in there committing it, because that is what they do. If prison is the society's way to punish the wrongdoers, they are the ones who will be in there taking up bed space.

Morton Lipscomb had been offended at Paul Iniko slapping him in the mouth with what he called his "guilt brush." Iniko nodded as he remembered the comment. Although he didn't realize it, Lipscomb had been entitled to deliver the rebuke. Paul Iniko figured he had more guilt than anyone else regarding the deeds of Maanka Dak. Back on the ship, he once had Maanka Dak under arrest.

The Overseers never placed murder aside to cover up a blunder, but Vuurot Iniko let a murderer go free for other reasons. Maanka Dak had been arrested for a murder—the murder of Overseer pain minister Torumeh and his family. Torumeh had been a monster, and the murder had been a *vikah ta* slaying of the *Ahvin Yin.* But no matter how just Maanka's act had seemed on the ship, or even here on Earth many years later, a murder is still a murder. A murderer is still a murderer.

Iniko looked down at his hands. His fingers were

wrapped around a metal railing and they were wringing it as though it was the neck of all of the world's problems. He took a breath, let it escape slowly, and glanced back at the security door to the area containing the conference room.

"A murderer is a murderer," he whispered. "And an accomplice is an accomplice."

He smacked the railing with his hands, glanced one last time toward the spin doctors behind the security door, then turned abruptly and headed for the security post that opened onto the parking area.

CHAPTER 21

IN A SUBURB called Friendship Heights, midway between CIA Headquarters in Langley, Virginia, and the Walter Reed Army Medical Center in Washington, D.C., Dr. Carrie Norcross sat in her home office, her gaze fixed to the office's television. She was watching C-Span's coverage of the Senate Intelligence Committee cutback hearings. On the hot seat was CIA Deputy Director Taylor Meade, and the DDI was showing the wear and tear of six hours of testimony. Dr. Norcross studied the image through narrowed eyes as she unconsciously nibbled at the skin on the inside of her lower lip.

"Senator Kinnison," continued DDI Meade, *"I doubt if there is a person in this room more aware of the collapse of the Soviet Union than I, nor more aware of the fiscal consequences. It has even come to my attention that the entire defense posture of the free world has changed, lowering the funding requirements for accu-*

rate intelligence from that area of the world. I do hope, however, that it has not escaped the notice of this committee that there is a vast universe out there peopled with possibly hostile powers whose technical military capabilities far exceed anything once possessed by the former soviets. There is a vast body of scientific—"

"Forgive me for interrupting, Deputy Director Meade," Senator Kinnison said, *"but as I understand the testimony that's been given before this committee, it is virtually impossible that the powers you mentioned know anything about us, Earth, or that a few of their people happened to stray here."*

"It is just as impossible," countered Meade, *"that to Earth is exactly where those people, as you called them, strayed."*

"Now, Senator Kinnison, Deputy Director Reed," interrupted Chairman Ransom Lloyd, *"I don't want to tie up the committee's valuable time with anything more about all those bald folks in Los Angeles. It's old news, twice-chewed cabbage."*

"Old news?" Reed's eyes went wide.

"That's what I said. Over the past few weeks, we've had very convincing testimony before us here, sir, that the whole Newcomer scare is nothing but that: a scare; a hoax. It's a perfectly explainable phenomenon that the media hyped into some kind of Star Wars blowout to sell more time to wig manufacturers. I hear now they even got a hair club for women!"

A wave of laughter met the chairman's words, and the camera panned until the screen filled with DDI Meade's face. The man's jaw was hanging open as his eyes blinked in disbelief. *"Senator Lloyd, are you serious? Do you really believe that the Tenctonese are simply a hoax? Bald people with spots? Over at the*

Smithsonian I can get you a hunk of their damned ship and drag it before this committee!"

"Yessir, I suppose you could. And would you believe we've had Air Force and NASA investigators who've done just that? The stuff just looked like junk to me." Chairman Lloyd raised a hand and shook a finger at the witness. *"And do you know what they told us that ship was made of, sir? Steel, titanium, plastic, and ceramic compounds, just like our own fighters and bombers. I mean, Lockheed could've built it, or maybe those folks with the mouse ears in Anaheim."*

The chairman allowed his joke to exhaust the laughter of the hearing room's audience. *"We're not gullible here in Washington, sir,"* he continued. *"You come in here, stick little green men in our faces, and tell us we have to spend ourselves into bankruptcy to prepare for some kind of funny-book war of the worlds. But, sir, you're goin' to have to do a whole lot better than current metallurgy and a bunch of skinheads to convince this committee. We have very real problems to deal with, sir. There're entire city blocks in Los Angeles and right here in Washington that are still rubble left over from city riots thirty years ago, not to mention the 'ninety-two riots."*

"Mr. Chairman, I cannot believe—" began the junior senator from Maine.

"I'm almost finished, Senator Easton. Now keep your shirt on." Chairman Lloyd faced the witness and clasped his hands as he raised his thin wisps of eyebrows. *"Deppity Director Meade, didn't it ever strike you as just a little bit coincidental that after traveling billions of miles through space, and with the entire two hundred million square miles of Earth's surface to crash on, your bald friends just happened to pile up outside Los Angeles, U.S.A., media center, film*

center, the entertainment capital of the world? Why do you suppose they didn't plow into the center of Siberia, the Pacific Ocean, or the Sahara Desert? I'll tell you why. There weren't any damned cameras on 'em, that's why. I know it's fashionable to treat this Newcomer matter like it's the real thing, but here in the United States Congress we have neither the time nor the money to engage in last year's bagwan moonie krishna space fantasies. Now—"

Dr. Norcross's telephone rang, and she cut off the television's sound, leaving Chairman Lloyd's mouth to flap silently at his witness. Picking up the receiver, she pressed the scrambler and held the receiver to her ear. "Yes?"

"This is Lipscomb."

"Yes, Mr. Lipscomb. What about the mayor's office?" she asked.

"The mayor won't play. Not for all the national security chips in Washington."

"Did you lean?"

"Like the proverbial tower, Doctor, but he won't play. The politics are all wrong. Election's too close, too many dead bodies, too many live bodies who know who's responsible, too many of them asking questions and demanding answers. Collins was right. We should've brought in Rand and the Bureau of Prisons from the beginning."

"That's ancient history. What about more juice?"

"Juice?"

"The mayor, Mr. Lipscomb. What if we used a bigger club?"

"Who're you talking about, Doctor? The President? That's what you'd need." There was a pause, then a short laugh. "You know something, Doctor? I don't think even the President could get the mayor to play.

Even if he could, I don't think the President wants the smell of this on his own fingers while his people sing 'Hail, Hail, the Gang's All Here' in front of a committee."

"Mr. Lipscomb, this is not going before any committee. The things at stake here are simply too important to the future of this nation and of the human race." She glanced at the television and saw the chairman and the junior senator from Maine silently exchanging heated insults. "Don't worry about Congress. There's nothing to worry about from that quarter. Is there anything else?"

"One more thing, Doctor. It might even be more of a problem. The rubberhead from the FBI, Paul Iniko?"

"What about him?"

"He took off on us today."

"Took off?" Dr. Norcross leaned forward and frowned at her phone. "What are you talking about?"

"Collins, Rittenhouse, and I were with Iniko at China Lake trying to hammer out an information management plan when Iniko took off. He left, split, made tracks, *adios muchacho*. Before he went, he came across just a little bit judgmental. You know what I mean?"

"He can't do that. He's under orders."

"He's an Overseer, Doctor. All he knows how to do is give orders. I don't exactly think he's worried about his pension."

"Where did he go? What do you think he'll do?"

"I don't know. He's one of Warden Rand's recruits, you know."

"Yes. I was aware of that."

"Well, Rand's dead. Add to that, two cops are dead and another two are critical. That doesn't even count a couple of dozen civilians. Iniko seems to have this soft spot in his head for cops."

"Soft spot? Don't be absurd, Mr. Lipscomb. As you said, Iniko is an Overseer."

"He's also a cop. According to his FBI personnel record, he's always been a cop. That's what he used to do for the slave drivers in space. He was what they called a watcher, and his job was figuring out who-done-it. According to the data recovered from the ship, he was quite good at it. Anyway, he might hurt us, Doctor. He can't prove much, but he knows who's who, what's what, and where a few of the bodies are buried. Blowhard finger pointing we don't have to sweat, but he's still an agent in the FBI. Rubberhead or not, that carries media weight." He paused for a moment, then said, "You do know who can prove a whole lot of embarrassing things should brother Iniko get his hands on him alive?"

"Are you suggesting we do something illegal, Mr. Lipscomb?"

Lipscomb chuckled. "No, ma'am. Not as long you keep that tape recorder running. All I was doing was making an observation on the life and times of *el fugitivo*. My job is editing truth for publication. I leave the icky jobs to those who enjoy that sort of thing. The editing would be a whole lot easier, though, if our boy should happen to fall off a cliff or get a sudden attack of lead poisoning. Just a thought."

She listened to the silence for a moment and then said, "Thank you for calling, Mr. Lipscomb. I think perhaps it's time for you and Mr. Rittenhouse to push your 'no comment' buttons and go home."

"I understand."

"You might suggest the same to Mr. Collins. We have no control over him, but we all have the same boss. I think he would find it in his own interests to take some time off for himself. Take the wife and kids to see the Grand Canyon, visit grandma in Vermont, that sort of thing."

"I'll tell him." There was a long silence on the other end of the line, then Lipscomb's quiet, "So long, Doctor." The connection was cut and Carrie Norcross hung up her phone.

Glancing at her watch, she closed her eyes, took a deep breath, and let it out slowly. Three times more she checked her watch, and exactly on the quarter hour she dialed a number and waited. There was no ringing, no beeps, no little messages of gratitude from multinational communications corporations. There was only silence, and then the click of a receiver being picked up. No voice answered.

"Very well," she said.

There was no answer. Instead the connection was cut. She listened to the hum for a moment, then hung up her phone.

CHAPTER 22

AT THE *RAMA VO,* Buck and his father stood in the garden before a paunchy human with a face the color of toffee. His hair, what there was left, was mostly gray and cut close to his scalp. He wore faded tan jeans and an aloha shirt that stressed the red end of the spectrum. His arms were heavily muscled and folded across his chest, and he introduced himself as Malcolm Bone. "Aman isn't in today."

"Isn't in?" Buck demanded. "He should be here. He's my Elder."

The human grinned widely and chuckled. "A boy lookin' for his guru. You just gotta be Buck Francisco, right?"

"Yes."

"This your father?"

"This is my father, yes. What I want to know is where is *my* Elder."

"Maybe I'm wrong, but according to the way I read that U.S. Constitution, young one, Aman Iri don't belong to no one but Aman Iri. Anyway, you should've called first. What's the matter? Don't you watch the telephone company commercials?"

"When will he be back?" Buck asked impatiently. "He wanted to see my father about something."

"He's gone for at least the next few days, doing his best to see if he can break his legs. He went out to some mountain yesterday afternoon, and tried downhill skiing for the first time today. Don't take it personal. It's a trip he's been planning for months."

Buck looked at his father and then back at the human. "Aman Iri is very old to be trying something like that. He's over a hundred."

"And it's so inconvenient for you too," Malcolm completed. He shrugged his wide shoulders and looked Buck in the eyes. "Just the same, he called a little while ago to say he's discovered up on his mountaintop everything from snow bunnies to the meaning of life." Malcolm Bone grinned. "I asked him what the people were like up there in snow city, and he said they're just a bunch of flakes. I guess he really likes skiing."

"Is there another *Hila* we can talk to, then?"

"Sure, kid."

"Where can we find one?"

Malcolm Bone held out his hands. "You're talking to one."

"A *Hila*," Buck repeated. "An Elder?"

"I know what the word means, kid. I'm a *Hila*. I am an Elder. I got the gray hairs and the baggy eyes to prove it."

"But you're *human*," Buck protested.

Malcolm Bone scratched the back of his neck,

shifted his weight from his right leg to his left and placed his hands on his hips. "You don't exactly have the hang of that flower and weed thing, do you?"

"And you do?" Buck demanded angrily.

The man's eyes were kind, even sympathetic. "I'd be a bum *Hila* if I didn't understand the flower and the weed."

"Look, mister, you can't be a *Hila*. You're not Tenctonese. You're human. You're not smart enough. There it is; I've said it."

"You certainly have." Malcolm Bone turned from Buck and faced George. Reaching out his hand, he said, "Hi. My name's Malcolm Bone."

"George Francisco," he answered, shaking the man's hand.

Malcolm Bone's greeting slowed for a foggy moment as the man frowned and raised an eyebrow at George. "The cop?"

"I'm a homicide detective."

Malcolm Bone released George's hand and pointed a finger at him. "I read about you, Detective Francisco. You know you made the papers today? The Thunderbolt Poet Killer? René Day? All kinds of congratulations."

"By the time I put two and two together it was all over."

"Aman said you might drop by with a few questions concerning *riana.*"

"You can help me with that?"

Malcolm Bone nodded. "Sure. I don't go through it myself, but—"

"I don't believe this," Buck interrupted. "You *can't* be a *Hila*. You're *human*. Humans simply don't have the mental capacity."

"Still lookin' for that red man, black man, yellow

man, white man, huh kid? Still huntin' for that little piece of something outside that makes you something inside?"

"I suppose you found yours."

"It's funny, Buck. You finally have the truth cornered, but you can't catch it 'cause you think it's a lie." The *Hila* pursed his lips and said, "I came to the *vo* three years ago, searching for answers, looking for truths, the same way I been doing since I lost my father in the sixties." He turned and pointed to the scorched wall of the garden perpendicular to the street. "The flames from that riot blackened those bricks. I was twenty years old." He lowered his hand. "Three decades later, I came here to be a student. They didn't want me as a student, though. The Elders here took me on as a teacher. See, I didn't need the paint chips. I already understood."

Buck, his eyes changing color from embarrassment and anger, glanced at his father and then looked at Malcolm Bone. "Okay, then, *Hila,* what do you call yourself? Black? Afro-American? Negro? Colored? What?"

"I'm a man, Buck. I look like one, act like one, and feel like one. If you call me a man, we'll get along just fine."

"What about your heritage? What about your culture?"

"Those are things that others have accomplished. As far as who I am matters, my only concern is with the acts, good and bad, committed by Malcolm Bone."

When Buck said nothing, the man turned slowly, squatted down and picked two pale blue blossoms from the nearest bed. As he stood he handed the blossoms to Buck. "I have to talk to your father, kid.

While I'm talking to him, I want you to take these, go to the back of the garden where there's a stone bench; I want you to sit your narrow ass down on that bench and rethink the flower and the weed."

"But you've given me two flowers."

Malcolm Bone lifted his hand, pointed toward the back of the garden, and bellowed, "Go!" Buck walked a few steps, and Malcolm said after him: "A hint. What you're looking for isn't in your hand or out there; what you're looking for is inside your own skin."

When Buck at last dragged himself out of sight among the plants, defiantly staying away from the granite bench, Malcolm turned to George. "How'd he injure his head?"

"Saving my life. He took a bullet meant for me."

"He's a good kid. Is the wound serious?"

"It's not a serious injury, but it'll leave a permanent scar."

"What a wonderful scar to have," Malcolm Bone declared. "It's like a medal for saving his father's life. Every time he sees it, he can remind himself of a good thing he did." The man raised an eyebrow and looked skeptically at George. "Providing you were worth saving. Were you?"

"I think so," George answered, his anger making Malcolm Bone's outline appear tinged with red.

"Good. Then, what a wonderful scar to have." Malcolm gestured with his fingers for George to continue, and George told the story of the *Ahvin Yin,* Maanka Dak, and the *vikah ta* that had already cost so many lives. Malcolm listened without comment, and by the time George had finished, they were inside one of the *vo*'s comfortable sitting rooms that opened onto the garden. While George sipped a cup of tea, Malcolm seemed to stare off into space. After a moment of this, he turned to George.

"Did you want to know about *riana?*"

George sat upright. "Yes. I believe I've fooled myself long enough."

"Okay. Good." The *Hila*'s eyebrows went up. "Understand, man, it does mean your child-bearing years are over. *Adios, sayonara, toucus,* and that's the way it goes. It's a lot like female human menopause in that respect, except the physical and mental symptoms are quite a bit more bizarre."

"Blindness, hallucinations?"

"You've gotten a few episodes of the light show?"

"Yes."

Malcolm nodded. "Okay, great. Then it's just about over. You might get a few more bouts, but they shouldn't last for more than a couple of days. Until you're sure they're over, though, I'd hang up the gun and let someone else do the driving."

"That much I already had figured out."

Malcolm scratched the back of his neck and frowned. "Now where was I?"

"Symptoms."

"Yeah." Malcolm leaned forward and pointed at George. "Some of those mental symptoms are things you can change."

"Change? What? Change how?"

"George, if you had to describe your feelings about *riana* with one word, what word would you pick?"

"Terror." The answer leaped from George's lips before he realized it. He paused to reconsider his answer, and when he had, he nodded and repeated, "Terror. *Riana* then you die. Right?"

"You tell me."

George looked into his feelings. "You can no longer

breed, physically you enter a period of decline. You cannot perform as well, and the costs of maintenance increase, reducing the net return. *Riana* then you die."

"That's something you can change, George."

"How?"

"Man, everything you just said in the present tense is ancient history. It's the past. The Overseers are emptying garbage cans for Lupini and Company, the ship is cut up and stuck in a museum someplace, and you live in a place that makes discrimination against someone because of age against the law."

George pondered what Malcolm had said. When he was finished, George shrugged and held out his hands. "The feeling is still terror."

"You ever hear the saying that a ten-mile walk into the woods is a ten-mile walk back out?"

"No."

"Well, you've heard it now. Time takes time. The point is that it took you a lot of years to learn to feel the way you do about *riana*. It's going to take some time to unlearn those feelings and begin feeling good about it."

"*Good* about it? How can anyone feel good about *riana?* I love children. Nothing has ever made me feel more fulfilled than conceiving and carrying my children."

"You've got children, George. More than that, the world is filled with children. No loss there. As far as actually conceiving and carrying children, part of *riana* is a gradual increase in the meaning and pleasure of lovemaking."

George's eyebrows went up. "Really?"

"Would your *Hila* lie to you, George?" Malcolm grinned and clasped his hands over his belly. The grin faded and the man nodded. "As for no longer being able to carry your own children, there are compensations."

"What could compensate for that?"

"Well, the way it was explained to me, George, you know that burst of brilliance, that super mental clarity you've been getting glimpses of recently?"

"You mean that amazing intelligence that fills in the cracks between those continents of absolute stupidity I've been experiencing? Yes," he replied warily, "what about them?"

"That's a peek at what your mental abilities will be like when you've gone through the changing all five or six times over the next sixty or seventy years."

"You mean I've got to go through this again?"

Malcolm nodded. "Sure, but the remaining times won't be quite so spectacular. And, like I said, it's all finished in the next fifty or sixty years. Maybe much sooner. Here at the *vo* we've heard from dozens who're going through the same thing, and the one thing you all have in common is that you're doing your first *riana* on average eighteen to twenty years earlier than when you were back on the ship. No one's figured out why yet. The air, pollen, L.A.'s water, rap music, it could be anything."

"Does that mean life span is also shortened?"

"Unknown." The *Hila*'s eyes misted over for a moment.

"Is there something wrong?"

Malcolm shrugged and raised his eyebrows. "Nobody's got a lock on the next ten minutes, George. I could be watching sunsets a hundred years from now or this second could be my last." He glanced at his hands then shifted his gaze to the garden. "What could be safer than working in a grocery store?

Stacking cans, doing inventory, and punching a cash register for a seventy-year-old grandmother. That's where my son was killed in the 'ninety-two riots. He was just seventeen years old. My boy's skin was very light-colored," said the man, his voice cracking. "He was working for a Korean-American. We and they, us and them. The store was looted, my boy was killed along with the owner of the store, and the whole thing was torched. I spent quite a while trying to figure out who to hate: cops, gangs, Koreans, the rich, the poor, the media, the government. Us and them. Us and them." His lips parted in a sad smile. "Red and yellow, black and white, we aren't labels in his sight. I'm grateful your son is still alive, George Francisco."

He shook his head, blinked his eyes, and appeared to throw the whole thing temporarily off his back. "Back to today, George. Every time you go through the changing, your mental speed will increase. It's like having another card thrown into a computer, expanding the memory, increasing the speed. As I said, *riana* has its compensations."

"Was Buck right, then? Are the Tenctonese as a race more intelligent than humans? They certainly do better in school."

Malcolm Bone looked out of the window onto the garden and watched Buck walk the paths among the trees, shrubs, and plants. " 'Intelligent' is one of those labels, George. To me all it means is what you do with the equipment you got. The statistical frog cutters, on average, figure Tencts have a little faster equipment than humans. What operators do with the equipment they have is something else, though. There are a lot of 'thems' that do better than the current 'us' depending on what someone wants to make out of it. But the winners of the past two national spelling bees were human boys. Does that make humans smarter than Tencts? Does that make boys smarter than girls? Flowers and weeds, George."

George Francisco nodded. "All it means is that two human boys worked very hard and won their respective spelling bees. They used what they had very well."

"See how smart you're getting?" Malcolm said with a grin. "One guy I threw out of here had a different response when I told him about the spelling bees. His response was to ask me, 'Were they black or white?'"

George laughed, then paused, then frowned. "Incredible," he muttered.

"What's incredible?"

"What you said about the person you threw out for asking if the boys who won the spelling bee were black or white. The first thing that popped into my mind was to ask, 'Was *he* black or white?'"

"As a matter of fact, he was sort of between a Malaysian beige and a Chippendale rose." Malcolm raised his eyebrows and closed his eyes. "A ten-mile walk into the woods, George," Malcolm Bone reminded him. The corners of his mouth turned down as he held out his hands and looked back at the garden. "Anyway, neither the Tencts or the humans use more than ten percent of their mental abilities, so I don't figure who's the smartest has much meaning."

Without taking his gaze off Buck, the *Hila* said, "George, have you solved the mystery of the flower and the weed?"

"I thought I had, until we had this little talk."

"What is it?"

"A flower is a weed that someone decided to keep," George answered. "A weed is a flower somebody decided to throw away. There are no weeds; there are no flowers."

Malcolm nodded. "You got it." He glanced at George. "You understand why Buck has to learn to say the same thing his own way?"

"Yes." George looked through the window, and among the several persons walking the paths was what looked to be an incredibly old human woman who was moving along with the aid of a walker. Over her pale blue morning dress she was wearing a bright red T-shirt printed in green, yellow, and silver, with huge letters that read: SMART RAT. "Is she a *Hila* too?"

"She's a student. Once she figures out the flower and the weed thing, I expect she'll be offered a position as an Elder here. She has over ninety years of experience to offer. She probably won't take it, though."

"Why do you suppose that?"

Malcolm turned from the window and leaned his elbows on his knees as he faced George. "Her name's Molly Grey. She's hung up on a label: age. Her label tells her that the older she gets, the stupider, uglier, and more useless she gets. As a result, the older she gets, the stupider, uglier, and more useless she becomes. Things got to where she could hardly remember her own name." He looked out the window and smiled as Molly bent over to touch a rhododendron blossom. "You ever hear of the smart rat, dumb rat study years ago?"

George frowned and harnessed his new abilities to retrieve an obscure bit of data. "That was the study where they found that a label stuck on a study group or sample will predetermine the results of the study?"

"That's the one. Tell a heap of grad students the bunch of rats they have to put through their maze is stupid, and the results will show that that bunch of rats is stupid. They did it with human students too. Instead of rats, they used kids. They told one teaching unit their kids had IQs in the eighties and the other unit that their kids had IQs of well over a hundred. Sure enough, the eighties group could only do eighty work and the hundreds bunch did hundred work. Both groups of kids were the same."

Malcolm nodded toward Molly Grey and her smart rat T-shirt. "She's working on solving her own version of the flower and the weed. With her, there are no races; only people. The divisions are according to age. The classes aren't black and white or rich and poor. They're young and old."

George frowned and leaned back in his chair. "Buck is just the opposite. He's almost reverent of the aged. He considers age where wisdom resides." He looked at Molly Grey and studied her as she moved her walker painfully down the path. "Maybe she and Buck will meet. They have much to learn from each other."

"Anything's possible," Malcolm answered. "We all have much to learn from each other."

"You haven't said why you think she wouldn't take on the job of *Hila*."

"Simple. Because of her dumb rat label, there's a lot of living she hasn't done. For over thirty years she's only gone out of her home four times for medical emergencies. Now that's what I call doing hard time. Once she gets free of that label, she has a lot of catching up to do. I wouldn't put it past Molly Grey to make Aman Iri take her up some mountain somewhere and send her down strapped to a snow board."

Malcolm paused for a moment, turned his head, and faced George. "Do you see the smart rat T-shirt you and the rest of the cops put on Maanka Dak's back?"

Taken back for a moment, George's eyebrows went

up as he tried to hammer out the meaning of Malcolm's question. "He is smart. Not just smart; he's brilliant. The things—"

"No doubt, George, no doubt. But I'm not talking about what he is. I'm not talking about what he thinks of himself. I'm talking about the label you and the cops put on him. See, it's not how the label makes him act; it's how the label makes the police department act. That's the thing you people can control. By himself, Maanka Dak is just one guy on the run without a friend in the world. But he scared the shit out of everybody with the way he busted out of China Lake, didn't he?"

"That's putting it mildly."

"And the next thing you know, he's the single most important threat to life on earth as we know it. After you stuck that label on him, he became that."

"I think you're overstating things a bit," George said.

"Oh, yeah? What's the first thing you people did when you decided to track him down and nab him?"

"The police?"

"No, the El Segundo Center for the Farting Impaired. Yeah, the cops. What'd they do?"

George held out his hands. "You mean setting up the command center?"

"Yeah, I mean setting up the command center. You made him brilliant. If you'd left the communications the same, he never would've been able to tie into everybody's lines and control them without owning the phone company. But to keep the smart rat down, you gathered all the wires in one place and handed the plug to Maanka Dak. I'm sure the guy has a few neurons chugging away up there, and I bet he got a whole row of gold stars in alien kindergarten up there in the ship, but you yahoos make him look like the brain that ate Chicago."

George frowned as he thought of something. "My wife and daughters."

"What about them? You give 'em some kind of special protection?"

"They're in a safe house." He looked up at Malcolm. "A super safe house. The department went out of its way to make certain no one could trace them. The place doesn't even have a telephone, so it wouldn't appear in the phone company records."

"And how many places in L.A. don't have phones?"

"Thousands and thousands."

Malcolm nodded. "And how many of them don't pay any property taxes, or pay them through the police department budget and have the funds rebated?"

George frowned as he intertwined his fingers. "And how many of them have three or more unmarked police cars parked in the neighborhood? Dumb rat, dumb rat, dumb rat."

Malcolm Bone stretched his arms over his head then nodded as he clasped his hands over his belly. "Don't be too hard on yourself. Your boy Maanka has a couple of big blind spots too. He's got a big smart rat T-shirt on himself, for one thing."

"Isn't that good?" George asked as he gestured toward Molly Grey.

"It can be used for shaking things up, for shattering dumb rat labels, but it's no view of the real world. Molly's going to have to ditch that shirt before she can be healthy. See George, wisdom is beyond labels. It's light years past black, white, wrong, right, smart, dumb, us, and them. Wisdom is seeing things for what they are and accepting that it is so."

George allowed the silence of the room to repeat the *Hila*'s words. When he had opened his entire mind to hear them, he said, *"Hila,* this is a fine place. The *Rama Vo;* it's a fine place. I think I'd like to return."

"The door's always open."

George looked at Malcolm. "You stated that Maanka had two blind spots. His view of his own brilliance was one. What's the other?"

"The *vikah ta,* of course. The destruction of you and the memory of you. It's a dumb rat program running, and ruining, a great piece of equipment. You're the label he's hung up on, George."

"That's it?"

Malcolm grinned. "It's an edge. Look, what's the first priority of the cops?"

"To catch or kill Maanka."

Malcolm nodded. "Yeah. You see, if Maanka Dak's only goal was to escape, I wouldn't give the LAPD one chance in a million of catching him. A flea gets around a whole lot easier than an elephant, and Maanka is one smart flea. But, see, escaping isn't his first priority. Killing you and the memory of you is his big goal, and that's where you've got him. See, all you got to do is switch the label tables on him."

"You make it sound very simple."

"Nothing complex about it. One thing, though. When you switch those labels, you're probably going to disrupt that guy's way of seeing things. It could change how he looks at you, at himself, at the universe."

George looked through the window at the garden and saw Buck talking with Molly Grey. They were splashed with iridescent purples, reds, and golds, but George knew that the color distortions would pass with time. Besides, he knew they were not real. He saw them, yet he knew and could act as though they were not real.

He held up a mental finger and corrected himself. The colors were real. They were symptoms of a real biological condition. Seeing the colors, however, didn't make Buck purple and Molly red and gold. Seeing things for what they are and accepting that it is so. Wisdom. The solution to every problem in the world; every problem in the universe.

Was wisdom a skill of Maanka Dak's? Could he see things for what they are and accept that it is so? George slowly shook his head as a wealth of answers flooded his mind. He knew that from that exact moment he would never see things exactly the same way again. The Buck he knew a few minutes ago was in the process of being replaced by an entirely new being, one who could see other beings without their destructive, meaningless labels. From moment to moment it was all changing, growing, becoming what the universe allowed. Everything was changing save Maanka Dak, and that was Dak's flaw.

George's attention came back to the present moment when he saw another person, a Tenctonese man, walk up to Buck and Molly. He seemed very familiar.

"Who's that?" the *Hila* asked.

The man held out his left arm, and George started at the tattoo surrounding his wrist. "Overseer!" George whispered. He looked at Malcolm Bone and smiled sheepishly as he said, "I may have some more work to do on the flower and the weed."

"We all do, brother." Malcolm nodded toward the garden. "Who is he?"

George studied the Overseer from his natty gray suit to his bracelet tattoo. The man's face showed no emotion, and possibly his being contained none. "His name's Iniko. Paul Iniko. He works for the FBI and was at the autopsy trying to limit the number of witnesses." George shifted his gaze to Malcolm Bone. "In answer to your question, *Hila,* I don't know who he is. Not yet."

CHAPTER 23

THAT NIGHT MAANKA Dak sat in the back of the van, routing calls through the police command center, responding to orders, and issuing a few orders of his own, all with voices synthesized from the voice prints of their owners. The city was a vast chessboard, and Maanka the master, playing both sides of the deadly game.

Thorough revenge.

In his *vikah ta* Dak had yet to settle which was more important: killing Nicto and his memory, or making Nicto wait for it, knowing that the fact, as well as the moment, of his death was within Maanka's power. On the one hand he entertained the staff of the command center, duping them into believing their orders were being carried out. On the other hand, he moved about the pieces in the field, directing force and skill into wells of impotence.

Yet Carrie Norcross, with her petty privileges and

nonbinding promises, presumed that *she* controlled *him*. Up until Maanka Dak, all authority understood was control. But control of any kind over Maanka Dak was rank fantasy. It was Maanka who was in control, who had always been in control, and who would continue in control until the death of all authority.

At precisely 10:05 P.M., however, the incoming calls ceased. In addition, none of Maanka's outgoing calls originating at the van could make a connection. Nothing worked. It was as though the entire universe of semiconductor theory had been proven false and every microchip in L.A. had pulled up its own pins and had withered away.

Another player had entered the game.

Maanka smiled. The new player had discovered his transceiver control package. That was all. "But one control does not a redundancy make," he sang to a Gilbert and Sullivan tune.

He pressed the voice delay. "I do believe that pulls the plug on the evil Maanka Dak," he said into the voice pickup mounted on his collar. Captain Grazer's voice came from a sound column, saying, "I do believe that pulls the plug on the evil Maanka Dak." Maanka grinned and turned to face the computer. The screen still had a spot of Brick Wahl's blood on it. He hadn't noticed that before. He licked the tip of a finger and wiped off the blood.

Placing his fingertips upon the keyboard, he gave the command to engage the backup control he had installed at the command center.

A warning prompt at the bottom of the screen flashed. The control would not engage. Maanka tried the command twice more before he leaned back against the inside wall of the van and frowned.

"They couldn't have found the backup," he whispered.

Most of the control had been software hidden in the operating programs. The receiver and engagement control was one of the reprogrammed Niyezian implants, barely the size of a clipped nose hair. It gave off no measurable energy emissions, and had been inserted beneath the edge of some tape that had been holding a sheet of typed instructions onto the central processing unit. It simply couldn't be found unless one knew exactly where to search and exactly what the object of the search looked like. Maanka Dak was the only one who knew that.

What else? All of the equipment replaced?

Why? For what reason?

His eyes studied the banks of lights and dials he had assembled from Radio Shack, industrial electronics, and telecommunications warehouses he had broken into. "Very well. No need to panic. Perhaps the other side has finally put someone competent on the team."

Maanka could feel his blood quicken. A challenge to his intellect of any kind was so rare, and he did so enjoy a true challenge. It could have only one possible outcome, but it was more exhilarating to track and chase the quarry through difficult terrain before killing it than simply dropping it in a zoo.

"I am the hunter," he said as he punched buttons on his keyboard, attempting to slave the video monitors at the center. "Where are you, little wabbit? Wubberhead Fudd has something for you."

None of his taps into the video monitor feed at the command center were operative. They not only wouldn't respond to being controlled, they didn't even indicate that they were there.

A power failure?

A power failure didn't make much sense, Maanka thought. Something as important as a police facility should have a backup generator. "Still, authority is just another way of saying a mind is a terrible thing to waste." A power failure was a possibility.

He did have audio monitors that were battery operated. He tried one, then the next. The one on Francisco's desk was dead, as was the one he had planted in Captain Grazer's command terminal. There was another battery-powered audio monitor, however. A bug he had placed in a light fixture above the command terminal. He punched in the command to activate it, and was surprised to find himself relieved that it, at least, still worked.

"—don't know, J.J. It sure looked to Officer Toledano like you were ripping off that appliance store. Now, maybe he was jumping to conclusions. You looked suspicious, though."

"Suspicious, hell. I don't know what you're talkin' about. Suspicious."

"Well, man, you were running down the street with a double armload of high definition TV. See what I mean?"

"No. You tell me."

"See, it wasn't like you had a flag or a sign protesting the oppression of the masses."

"Climb outta my face, Tom boy. I was makin' a political statement. You know what whitey's been doin' for the last four hundred years. I'm just gettin' a little back for the brothers, see?"

"Four hundred years, man?"

"That's right."

"You don't look that old, J.J."

"Man, don't give me this shit. If your great-granddaddy raped my great-grandmama, the guilt's yours! You hear me?"

"Not under this country's constitution, Spartacus." There was the sound of a chair being pulled out. "J.J., J.J."

"Don't call me J.J. My name's Jamil Jafar!"

"Ah, J.J., J.J. We searched your apartment, J.J. You been makin' a lot of political statements lately, haven't you? You just about nailed Simon Legree's hide to the wall with this haul." There was the crackle of pages being turned. "Twenty-three color televisions, forty-four VCRs in their original packing boxes, sixteen microwave ovens, eleven laptop computers . . . Fifty gift sets of the *Alien* trilogy? You got a thing for Sigourney Weaver, J.J., or do you like 'em gray, slimy, and full of drool—"

Maanka Dak shut off the sound and continued staring at the paddle switch he had just thrown. The command center had been set up in an interrogation room. The evidence seemed to support that it was an interrogation room once again. That, however, made absolutely no sense whatever. He threw the switch on again.

"—the oppression of the people's all the justification I need, man. Now, I don't wanna say nothin' more till my lawyer gets here."

"J.J., J.J.—"

Once more Maanka turned off the switch. The command center must have been moved. But it would have to be set up with all new equipment. Had it been done without notifying any of the principals? Perhaps they had done it outside the command net. Perhaps the police really had put someone on the job who knew what he was doing.

They had discovered he controlled the center. Did they know how far-reaching his control was? Where was the new center? It couldn't have been set up with all new personnel. At the very least, someone from the previous center had to be there to brief the new team.

Wheels turned and connections were made as Maanka's mind pieced together a counter plan at top speed. He reached out his hand and switched the function of the voice synthesizer to voice-print matching. He had the voice prints of all three shifts of cops that worked out of the command center and every principal connected with his escape, the massacres on Soto and Wilshire, and the family, friends, associates, and acquaintances of George Francisco.

His fingers flew over the keyboard as he entered the commands to begin a print search of the phone lines of the likely divisions. Enough voice identifications and routes would show a pattern pointing right at the new location of the command center, unless the new opposition was very sophisticated indeed.

On his screen, print identifications slowly began registering: Bradley was calling someone. Watkins, Rolfe, Yamato. It was late. The second team was on. Except there were problems with the call origins and destinations. Lieutenant Yamato's call had originated at University Division. The call he made was to a number in El Centro. Police line, official call, absolutely nothing to do with the command center. Dak punched the keys and called up the data on the Watkins print.

Sergeant Watkins had called from a phone box. He was back on the streets in Hollenbeck. The call was to his watch commander.

Sergeant Rolfe was back with the SWATs. His call

had been to his own home. Lieutenant Bradley from homicide also called home.

Dak frowned as he continued the search. There were three more calls: Weyl, Llada, and Macdonald. Weyl was back in University Division making a call to the airport. Llada, calling his home from the Hollenbeck station, was still on the line. Maanka cut in and listened.

"—call, Rafael?"

"Lisa, Lisa! I got the transfer to West Hollywood!"

Thence emanated from Lisa Llada a high, ear-piercing scream that would have dogs and bats for a six-block radius calling their therapists. "We can get it, then, the house in Santa Monica! Right?"

"Right, baby! We are on our way to the ocean!"

Another bat-shattering scream and Maanka cut off the switch. He sat there for a moment, staring at the sound column. "What in the hell is going on?" he muttered. He reached out, switched the call selector, and flipped on the monitor.

Macdonald was still on the line, waiting for the results from the lab on some suspected cocaine nabbed in a bust outside the police station on First and St. Louis.

A strange feeling ate at Maanka's stomach. It was a eccentric feeling, something akin to what he always imagined fear to be like. He switched the selector to another line. Lieutenant Yamato was calling El Centro again, and Maanka cut in to listen to the call.

"—to catch you in, Chief. Look, we're trying to get a line on a perp named Rico Fontana, five-foot-seven, a hundred and twenty soaking wet, brown and black. He's an alky with a child-molesting rap sheet down to his ankles. He's on the computer, and I faxed his face and specs down to your Sergeant Rayburn. We've gotten word he might be in your area."

"I got the fax, Lieutenant," came the voice from El Centro. "Ugly dude. What's the warrant?"

"Rico's graduated to the big time, Chief. Murder *uno.*"

"We don't have him, but I'll pass this around, Lieutenant, and—"

Maanka cut off the switch and glowered at the screen before him. Had they scripted out an enormous citywide charade—statewide charade—to trap him? Had they set up an entirely new command center manned with entirely different personnel? It would have to use all new equipment and be in a different location, but that would answer it all.

There was another print ID on the screen, Captain Milton J. Grazer. Whatever was going on, he'd have to be connected with it. The call was from Grazer's home in South Pasadena to an address on Mission. Maanka selected the call and switched on the audio monitor.

"—any pumpkin ice cream?"

"Pumpkin?"

"Pumpkin ice cream," Grazer pleaded. "It tastes just like pumpkin pie. I have to get some."

"I never heard of pumpkin ice cream. If the stuff tastes like pumpkin pie, why not get your wife a pumpkin pie?"

"Pumpkin pie?"

"Yeah, you said it tastes like pumpkin pie. Why not get your old lady a pumpkin pie?"

"I don't get her goddamned pumpkin pie instead of pumpkin ice cream, you dip, for the same goddamned reason that you buy cherry ice cream when you want cherry ice cream instead of goddamned cherry pie! And let me tell—"

Maanka cut off the switch and frowned. How long could everyone keep up the act? But then, perhaps it was no act. If that were so . . .

Maanka smiled thinly as he activated one of his remote telephone transceivers and switched back to the voice synthesizer, disguising his own voice print. He dialed the COP FINK number, energized his trace detector, and punched his elapsed time meter.

"Perhaps it's time to dangle some bait," he whispered.

"LAPD Hotline," answered a voice after the third ring. Three rings was just the right amount of time not to appear too eager; not to appear too obviously unconcerned. Maanka wondered if somewhere there was a federally funded study on how long to wait upon answering a suspect's telephone call to produce what effect.

"Yes," he said into his collar pickup. "My name is Norman Lewis. I have some important information concerning the mass killings on Wilshire and on Soto. Could you connect me with the proper authorities?"

"One moment."

No click, no hum, no reverb vibrations. The trace detector worked both ways: catching the attempt to trace him and allowing him to trace anyone on the other end of the line. It worked very well at detecting taps too. COP FINK recorded all of its incoming calls for insurance reasons, the same as did all emergency services. "That's right, friends," said Maanka to himself, "sixty-four cents out of every tax dollar goes to a lawyer."

He could hear the hollow rattle of a keyboard being

punched as he hummed another line from his prison composition, "Kill a Lawyer for Jesus."

Funny how that had worked out when Rand freaked in the Bucky McBeaver's. "Kill a lawyer for Jesus!" he had screamed, making the patrons scream with him. "Kill a lawyer for Jesus."

According to the news, he had started a movement. Supposedly there were men and women picketing in Sacramento carrying Kill a Lawyer for Jesus signs.

The COP FINK voice came back with, "Neither one of those cases have special lines, sir. Our records show that both of those investigations have been dropped in grade. No special command center or task force. In such cases, any follow-up would be handled by homicide or the division in which the incident occurred. If you have something to add to either investigation, I can give you the number of the appropriate divisions, or I can take the information myself. Whatever you prefer, sir."

Maanka frowned, trying to anticipate his opponent's next step. Actually, he was attempting to anticipate his opponent's anticipation of his next step. "Perhaps the people I want are listed differently," he said at last. "Is there a command center organized to apprehend Maanka Dak, an escapee from China Lake? The information I have relates to his location."

"One moment." Again the sounds of fingertips working a keyboard. A pause, a small curse, another pause. "How do you spell that?"

Maanka spelled his own name and checked the trace detector. Nothing was being run on the line. At least, it was nothing he could detect.

"I'm sorry, sir. There is no Maanka Dak on our register, not with that spelling, at least."

"I said he escaped from China Lake."

"Let me check the federal register." More keys being punched, more delay, very skillful. Still the trace detector showed nothing. Yet no one knew better than Maanka that any electronic measure was little more than an invitation to a future countermeasure, which was in turn an invitation to still another countermeasure.

He rose from his seat, poked his head through the blackout curtain to the cab and examined the dark service alley. He could see the wrapped remains of the two winos he had killed for reasons of privacy. There were no flashing lights, no indications from the motion detectors mounted on the outside of the van. He heard the telephone operator burst out with an involuntary laugh, and he pulled his head back through the curtain.

"Mr. Lewis?" the operator said.

"Yes?"

"According to our records, Mr. Lewis, Maanka Dak, also known as Pete Moss—" She gasped another laugh. "Sorry. He was a federal prisoner. So he'd fall under the jurisdiction of the federal authorities. Would you like me to give you the number of the Justice Department?"

"No. Thank you."

He cut off the connection and stared with hatred at the sound column. Pete Moss. The name still rankled. What a strange person Tom Rand had been to insist that all of his Tenctonese prisoners use their Tenctonese names.

Maanka blinked his eyes and looked around at the equipment he had put together. This was trustworthy. Rand was a child. He was part of the authority.

Did the operator know he was Maanka Dak? Was there no command center? Had everything been downgraded despite the media furor demanding everything from the recall of the chief of police to the return of the National Guard?

Someone who knew what he was doing was running things, he was certain. It was virtually impossible for them to triangulate on the shielded signal his equipment had made for the purposes of calling the hotline, but that depended upon yesterday's technology having stood still.

He looked at the equipment in his van, every corner packed with wonders considered improbable or impossible by those heavy with current wisdom. Maanka knew from experience that such impossibilities, and how one reacted to them, were the avenues toward either success or failure. Only twice before had he regarded a very high improbability as an impossibility. The second time he had been wounded and arrested by George Francisco. The first time he had been arrested and set free by the watcher, Vuurot Iniko.

"Iniko," Maanka said out loud, his eyes widening. "Iniko," he repeated.

Vuurot Iniko, *charkah*.

Watcher.

Iniko: the Overseer whose motives were as obscure to Maanka today as they had been years ago on the ship. Iniko had caught him, had him under arrest, and had had enough evidence to prove him guilty of the murders of the pain minister, Torumeh, and his family.

But the watcher had done nothing.

He had said nothing.

He had only looked into Maanka's eyes with a gaze that declared, "I caught you."

Then the watcher had released him, never saying a word.

Iniko.

What had happened to Iniko?

Maanka Dak reached to his keyboard and punched in the command slaving the Department of Immigration files. That link, at least, was still functioning. He entered the command for a search on Vuurot Iniko. "The watcher with the strange sense of justice."

While the search ran, Maanka frowned and stared at a dark corner as he thought of the watcher. Iniko had caught him because he'd been careless for a split second. No one else, no normal person, would have noticed it: a tiny sliver of metal where a tiny sliver of that particular kind of metal should not have been. Most of the watchers would, and did, miss it. Those who wouldn't have missed it would've explained it away or ignored it. Vuurot Iniko had not missed it, and he had not rationalized away its existence. He had refused to put it down until he knew why it was where it was. He had found out the answer to his question. That answer led to another question, and that question to another answer. Moments later Maanka Dak was under arrest, facing certain death by torture.

A moment after his arrest, however, Iniko had let Maanka go. No comment, unless the capture itself and that table covered with evidence was a comment.

Nothing.

Iniko had been clever enough once to catch the elusive avenging ghost of the *Ahvin Yin*. Perhaps he was on the job again. Possibly Iniko was trying to make up for letting him loose back on the ship.

Maanka smiled at his own foolishness. When was guilt or conscience or any other feeling aside from a desire for power an Overseer's motive for anything?

Overseers just did. They were, in their own way, robots of a sort: automatons responding to their own genetic codes and training programs. After the Chooser selected a child for the black tattoo, the future Overseer's feelings were deadened and trained away.

"Guilt?" Maanka muttered. "Overseer guilt?" The thought of it made him want to laugh. An Overseer who could feel compassion or guilt would not be an Overseer. No, if Vuurot Iniko was after him, it had less to do with guilt than with the thrill of the hunt.

Maanka closed his eyes and brought back the image of the ship, that room, Vuurot Iniko in his black uniform. The watcher's face; his eyes. Iniko's look had said more than "I caught you." It had said, "I can catch you again."

The audio tone beeped, signaling the end of the search. Maanka punched for the information to appear and sat back as the image and the sketchy immigration disposition record of the watcher filled the screen.

Paul (Vuurot) Iniko's testing scores had been quite extraordinary, although nowhere near as high as Maanka's. After the Newcomers had been released from quarantine, Iniko had gone away to college. He graduated from Northwestern University, and then, because no other law school would take an Overseer, he was admitted to the University of Maine Law School, which had been, as usual, short on funds and hungry for any applicants who could pay tuition and tie their own shoes.

After graduating with what that institution considered honors, he had applied for the FBI Academy. Thanks to the intervention and encouragement of Thomas Rand, warden at China Lake, he had been accepted and had gone to Quantico. There the Department of Immigration record ended.

It wasn't worth going after the federal records on the watcher. "It's Iniko," Dak declared to the confines of the empty van. "It has to be Iniko."

Maanka shut down his equipment and climbed into the driver's seat. He knew where he had to go. The van coughed to life, and he backed out of the service alley onto Fraser. Throwing the vehicle into drive, he headed north until he reached Eagle. He turned right onto Eagle and nodded to himself. Perhaps Francisco and Iniko had caught him unaware for a moment. Very well, it would take him time to locate and take over the new command center, but he knew he could do it. Also, there were several cards he hadn't yet played. Francisco's family at the safe house in Montebello was one of them. He knew where Susan, Emily, and Vessna Francisco were being hidden.

"The memory of him," whispered Maanka. "The memory of him."

All he would have to do would be to slave one or two of the outside guards. He pressed his fingers against his jacket and felt the shape of the *tivati urih*. This time he would be certain to leave enough officers there guarding things on the outside. They would delay any kind of help that might arrive accidentally or on purpose, as the Frankel woman had done at the Francisco home, with that bloody frying pan.

Twenty minutes later he silently braked his darkened van a few numbers away from the safe house, turned off the ignition, got out, and examined his surroundings. Everything was quiet, no one on the street, most of the houses dark. Here and there a porch light, streetlight, or the bluish glow of a television touched the night.

His sensitive ears listened to the program being viewed in the house next to where he was standing. He went to the shadow of a fence and crept closer. He had seen the program before at China Lake. It was a very popular soap reworked for late night Newcomers. Rodney and Betty were fighting once again over Rodney's half brother (Betty's second husband after her first marriage to Rodney had been annulled), Steven, who was intent on breaking up Rodney and Betty's second marriage in order to remarry Betty and divorce her, thereby qualifying for alimony to be drawn on the vast sum Betty was supposed to inherit from Steven's and Rodney's manipulating grandfather, Martin, who was gasping out his last in a Boston hospital while secretly making out a new will. Cynics referred to the serial as "Rubberhead Place" or "Slag's Landing." He crossed the heavily shrubbed lawn, got into position, and peered through the blinds.

It was no ruse. There were viewers watching the program: a man, a woman, three girls, and a young boy. They were all human and laughing themselves sick. Maanka frowned as he squatted down. The man and the woman could be undercover officers, but not the four children.

The block hadn't been evacuated. Perhaps they thought evacuating the block would've been too obvious, tipping their hands. Still, the block should've been evacuated. If it came to shooting, poison, or explosives, the survivors would sue. Fiscal responsibility indicated an evacuation. Someone wasn't doing a good job of following the rules. Had the lawyers given the police department back to the cops? Not bloody damned likely.

Going back to the van, Maanka reached in and picked up a machine pistol and a five-pound block of J-26 molded around a programmable fuse built into the handle of a dead man's switch. He checked to make certain his neural controllers and the implantation instrument were attached inside his jacket, then, gently closing the van door, he vanished into the shadows and began working his way toward the safe house.

He glided through the night, his feet making no sound, his eyes and ear folds absorbing data, his magnificent brain collating at top speed.

Vikah ta.

It was the ship. Itri vi and the Niyez, the *Ahvin Yin* and its torch of justice against the minions of pain and suffering. This time, however, the playing field was worlds away and the opponent exceedingly clever.

He checked another house and another. A Tenctonese couple arguing about money, an elderly human couple arguing about money, a gay human and his Tenctonese lover arguing about money, a Tenctonese family watching "Slag's Landing," rolling on the floor, laughing.

As near as he could determine, all of the houses but one were occupied, and that one was for sale. The one house he knew for certain was occupied, the safe house, was dark.

"So clever," Maanka mocked.

All of his redundant systems had been countered, each of his backup plans had been anticipated. But would they be foolish enough to move the Francisco family, suspecting, as they must, that he would notice and then strike?

Each time he had checked before, Susan Francisco and her two daughters had been at the Montebello address, along with six police officers. Two of the officers had always been within the structure. Four were always outside, pretending to be doing anything but guarding the house.

Imbeciles.

Children.

Fear-riddled, thick-headed fools.

Yet, thought Maanka, there is another player on the field. Iniko? Possibly, but there was something spiritual, something mystical, about the power currently aligned against him. It was as though his enemy could see into his mind and read his thoughts. It was the feeling of someone knowing your thoughts before you've had a chance to think them yourself.

It was dangerous. Terrifying. Terribly exciting. It made Maanka's blood rush, brought all of his senses into sharp focus, drew upon all of his vast powers of intellect. He studied with his eyes every shade and shadow. He weighed with his ears every scrape and breath of sound. He sniffed at the air and felt the wind currents and humidity with his skin. The data absorbed by these measures brought a frown to Maanka's face.

None of the outside officers were there. Nowhere on the street were any of the outside officers. None of the unmarked police cars were parked in the area. There was no one. The houses hadn't been evacuated, and no one was outside guarding the safe house.

A snare.

A clumsy, very obvious ambush.

It played before his eyes like the steps of a dance. The safe house was the vortex of a clever trap, spring set, bait ready, jaws sharpened, waiting for him to insert his foot. Maanka squatted behind a bush, reached within himself, and called upon his mind, his courage, his center.

It was certainly a trap. The tip of every nerve ending told him so. But traps depend upon the prey acting as predicted. Maanka had to react unexpectedly. He had to foil the maze, confuse and confound the big hand with the cheese, make certain that this rat didn't get snapped.

But there was something else.

No officers were guarding the outside. There were none on the street. The house itself was dark. It was a gigantic maw waiting to snap shut upon whoever or whatever approached.

That is what it appeared to be.

Obviously a trap.

Obviously.

Patently.

Hence, his diabolical enemy knew that he would see the apparent trap and run in the opposite direction. He was supposed to look upon that clumsy arrangement, conclude that it had to be an ambush, and then run, leaving the inhabitants within unmolested.

"One thing I'm not going to do is leave them unmolested," he muttered to himself with satisfaction. Maanka Dak felt almost intoxicated as he looked from behind the bush and engaged the program on his bomb. The program entered and verified, he gripped the handle and depressed the dead man's switch. The dull blinking of the red activation indicator would help make him an easy target.

How dare they insult him with such a clumsy ruse? He stepped away from the shrub.

Was killing George Francisco the goal?

He shook his head. No. The goal was *vikah ta:* thorough revenge. There was much more pain to inflict on Francisco beside his own death.

Look at the pain he had caused by slaving George's human partner with an implant. The likely death of Matthew Sikes was eating George Francisco alive. How much more pain was there to inflict? There was the torture and death of Susan Francisco. If he could capture her alive, perhaps he could videotape her demise.

The rape, torture, and death of his wife, his daughter Emily, his son. His baby daughter Vessna. That would drive the traitor mad, choking on his own rage for eternity.

But the trap was too well set for that. Kidnapping was probably not possible. Nothing could stop him from killing Susan Francisco and her two daughters, though. That much was written. No need to become greedy.

Maanka nodded. Dead Susan. Dead Emily. Dead Vessna. The pain of that would indeed be a more thorough revenge on his brother Nicto than death. Death was so quick, so final. The end of everything, including feeling.

Horrible, excruciating feeling without end. Life, then, would be revenge. That would be *vikah ta.* Live long and suffer.

He walked until he stood in the center of the street. Turning to his right, he walked the center line until he was opposite the safe house. He stopped, faced the house, and waited. If the SWATs dropped him right there, the bomb contained enough high explosive to flatten the safe house and everything else within an eighty-meter radius. "There is no stopping me," he whispered as he began walking toward the safe house. "No stopping me."

He felt his skin tingle as he approached the house, waiting to see the muzzle flashes an instant before the hot metal flew through his body. He doubted that he would be alive long enough to suffer any significant amount of pain. Especially, he reminded himself, when he would be laughing, thinking about the deaths of his slayers, a surprised look on the dismembered face of every corpse.

Step by step he approached, visualizing the pain in Nicto's face as he heard of his wife and daughters' deaths; as he mulled it over in his mind for the remaining years of his wretched life; as the thought of it corrupted the last moment before his death.

"Kill me, kill me, kill me," Maanka prayed to the shadows beneath the trees, to the dark windows facing him. He would die, his finger would relax, the switch would close, and the neighborhood's silence would be shattered by the explosion.

Worried eyes would peer from behind curtains and through vertical blinds to see what had happened. There would be dust, smoke, possibly a column of flames lighting the sky. But what had happened? Few would know. Even fewer would care. Certainly his brother Nicto would be one of the rare exceptions, Maanka thought, as well as whoever was captaining the other side.

Iniko.

Failure would be his punishment for aligning himself against the *Ahvin Yin*.

Maanka Dak stood upon the flagstones before the front door. He felt light-headed, not having expected to be alive at that point in time. Holding the bomb in his left hand, he thrust the machine pistol into his belt and tried the doorknob. Finding the door locked, he smirked as he pushed the button for the doorbell and listened with satisfaction to the tacky bing-bong from inside. When no one answered, Maanka pressed the button again and again.

Silence.

"A trap isn't a trap, you idiots, unless there's some way in," he muttered angrily.

With his fist he pounded on the door until his hand ached. A light went on in a window next door and a porch light went on across the street.

"It's me!" he bellowed. "How easy can I make it for you?"

"Hey, fella!" came a shout from next door. "Nobody's there." Maanka pounded on the door again. "You deaf, asshole? Nobody's there. Go away or I'm calling the cops." The face went back into its hole and Maanka stared at the safe house door. A sinking feeling pulled at his hearts.

Nothing could be more obvious.

Susan Francisco, her two daughters, all of the police officers, were gone.

No one was in the house.

It explained everything. No big convoluted scheme; no intricately designed trap; there was simply no one there. They'd moved.

"No one's there," he said out loud. He knew it, but it was like that card game, poker, he played with some of the other inmates at China Lake. So many times he just knew what the cards were, but he just had to see them. The thought of possibly being bluffed out of a pot enraged him. He always called; always saw those cards; always paid his money to do so. Sucker bets. He could not resist a sucker bet. That was why he'd given up poker.

But why?

If they were gone, why?

They couldn't be there, but they had to be there.

Sucker bet.

He took a step back, renewed his grip on the dead man's switch, and then ran at the door with his shoulder, splintering the door frame on the first attempt. Inside it was silent, and he reached his hand to the switch and flipped on the hall light. He squinted against the glare and observed the cheap furniture, coffee-stained rugs, cigarette burns on the edges of everything, the aroma of wall-to-wall ashtray. It was a place where many cops had spent endless hours.

He checked the back, ran up the stairs and checked the two tiny bedrooms there. There was a crib in one of them. The house was deserted. From one of the upstairs windows he saw a black-and-white slowly cruising down the street. The unit pulled over to the curb and stopped. It wasn't a regular patrol or drive-by. The neighbor must have called the cops just like he said he would. Was that the trap?.

"This trap is apparently full of holes," he said as he reminded himself that the gift of the apparent is to make a trap look like a free meal or a route of escape. Yet, there is the apparent, and the apparently apparent. A hidden door looks more like a door to the fugitive than a door in the open. A hidden door that is hidden to make it look like a hidden door, however, can be the entrance to death's maze.

246

Door or lure?

It was time to get some answers from the opposition.

Maanka looked down at the bomb in his hand, canceled the program, and quietly padded downstairs as he reached into his jacket and withdrew the implantation device. Once he was in the kitchen, he backed himself against the wall and fitted an implant into the device. He entered his basic slave control program into the device, waited for a moment, then glanced around the corner and watched through the living room windows as the officers emerged from the black-and-white. Both of them remained hatless as they put their batons in their belts and drew their revolvers.

While one officer approached the front door, the other should've streaked for the back door. It made sense. If the cops come running in the front, the suspect escapes from the rear. But the officers weren't doing what was smart. They stayed together as they both approached the front door. There was no way to implant one of the officers without getting him alone. Maanka felt the grip of the machine pistol stuck in his belt. Perhaps he could take out one officer and subdue the other, but they both had their weapons out. Maanka demanded of himself an answer. Would he risk throwing away his chance at *vikah ta* to take out one officer in the hopes of slaving another for a purpose that he hadn't quite thought out?

There was another black-and-white on the street, and Maanka felt his hearts beat out of sync as he realized the second pair would attempt to cover the rear of the house. In a matter of moments the first pair of cops were through the front door and Maanka Dak was out the kitchen door and back into the shadows.

He pushed his way through a hedge, crossed over to an adjoining backyard, and crossed between the houses to another street, his breath coming hard.

Moments later, his hands shaking, he was in his van, driving west on Beverly. Maanka Dak knew he could play any game and win, yet to do so he needed to know the game. To know the game is to know which rules to break. Without knowing the game, breaking the rules can be playing into the hands of the opposition.

The Francisco family had been moved. There was no cause for panic. Maanka had identified four other safe houses that would be good possibilities. The Franciscos had to be somewhere, but that somewhere might be entirely out of the area. If that were the case, it would be back to combing the credit card data banks to pick up the trail. Susan Francisco and her daughters had been moved. That's all there was to it.

Yet even at the height of his fear, George Francisco hadn't left his home. His son had even arrived very late. Somehow Buck Francisco had evaded the security surrounding the house. Have to think about that.

Nevertheless, George Francisco had stayed home. Was he offering himself as bait?

Possibly.

He wasn't the kind to thumb his nose at his enemies, if the enemy in question was after his friends and family. But the new adversary, Iniko or whoever it was, had thrown all of Maanka's equations into imbalance. The old limits were out of sight.

Before Maanka's van reached Atlantic Boulevard, he turned off Beverly onto a side street and pulled up behind the husk of an abandoned Ford Galaxy. He sat shaking behind the wheel for several minutes before he scanned the street and found it deserted. He took a deep breath, engaged the motion detectors, and turned to enter the rear of the van. Once there, he pulled the blackout curtain shut, sat down, energized his equipment, and locked into his telephone remotes. Concentrating his attention on one number in North Belvedere, he stared at the screen, his eyes almost glazing as his mind worked at a furious pace, sorting and collating the new data, trying to get a step ahead of the opposition.

The Francisco number came on the screen. Route identification: Mount Andarko Hospital. He was still at his home. Francisco would be on the telephone checking on his partner's failing progress. Maanka's mouth opened and a hiss came from his throat as the voice-print identifications came on the screen: Susan Francisco, then Cathy Frankel.

He cut on the switch to monitor the call. "—stable, but they can't keep him like this for much longer. They're getting ready to operate. Are you and the girls all right back home?"

"The house is just a wreck, Cathy. You should see the hall mirror, the walls. We'd just painted." She laughed nervously. "I'm being terribly silly. I'm so happy just to have the family together; so happy that we're alive. This has been such a nightmare, I'm just grateful it's over—"

"Over?" Maanka repeated.

He cut off the switch and stared at the screen. There seemed to be an odd warp in reality's main strut. The voice-print identification of George Francisco appeared on the screen, and Maanka lifted his hand to cut on the monitor, when the motion detectors began flashing.

There was a sound. Maanka turned his head as he heard a rattle from the back of the van. A scrape, a voice muttering, another voice answering.

Maanka watched as the lights in the compartment took on a purple tinge and went slightly out of focus. There was irritation, pique, anger, and rage. What rode through Maanka Dak's mind right then was off the scale.

It was too much.

Everything was a bit too complicated, a bit too delicate, to have to bother with ants.

It was just a bit too much.

Another rattle, and Maanka pulled his machine pistol. He aimed it in the direction of the back door and stood up as he listened to someone work at the lock with a pry bar. There was a snap and a clunk; flesh and bone striking sheet metal.

"Damn!" cursed a voice in a loud whisper.

"What is it, Rody?" whispered another voice.

"Shit! Look! Tore my goddamned fingernail!"

"Fingernail? Jeez, Rody, get on with it."

"Lookit it! Lookit my damned fingernail!"

"Jeez, Rody. Open it up! C'mon, man! We gotta go."

"Dammit, Buggy, it hurts!"

"Forget the fuckin' fingernail, okay, Rody? We gotta go!"

"Awright, Buggy. Don't pee in your pants. It just hurts like hell."

"Okay, Rody. I acknowledge that."

"Fuck you."

There was a wrenching, groaning sound, then a snap. The door opened slowly and the ones called Rody and Buggy cried out as they saw the machine pistol pointed at their faces. Maanka pulled the trigger, the pistol roared, then he reached back, pulled shut the door, and the van squealed away from the curb, leaving the pair of thieves with the remains of their faces staring up wide-eyed at the night sky. As the life ebbed from him, the one called Rody peed in his own pants.

CHAPTER 24

GEORGE FRANCISCO LOOKED out of the living room window at the street's night sights. No cops, no traps, no special anything. Mrs. Rothenberg was walking her evil-tempered pit bull, Satan. The animal was so mean and uncontrollable that late at night was the only time she could walk him. Nate Robeson, as usual, jogged by her and Satan. As he usually did, Satan pulled loose from Mrs. Rothenberg's grasp and chased Nate. Both Nate and Satan loved to run together.

Across the street Polly Wexler's cat was on the roof again, singing at the top of its lungs. Chances were, Ramon Gutierrez, her next door neighbor, was dialing 911, although Emily might have been right about what she said regarding Ramon's feelings toward Polly. The last time George had seen Ramon and Polly together in the daylight, Ramon had neglected to mention the cat, so concentrated was he on sucking in his gut. Things were normal. That was the abnormality.

"It was a *Hila* at the *Rama Vo* who suggested turning the label tables on Maanka," George said to Paul Iniko. "We made Maanka brilliant by treating him as though he were brilliant. Canceling the command organization and quitting the safe house ended the brilliance."

"And now," Iniko said, "you're treating him as though he's stupid?"

"No. I had the captain cancel everything and go back to normal operating procedures." He turned his head and looked at the former Overseer. "We're treating him as though he is nothing."

Paul Iniko was sitting in the overstuffed chair next to the couch where Susan and Buck sat. Susan sipped at a cup of tea, while Buck, lost in thought, stared silently at the FBI agent. Emily and Vessna were upstairs, asleep. Susan placed her cup and saucer on the coffee table. As she did so, her hands shook, slopping a bit of tea into the saucer.

"I'm sorry," she said to no one in particular. "It's been a harrowing couple of days. I'm still frightened."

"It's all right," George said.

She glanced nervously at Iniko, and shifted her gaze to George. "Darling, are you saying we have no protection against this Maanka Dak?"

George turned his head and faced the window once more. "There are Agent Iniko and myself. I have my pistol." He glanced at Paul Iniko and raised his eyebrows.

"Yes. I have a weapon, as well."

"We have two pistols, then. Perhaps we also have Maanka Dak's imagination working for us."

Susan glanced at Buck, frowned, and held out her hands as she looked again at her husband. "George, please explain something to me."

"If I can."

Susan moistened her lips and forced her voice to calm down. "If all of those dozens police officers last night, armed to the teeth and watching every blade of grass, couldn't stop Dak, I don't see how just the two of you can manage from in here with nothing but your street clothes."

For the first time Paul Iniko cracked a tiny smile. "I think, Mrs. Francisco, it's more like no defense at all can't do much worse than last night's super effort by the department."

"This is hardly the time for levity, Agent Iniko," Susan snapped, the anger and acid resentment in her voice at last obvious. She faced George and said, "When you said this man was coming over, you told me he had some important information. You didn't tell me he was an Overseer! I think I'd best know what this important information is." George glanced at Buck, but Susan placed her hand on her son's shoulder. "I think Buck's paid his dues for this meeting."

"Quite so," George said. "I was just wondering at his reaction to sitting down to tea with a black tattoo." George looked around and fixed his gaze on Paul Iniko. "It's your intention to get the information out, isn't it?"

"In an effective manner."

"Go ahead, then. Tell them about MDQ."

Susan looked at the FBI agent. Iniko's face became wooden as he debated something within himself. The debate concluded, he began talking in a deep monotone, his face revealing nothing about his feelings. He sat motionless in his chair, seemingly more rock than living being.

"There are no more Overseers, Mrs. Francisco.

There are no more slaves." He steadied his gaze on her. "I am not your enemy."

"You have been my enemy since I was born, *Overseer*! You can't come in here wearing a coat and tie, sit down in my living room, and tell me all those decades of horror didn't happen."

"No," he answered. "I won't tell you they never happened. Neither will I tell you they were better than you remember them, nor that I am to be excused my role. I will tell you two things, however."

"Two things?"

Iniko nodded. "First, those decades of horror are in the past, not the present. The pain you feel now you inflict on yourself. No Overseer is inflicting it. Second, on the ship I had precisely the same amount of choice as to what I became as you did in what you became: none."

Susan was silent for a long time. At last she said, "What about this MDQ and what does it have to do with us?"

Iniko gripped the armrests of his chair, leaned back and began. "It stands for Medical Q. I don't think the Q stands for any particular word. It simply represents intelligence as in intelligence community. MDQ's an anachronism left over from the Cold War; a secret government organization that studies and conducts experiments in the medical and psychological aspects of intelligence work."

"You mean drugs and stuff like that?" Buck asked. "Secret experiments with LSD?"

"Among other things," Iniko answered. "MDQ was organized under the authority of the Clandestine Offices Act back in the sixties; its funding appears on no departmental budget."

George Francisco leaned his back against the wall, folded his arms and watched as Paul Iniko appeared to hammer the last few nails into the coffin of his FBI career. Malcolm Bone's comments regarding labels played before George's mental eye as he studied the former Overseer.

Former Overseer, George thought to himself. Could such a thing be possible? Were the Overseers simply an occupation, an organization, an association that could be terminated by withdrawing, by ending the reason for the association's existence? Or, instead, were the Overseers a race unto themselves, genetically fixed to be arrogant, unfeeling monsters for life?

They were chosen young to have their feelings of compassion, love, and pity cauterized, a vicious program of right and wrong hammered in the gaps to replace them. They were educated separately in disciplines designed to equip them to wield power. In exchange they were given authority, power, and privilege.

Race or occupation? Label or fact? Perception or prejudice? It seemed stupid to say it, but nothing changed without change. George wanted very much to be changed, to have the peace in his hearts that came from having no hates, having no resentments. But Overseers were a different kind of test. George had a lot of old scores that clamored to be settled before anything like forgiveness could be approached.

There was that tattoo around Iniko's left wrist. What did he see there? George asked himself. To see things for what they were, he would have to say that all he saw was a tattoo. But that mark, that label of all labels, meant so many things: pain, frustration, oppression, cruelty. Was a ten-mile walk into the woods but a mere ten miles back out? The question hung before him like a challenge.

"George," Susan interrupted.

He looked up and saw that his wife, Paul Iniko, and Buck were looking at him. "What?"

Susan stood, walked over, and placed a hand on his arm. "You looked terribly upset."

"Upset." He closed his eyes as his murderous wave of anger left, to be replaced by a flood of depression. "It's nothing; a physical thing I'm going through."

"Did you have a doctor examine you?"

George nodded. "Yes, I did."

"Is it *nia?*"

George took an angry deep breath and let it out as he shook his head. "No. It's not *nia.*"

"Well, George? What is it? Is it something more serious? You can tell me. In fact, you'd better tell me."

He glanced at Iniko and Buck, both of whom already knew. Susan was the only one who didn't. "I'm sorry for getting angry. Getting angry is part of the problem, as well as sadness, the giggles, hallucinations, and who knows what else. It's *riana.*" As Susan took a step back and covered her mouth with her hand, George nodded at Iniko. "Go ahead."

Iniko studied George for a moment and nodded as he shifted his gaze to Susan. "Shall I continue?"

She looked at her husband for a long time, her eyes wide and filled with tears. *"Riana?"*

George giggled, shook his head and said, "That's right, and I'm not going to die. At least, it won't be from *riana.* We can talk about it later. Let Agent Iniko tell you about MDQ."

Iniko raised his eyebrows, and Susan nodded as she sat in the straight-back chair next to the window. "Very well."

Iniko stared at George for a second, then looked at Susan. "Perhaps it's not my place to say this, Mrs. Francisco, but your husband is right. There is nothing to fear from *riana*. I've been through it twice myself."

"On the ship," Susan said, *"riana* meant that you died!"

Buck reached out his hand and placed it on his mother's arm. "Mom? Mom?"

She looked at her son, her eyes filled with anger and fear. "What?"

"Mom, don't worry about it. We're not on the ship anymore."

"I know we're not on the ship," she repeated, sarcasm creeping into her voice. "We're not on the ship, we're having an Overseer over for tea, and the *Ahvin Yin* is trying to slay your father and his family as traitors. Nothing to worry about at all."

"I meant there's nothing to worry about from Dad going through *riana.*"

Susan stared at her son for a moment, then faced Paul Iniko. "Very well, Agent Iniko. What does this secret intelligence organization have to do with the nightmare my family's been put through since yesterday?"

"They organized MDQ, funded it, and did everything to bring it into being except plan to. It was simply there for decades, harmlessly drawing funds, employing a few hundred bureaucrats, churning out classified reports that no one cared to read. I believe the Senate oversight committee was planning on eliminating the funding for MDQ. Then our ship landed."

"Monsters from outer space," Buck said. "There really *is* someone out there."

"Yes." Iniko clasped his fingers together in his lap

and leaned forward, resting his weight upon his forearms. "Once the ship came under the control of the U.S. government, MDQ immediately took control of the medical equipment, supplies, and data. As you remember, most of the medical staff were killed in the crash. Those that remained were thoroughly investigated. Considering the mission of MDQ, I can only imagine the reaction once they learned about the Niyezian neural transmitter technology. In any event, Maanka and Sita Dak and Sing Fangan were the three most experienced technicians who remained from the original implant teams. However, by the time MDQ had pieced that together, the Dak brothers and Sing Fangan had already entered the exciting world of direct-withdrawal banking."

"He was arrested for bank robbery," George said to Susan. "I was one of the arresting officers."

Iniko leaned back in his chair. "The apprehension of the Daks and Sing Fangan was supposed to be a bureau operation with minimal LAPD support. I believe it was very important for the FBI to arrest all three men alive and out of sight of any other authority. The bureau, of course, is a part of MDQ. With the leverage of hard time in the balance, the chief of the organization—"

"Dr. Carrie Norcross," George completed.

Paul Iniko nodded. "Yes. She could've worked a deal with the Daks and Fangan."

Susan slowly shook her head. "They'd tell MDQ how to manufacture controllers and stick them in humans in exchange for failing to prosecute, right?"

Iniko smiled. "That's right." He pointed at George. "Except your husband and his partner, Bill Duncan, shattered the whole plan. The short of it is the FBI thought Maanka and his gang would hit one place, and those two cops on backup figured Maanka would hit someplace else." He nodded his head respectfully at George. "I've seen the files. It was a brilliant deduction."

"I didn't make it," George said, sadness entering his voice. "A big, dumb, bigoted, Scot son of a bitch named Duncan figured it out."

"How?"

"He's a cop. He was a cop. He said his bunions hurt, so we left our post blocking a street and raced to the Third Street Penny Bank. The three of them were coming out the door of the armored truck just as we arrived. Maanka's biological brother was killed during the arrest. I killed him."

"The *vikah ta*," Susan said. Turning to Iniko, she asked, "And what does this MDQ have to do with what's going on now?"

"They couldn't hide the arrest or otherwise work the same deal. A shootout in front of a bank? Amanda Reckonwith and the media were on it like chains on . . ." Iniko's eyes changed color from embarrassment. "The media were all over it. There was no jiggle room for a deal. MDQ did the best they could. Under the guise of investigating the applications of Tenctonese science to mental health, they've been working with Maanka Dak over the past few years, attempting to recreate the Niyezian neural control technology and adapt it to controlling humans. Right now media representatives of Central Intelligence, the National Security Agency, and a number of other institutions are busily doing their best to make certain that no one responsible gets identified as responsible. Polishing perceptions, as one fellow put it." Iniko stood and walked to the picture window. He folded his arms and stared at the streetlights outside. "To a large degree, MDQ is responsible for Maanka Dak's escape, and for everything that's happened as a result."

"I don't get it," Buck said. "Stuff like that isn't legal. Why haven't you or someone else blown the whistle on this?"

Paul Iniko's gaze shifted until he was looking at Buck. "Everything I've told you about MDQ is hearsay; my unsupported opinion. I have a few memos and can remember a few names, but there's nothing worth bringing into court."

"What about the media? Go on the talk shows, CNN, Fox Fire?"

"To many, Buck, I'm just an Overseer. Whatever I have to say is a lie." He looked at Susan. "I wouldn't just be sipping on a cup of tea. I'd be telling them that their very own government, of some of the humans, by a few of the humans, for a few of the humans, is corrupt, operates outside of the law, and got a lot of good people killed through suspicion, avarice, and plain stupidity. How many would listen?"

"Then what're you doing here?" she asked.

Iniko looked back at the street. "I have my own piece of responsibility regarding Dak. I had him back on the ship. He was a murderer, I had him, and I let him go."

"Murderer?" Buck asked. "Who did he murder?"

"It doesn't matter who he murdered," Paul Iniko answered. "I used to think it made a difference. I used to think it was justified to kill someone if he was a big enough monster and in a place where he could not be touched within the rules. I loathed the person Dak killed. I despised him so much I excused the murders of his entire family and violated my duty as both *charkah* and Overseer. Indeed, he was a monster. But it doesn't make a difference. A murder is a murder. A murderer is a murderer. An accomplice is as equally guilty."

"Who did he murder?" Buck insisted. "It does make a difference." He glanced at his father. "Was it on Itri Vi? Was it the pain minister, Mro Sheviat? We all knew about his death. Did Maanka Dak kill Mro Sheviat?"

"No, Buck," George interrupted.

Susan allowed her arms to fall to her sides. "Buck, what do you know about that? You weren't but six or seven."

"The *Ahvin Yin,* Mom. We—the children—we worshiped the *Ahvin Yin.* When Mro was killed, we all knew the *Ahvin Yin* did it. They were our heroes. If Maanka killed Mro, I can see why this Overseer let him—"

"No, Buck," George interrupted a second time. "Dak didn't kill Mro Sheviat. You know he didn't."

"No, Dad. As always, all I know is what I've proven to myself. Everything else is somebody else's opinion."

George glanced at Susan, shifted his gaze to Paul Iniko, then let his gaze come to rest upon his son. "I told Buck before that Maanka didn't kill Mro Sheviat. I did."

Susan's eyes widened. "You?"

"Me." George refused to look back at Susan. Instead he looked at the floor before Buck's feet. "There's nothing pretty about it. I executed him. He was bound, helpless, and pleading for his life. In my hearts I had nothing but hate, revenge, pain. He had been responsible for the torture deaths of my parents, my *binnaum,* so many friends. Executing him was part of my initiation into the resistance." George lifted his gaze until he was looking in his son's eyes. "I ripped out his throat with a knife."

"That isn't murder, Dad," Buck protested. "That's —That's—"

"Murder," George completed and smiled slightly. "I did it for many reasons I thought were sufficient at the time. Perhaps it was. I've gone over it a hundred thousand times since, and I'd do the same given the same set of circumstances. But it wasn't revolution, a political statement, or anything else. It was punishment, revenge, murder." George's lips were touched by a sad little smile. "Buck, don't let your *Hila* catch you playing label games like that with your own head."

"What of the other murder?" Susan asked.

George glanced at Iniko, then leveled his gaze on Susan. "It was on the ship, after Itri Vi. Maanka killed the Overseer pain minister Torumeh and his family."

"Torumeh?" Susan repeated, her eyes wide. "That was no murder! Torumeh was—was an incredible monster! How many men, women, and children endured intolerable suffering because of him? I remember his death. I remember blessing whoever it was that had done it." She faced Iniko. "Letting him go, Overseer, made you as close to a saint as anything could have been on that ship. Maanka Dak was a hero."

He raised an eyebrow as he said, "And now Maanka Dak's killed Tom Rand, Bill Duncan, dozens of innocent bystanders, and unless we can capture him and his equipment intact, it's likely that Matthew Sikes will die, as well. He's a murderer, Mrs. Francisco. He's a psychopathic killer whose killings have only recently become distasteful. He's always been a psychopathic killer, and I let him go." He turned to the window and stood next to George as he studied the night. "I wonder where he is, now that he's no longer brilliant."

"I wonder what else is coming at us," George added.

"Whatever it is, Dad," Buck whispered, "it's coming through the basement." He pointed down toward the floor. "Emily's toys. I heard something move."

Paul Iniko reached out and cut off the lights as George pulled his pistol and rushed to Susan's side. "George," she said, her voice edging into panic. "I told Emily to put those toys away before she went to bed. I swear I did. I'll—"

"Susan," he whispered, "it's all right. He's not company. We don't care what he thinks of the basement. Okay?"

"Okay." She giggled nervously, nodded in the dark, and grasped her husband's left arm with both of her hands. "How did he get into the basement? There're no windows or outside doors."

George held his lips next to her ear fold and whispered, "You can ask Buck while both of you are hiding upstairs with Emily and Vessna. If there's shooting, I want to know where all of you are."

"Shooting?"

"There shouldn't be any. Paul and I rigged a little welcome down there."

"George, please be careful." She glanced into the dark, her eyes not finding the FBI agent. "Paul too."

George kissed her cheek and gave her and Buck a shove toward the stairs. Walking past the stairway, he came up behind Iniko.

The FBI agent held up his hand, showing four fingers. Checking to make certain that George understood, he made a fist, pointed at George, then pointed toward the shadow beneath the sink, where George had cowered the night before. As quietly as he could, George tiptoed to the spot and squatted facing the door. The door was padlocked and had two metal bars braced across it, one at chest height, the other at knee height. Concealed deep inside Buck's tunnel, Iniko had placed a small explosive charge that he could set off by means of the remote control attached to his belt. Once the charge exploded, the tunnel would collapse, and whoever was inside the basement would be trapped. At least, that was the plan.

Iniko pressed himself into the dark corner of the kitchen to the left of the door, held out his automatic and froze. George aimed his own weapon at the door, cupped his grip with his left hand and listened past the beating of his hearts to the sounds from the basement.

Who would it be this time?

Maanka himself, or more of his enslaved police officers? George hadn't expected anything tonight. If Maanka had been as two dimensional as Malcolm Bone seemed to think he was, bringing Susan and the girls home and shutting down the command center should have shuffled enough labels to grind him to at least a temporary halt.

He hadn't really believed in the label game. He had been at a loss, however, as to what else to do. Besides, Iniko had gone along with it.

George glanced at the shadow opposite his. Iniko, an Overseer, had gone along with the *Hila's* suggestion. For a thousand reasons George could think of, he should have found that reason enough to reconsider the whole thing. Yet, there was a part of him, something new that had grown within him, that had trusted Paul Iniko. And now the wisdom of that choice was about to reveal itself.

As a foot made the bottom stair squeak, George looked at the blacks and grays in the kitchen, grateful that there were, at least, no psychedelic light shows or stretches of blindness with which to contend. The third stair from the bottom squeaked, and he fixed his gaze on the door, his pistol sighted dead center. There was a bit of a gold tinge to the shadows, and the taste of copper in his mouth. The gold quickly faded to garnet, and the copper taste mutated to something resembling celery.

Tension, he silently told himself. Stress brought on the light show; therefore, it was up to him to manage his stress. Relax. Take it easy. The next set of feet had yet to step upon the bottom stair.

Why?

The garnet began to sparkle with scarlet blooms. Why wasn't the next guy in line on the stairs? From the sounds below, the other three intruders were waiting amidst Emily's toys while the fourth climbed the stairs.

A rush of all four would have made more sense. While he and Paul Iniko were occupied killing off the first two of Maanka's slaved beings, the remaining two could open up with rapid-fire weapons, providing they could get through the door, of course.

There was something wrong.

The intruders appeared cautious.

They seemed to care whether they lived or died.

The blindness touched him for a moment as windows opened in his mind. Keeping his weapon pointed at the door, somehow he knew that the intruders were not under Dak's control, nor were any of them Maanka Dak.

The images came back to his eyes painted in vibrant blues and greens.

Professionals. Quick. Silent. The almost inaudible click of a bubble switch, the third stair squeaking, then the bottom stair squeaked.

MDQ.

They were after Iniko.

That bubble switch signaled an explosive charge set against the door. "MDQ, Paul!" George screamed. "Fire in the hole!"

George turned toward the back door as he saw Iniko begin to spring for the living room. Just then the room filled with a flash and a sound beyond hearing as a giant hand picked up George and slammed him into the wall.

The world kept spinning, feet over head backward. His head felt unpleasantly drunk; as though every fiber of his being was about to be puked out into the celestial commode. He could hear nothing. All he could see were lights and blobs whirling about. Some smell, acid and bitter, filled his nostrils.

He tried to move and there was a numbness in his leg. He reached down with his hand and felt a piece of metal protruding from the fleshy part of his thigh. Another window in his mind opened.

They weren't just after Paul Iniko. To eliminate Paul, the four intruders would have to take out George and his entire family. No witnesses, no one left behind to tell tales about people and organizations back in Washington. Just another tragedy caused by that rash of unexplained mass killings out there in L.A. Perhaps it was El Niño, the Santa Anas, the cops freaking, or another grassroots political statement burning the damned city down, blowing it up, shooting it to pieces. Who the hell cared? It's on the other end of the country, the home of Flakes R Us, and anyway, it's only a bunch of rubberheads who were wasted.

They're taking our jobs and raising a bunch of terribly uncomfortable civil rights, defense, and space exploration questions. Good riddance.

The metal was a piece of the crossbar George had spent part of the afternoon installing on the door to the basement while Paul set the charge in the tunnel. He didn't know whether it made more sense to leave the bar stuck in his leg or to yank it out. Left in, it plugged up the hole rather well. However, it also left a foot or more of bent metal sticking out of his leg like a great fishhook looking for things upon which to snag.

To yank or not to yank, that is the question.

It made sense to yank out the metal while the leg was still numb. Waiting until the lights stopped dancing in front of his eyes and the paramedics arrived would mean having it yanked out when feeling had come back to his leg and he was screaming with the pain.

George reached down, intending to explore the rod with his fingers. That's when he found he still had his pistol in his hand.

Another explosion, smaller, a pistol shot, made George look up. A lavender shape was standing in the bright red door to the living room. In its hand was a pistol. It had just fired at the crumpled form of Paul Iniko on the floor.

The figure aimed again, and George lifted his pistol and fired twice at the lavender shape, bringing the figure down. Another figure, also lavender, fired at George from the basement door, and George emptied his weapon in the shape's direction. He heard the person's footsteps running down the basement stairs. He spoke to another person in the basement, then they fell silent.

George pulled the metal rod from his thigh, surprised that feeling had come back to his leg. He reached up to the counter and pulled himself up to his feet. Hobbling over to Iniko's side, he looked down to see Iniko holding a hand over his left heart. He was breathing hard and was barely conscious. "Iniko. Can you hold it together for a bit?"

The FBI agent closed and opened his eyes in assent. George reached to his belt, took the remote, and dizzily listened to the two shooters in the basement. When it was silent in the basement, he waited another minute and pushed the trigger. There was a whump sound followed by more silence. George slumped against the doorjamb and let the control fall to the floor. "Hope I had that timed accurately."

He felt Iniko's hand gripping his arm. He opened his eyes and looked down at him. "What?"

Iniko was holding up four fingers. He cocked his head and gestured toward the living room and the stairway to the second floor.

The fourth one.

One dead on the floor, two down in the tunnel. Where was the fourth?

Panic gripped George's throat as he dropped his own revolver and took Iniko's automatic from the man's fingers. He couldn't seem to pull himself to his feet. Instead he dragged himself through the door and turned his head to look up the stairs. He saw a white jogging shoe vanish from view as it left the opening to the second floor landing. There was no way he could get a shot at its owner. He pulled himself up and stumbled, collapsing at the foot of the stairs as a loud "bong" came from the top of the stairs. As he pulled himself to his feet, a lavender shape tumbled down the stairs and piled up into a heap before him. Susan came running down after, crying, and brandishing a skillet that George was beginning to look upon as an old friend.

"George," Susan cried, "damn it, I told Emily to put this away! I swear I told her!"

"I know." He held her in his arms, allowed himself a breath and his own eyes to fill with tears. "I know." He giggled and said, "I'll talk to her about it." He sobbed out another laugh and looked up to see Buck standing at the head of the stairs with Emily at his side and Vessna in his arms. George brushed Susan's temples with his fingers and repeated, "Yeah, I'll talk to her about it."

CHAPTER 25

DIFFERENT.

Changed.

The rules changed.

It was all different from what had been intended. The event, the city, the planet, the universe, the life of Maanka Dak. Different.

It was a new thought; as though a hitherto sealed door had been opened, allowing light to enter where no light had ever before been. The light showed that rules are made and rules are unmade. Rules are not physical laws of the universe. They're creatures of choice, custom, ignorance, panic, prejudice, the idle selection of the moment. The rules chosen, the rules imposed, made the difference between freedom and slavery; war and diplomacy; cop and criminal.

He had always known it, but had not known it. The night had opened a door.

Except there are some doors that should not be opened. Maanka had a headache. It kept growing worse.

The open door had revealed to Maanka worlds of possibilities that he had never imagined, possibilities that were no longer possible for Maanka Dak.

Because of other rules.

Important rules.

Not material things. He had the ability to control others to provide him with whatever material objects he might desire. There were none, however, that he desired. The possibilities that were newly revealed to him were things of a more spiritual cast: different views of himself, goals to which he could have aspired, feelings he could have had. All beyond him now.

Maanka pulled back the blackout curtain, allowing the dirty yellow haze of the new morning to filter into the back of the van. The sun hung apparently motionless, floating in a sea of pollution.

"What a monument is a star," he whispered to the emptiness surrounding him. He turned his head and looked through hooded eyes at the equipment he had pieced together since his arrest; machines that he had invested with the programs he had designed over his years at China Lake. He reached out a hand and touched the screen of the holographic imager, the invention of which had brought him to the attention of the world's health services community. Now they could, in effect, take an organ completely out of the patient's body, hold it up to the light, and examine it. The organ could be sectioned, its parts function cycled, its composition and condition determined down to the molecular level.

In recognition of his achievement, the American Medical Association had established a scholarship fund in his name. Back in his cell were plaques, certificates, and framed letters of commendation from medical associations and academies around the world for that and other achievements of his. Before his escape, he had seen none of them. To Maanka they had been props lulling warden, guards, and parole board into a sort of stupor that would allow him to escape and work *vikah ta* on Nicto.

He had done things that no one had ever before done. The evidence of that sat before him, silently flashing its lights. Controlling humans, preparing for some kind of invasion from outer space, superior interrogation techniques, this was the monument, clandestine though it would be, that MDQ had held before him.

Insanity.

The monument was too small; too well hidden; the need of the author too great to be fed by such concealed testimonials.

Insanity.

What of that? What of MDQ's cover story? So many cures for so many mental and physical conditions? They were possible. He had done the work himself. To learn how to control a human, he had found it necessary to learn how to cure them. If only he could have figured out a new biofilament medium. The answer, he suspected, was somewhere in the enzyme attack on proteins, but he just didn't have the background to know, even to find out. He, Maanka Dak, could have gone down in the chronicles of Planet Earth as the bringer of health, the end of insanity, the end of so many diseases.

He could've spent those years since the crash studying, learning. . . .

Too late. Too late.

Barry B. Longyear

The new player was on to him.

There are choices that cannot be taken back.

Why had that door opened?

Something before his eyes changed. A flash, a new trace.

He focused his eyes and looked at the screen. Voice-print identification, a line in yellow letters upon a red stripe: George Francisco. The route identification was from Mount Andarko Hospital to Francisco's own home. Maanka Dak turned on the audio monitor.

"Maanka? Maanka?" the voice of George Francisco called. "Maanka?"

Maanka smiled and activated his collar pickup. "I'm here, Nicto."

There was a pause on the other end, and then Francisco said, "Okay, Buck. You can hang up."

"Dad, I just—"

"I know, son. It's going to be all right. Just hang up." Another pause, then the receiver at the Francisco home was hung up. "Maanka?"

The headache was growing worse. "I'm here. Nicto, I want you to know that it was not I who broke into your home last night."

"I know."

"Do you know who they were?"

"They carried no identification, but I assume they were under orders from someone connected to MDQ. There were four of them. We took in two alive. Neither one is talking, but all four have organized crime records. The two we captured are looking at a lot of time. Perhaps we can persuade them to testify."

Maanka smiled to himself. "Not them. Their guild has an obsession with *vikah ta*. It's too bad I can't implant them for you, although I doubt if it would

274

stand up in court." He leaned his elbows on the table edge and rubbed his eyes. "I want to know something, Nicto. Will you tell me?"

"If I can."

"Do you know Vuurot Iniko? An Overseer. He's in the FBI now."

"He was with me and my family at the house last night."

"Is he alive?"

"He was seriously wounded, but he's in fair condition here at Mount Andarko. They expect a complete recovery, if anyone can completely recover after having his guts torn to shreds."

Maanka Dak sat back and looked at the trace detector. Nothing was being run on the line. No one was trying anything. "Why did you call me, Nicto?"

"I want to make a deal with you: I want to swap me for the *tivati urih*. I want the Niyezian implantation awl."

Maanka felt his head split with pain. "That would be for Matthew Sikes, your partner."

"That's right. We'll meet, you turn over the device to someone there, and I'm yours. The only condition I have is that the *vikah ta* ends with me. Once you've finished with me, it's over."

"You wouldn't try to con an old con, would you, Nicto?" Maanka Dak shut off the pickup and held his head with his hands. "I don't understand," he said to himself. "I don't understand any of it."

Would Nicto try for an ambush?

A trick?

It made sense, if anything made sense, but when had anything ever made sense? Only in the depths of deepest madness was there sense. There, the answers could be relied upon not to change.

Had Nicto gone mad? The player's hand was in all of this unctuous self-sacrifice, wasn't it?

It was all a game, after all. But what was winning to Nicto? Maanka wondered. His own death? Nicto's partner's life? His partner's life in exchange for his own life? Would he throw away his future, his family, for a human? A cop? A piece of that hated authority that they had all sworn themselves to destroy?

That had changed. Where his obsessive hate for authority had resided, there was but a void. Now, what was winning to him, Maanka Dak?

The *vikah ta?*

It had been the *vikah ta,* but that had changed. So many things had changed.

He engaged the pickup. "Nicto, listen. I want you to know something. I'm sorry. About your partner. About Duncan. About Kavit. About Tom Rand. About them all."

"Sorry?" Nicto's voice exploded. "Sorry? How can you say that? How can you kill and injure all those men, women, and children and expect me to believe that you're sorry! By Celine's wrath, you monster! You raped Kavit! Do you know what she's going through right now? My partner is just this side of death! My family, all of those innocent men and women! All of the dead! And you're sorry?"

Reaching out his hand, Maanka stared at the sound column as a thousand faces seemed to peer at him, scream at him, accuse him. "Quiet! Quiet! All of you, quiet!" He squinted and pressed his palms against his temples until the faces stopped screaming at him.

"I don't know," he whispered. "I don't know, Nicto. I'm sorry. I'm sorry. That's all I know." He nodded at the faces. They were whispering at him, and he had heard what they had said.

"Nicto, I know you're undergoing *riana.*"

There was a moment of confusion at the other end, an audio stumble over the abrupt change of subject. "Yes," Nicto said at last. "Yes, I am."

"Does it truly make you more intelligent? On the ship the Overseers who'd gone through it said that it made them more intelligent."

There was a silence followed by a sigh, a tired laugh. "Yes, in widely spaced touches, I suppose it does. Whether it's going to be a net gain is still to be decided. Right now I feel quite stupid."

Maanka moistened his lips and let his chin rest on his chest. "I find myself in a strange corner. Is it you, Nicto? Are you the new player?"

"No, Maanka. You're still light-years beyond me in intelligence."

"Who, then? Who is my opponent? It's not Grazer. Is it Iniko? I remember the watcher. I've searched the records. I know he's in the FBI."

"No. He helped me last night, but it's not Iniko. The player is much more brilliant than the watcher."

Maanka Dak seemed to weave in place as reality began losing its grip on planet Earth. "Everything exploded in my face last night, Nicto. Every move, everything I tried, was anticipated. I could not make a move without it having been thought of first by someone else. It's destroyed something within me. Changed me. Who is the player?"

"You are, Maanka. You've been playing against yourself. All we did was back off."

"Back off?"

"We shut down the command center, moved my family back home, went back to normal operating procedures. The only unusual order given was that officers were forbidden to separate when answering calls, and that's because of another serial killer we're after called the Black Slayer. He's a very unhappy fellow who kills only police officers."

"Black Slayer?" Maanka wrestled his headache down to a place where his ears weren't screaming. "If all he kills are cops, why Black Slayer? Why not Blue Slayer, or Officer Off?"

"He's just like you, Maanka. He's hung up on a label. All he kills are what he thinks are black officers. His label includes anyone with a dark skin, which, thus far, has saved a number of folks who call themselves black, and has cost the lives of seven others, including an officer in Newton whose parents emigrated here from Calcutta, and an overtanned beach blondie on North Figueroa named Poswinski."

"What do you mean about me being hung up on a label?"

"Vikah ta, brother! This is not the ship; this is not Itri Vi. Torumeh and the pain ministers are long dead. *Vikah ta* is your label, Maanka."

"The player! Who is the player?"

Nicto paused for a moment, then said, "Perhaps there is a player. If it's anyone, I'd say it's a fifty-five-year-old human in an aloha shirt named Malcolm."

"Malcolm? Is he a genius?"

"No. He simply uses what he has very well; he remains always teachable. When was the last time you could be taught anything, Maanka?"

"Forever," Maanka muttered to himself. "Forever is forever."

"Maanka, what about the implantation instrument? The *tivati urih.* If you're really sorry for what you've done, that could make up for a little."

Maanka Dak laughed as everything in the universe suddenly fell into place. The new goals, the new view of himself, the new feelings, they were all still possible. That's the lesson today, he thought. Nothing is forever.

He stopped laughing and gasped to get back his breath. "Yes, Nicto. I'll give it to you. I'll give you the implantation awl. The Niyezian neural controllers." He reached out his hand and touched the keyboard he had taken from the corpse of Brick Wahl. "Instructions. All my data. Everything I know. Do you understand, Nicto? Everything I know."

"Where? When?"

"Patience, my brother. Have patience. There are things to do, people to see."

"Maanka, there won't be much point to this exercise unless it happens soon. The doctors at Mount Andarko don't think they can keep Matt Sikes alive much longer."

"Stay close to the phone, Nicto. I'll call you and tell you where and when to meet."

He cut off the connection and took a breath as he slaved a remote and punched in a call. The headache was fading. It was gone.

CHAPTER 26

RUMA KAVIT KEPT her gaze away from dark corners. Outside the window she could see the tops of three palm trees moving in the slight morning breeze. When she was released from the hospital, perhaps she'd go on a trip—somewhere quiet. The police therapist, a recovering rape victim herself, said that there were predictable stages of recovery. Denial was her current stage, moving over rapidly into anger. The feelings were scrambled, the pains so much deeper and sicker than the bullet wounds in her leg and arm.

Time. It would take time.

Her thoughts drifted back to Duncan. She had known him for less than an hour, yet she had known of him since she was accepted by the academy. He had been an anti-legend; a blue bogeyman. She saw the image of the palm trees smear with her tears, and she chased off the mental shadows once again. She tried to move her leg and winced at the pain in her thigh. The pain in the side of her head from the implant extraction acted as though it would never leave.

The operation had been successful. There wouldn't even be a visible scar. The same with her bullet wounds. There would be no visible scars. All of the scars would be inside. A yawning emptiness inside her knew something that others did not: the neural controllers had the potential to reach within the complexities of a nervous system and heal those scars. The strength that was needed to withstand the grieving that needed to be done could be bolstered. Perhaps the need for the grieving itself could be circumvented. Perhaps that might be an interesting area in which to work. The thought of wearing a uniform again was an instant trigger for more bouts of uncontrollable crying. Better to think of something else.

The door to the private room opened and a nurse looked in. "She's awake. Go ahead."

The nurse opened the door all of the way, revealing a Tenctonese male. The sight of him caused an automatic streak of fear, then anger, then resentment. The man, she recognized, was George Francisco. The fear, anger, and resentment remained.

He limped over and stopped next to her bed as the nurse left the room, closing the door behind her. Francisco's face was deeply lined, tired, the eyes sunken. "Officer Kavit, the nurse said you wanted to see me. How do you feel?"

"I'm mending," she managed to struggle out. "How's your partner?"

George closed his eyes and shrugged. "There's not much hope unless we can get the killer to turn over his equipment. Is there something I can do for you?" He reached out his hand to place it upon her arm, but she shrank away from his touch.

"Men aren't my favorite creatures on the planet right now, Sergeant."

"Sorry. I understand."

"Understand?" She felt her eyes fill with tears and she damned her own eyes for crying. "How can you possibly understand?"

"I understand enough to know why you don't want me to touch you. Do you want me to leave?"

"Yes! No! No. There's something I needed to tell you, first. Bill Duncan?"

"Yes?"

Ruma Kavit laughed involuntarily. "Duncan. Christ, what a pig. Filthy-mouthed, fat, foul-smelling, bigoted son of a bitch."

"He was all of that." George nodded and winced as he shifted his weight from his wounded leg. "Those cigars."

"That after-shave."

"Ya wanna bag of otter noses?"

Ruma laughed again. "I wouldn't let my daughter marry one, if I had a daughter—"

"—and believed in marriage," George completed. "What about him?"

She turned her head on her pillow until she was looking into George's eyes. "I found out something about Bill Duncan that you should know. The only reason I'm telling it to you is because it will make Duncan spin in his grave for you to know."

"What?"

"Bill Duncan was proud of you. Very proud."

George's eyebrows went up. "Are you joking?"

"No. I'm not joking. If there's anything in this universe you need to believe, it's this: Bill Duncan was proud of you."

Ruma watched as George turned away for a moment and folded his arms. "You sure I can't get you something, Officer Kavit?"

"Nothing. It's all right. You can call me Ruma, if you want."

He glanced back at her. "What are you going to do, Ruma Kavit? Once you get out of here, what will become of you?"

She turned her head and looked again at the tops of the three palm trees. "Duncan was a pig, wasn't he?"

"Yes. He was also one hell of a police officer."

The door opened and a uniformed officer stuck in his head and said, "Sergeant Francisco?"

"Yes?"

"Telephone call at the nurse's station. It's the one you've been expecting."

"Thank you." He turned and faced Kavit. "I have to go now. Maybe my partner still has a chance."

She reached out her hand. "Good luck, Sergeant."

He held her hand in both of his and nodded. "Good luck, Ruma. Good luck to us all."

She didn't release his hand. She'd seen something in George Francisco's face. "What are you up against, Sarge?" she asked.

"I'm not sure. Maybe nothing. Maybe I can buy my partner a chancc at retirement."

"Remember Duncan's rule number one."

"Right. Get home alive." He nodded at her. "You're going to do all right."

He released her hand and left the room, the door closing silently behind him. She watched the closed door for a moment, then let the tears come.

CHAPTER 27

Rogers Dry Lake, Edwards Air Force Base

"AMANDA, THIS BETTER be good. Middle of the night, stuck in this mobile unit out in the damned desert, freezing my ass off."

"Your ass could stand to lose about sixty percent, Jack."

Jack Rovitch rolled his fundament in the chair before the remote monitors and sneered out a laugh. "We'll see how funny this all is when Ronnie Glass calls us in to explain why we spent the night sitting in world's largest pile of kitty litter instead of following up on the Rand story at China Lake. I tell you, that's where the shit's at." He pointed a chubby finger at the monitors. They showed nothing but dark rooms and empty halls.

Amanda Reckonwith raised an eyebrow and nodded toward the monitors. "There's a story here, Jack. I'd stake my reputation on it."

"Reputation? The late night queen of the Slagtown beat? Don't make me laugh. What's this going to be, another where-are-they-now retrospective? A few years ago just huddled masses yearning to eat weasel jerky, now owner of his own dry cleaning establishment?"

"I trust my lead. This shit is going to be good. Count on it."

"Hell, there're ruts ten feet deep on the way to Roger's Dry Lake from all the heads that've done pieces on the camp, related to the camp, looking back at the camp, looking forward from the camp, and just plain camp. Nobody cares anymore. People're so bored about crap like that, they're already talking like the Tencts are a cult or the result of some kind of disease. They're bored."

"I don't think this story'll bore them, Jack."

"Really? Well, remember Father Maxwell's dictum: to be good shit, it has to stick, it has to stink, and it has to smear. Who's the lead? You can tell me now, can't you?"

"Now that we're here, I can. It was Maanka Dak."

Jack Rovitch frowned. "The con who busted out of China Lake? So what? He's yesterday's cold potatoes."

"What if I told you he was the engineer behind the China Lake story you want to follow up?"

"Eh?"

"That's right. He's the one who turned Warden Rand into a killer. Which also means the McBeaver Massacre and the Wilshire Waste are his. The potatoes warming up for you, Jack?"

"A bit. But for all you know, this caller is a crank, right? If it is Dak, that might even be worse. Maanka

Dak's a psycho, right? What if he's been watching your show all the time he was behind bars and he's got a real resentment?"

Amanda flashed her famous smile and held out her hands. "He managed to blank out base security, didn't he? All we had to do was hook up the feed, just the way he instructed."

"Amanda, baby, we already knew he was good with electrons. What we don't know—"

"A car is approaching now," Maanka Dak's voice said from an audio monitor. *"It's heading for the camp's old administration area."*

Jack froze for a second, then he reached out his hand and slapped the roof of the van. "Carlo! You see anything out there?"

"No, man," came the answer through the audio system. "And don't slap the roof like that, okay, Jack? You scared the—" There was a pause, then one of the blank video monitors filled with noise, then settled down, showing a pair of headlights moving through the darkness. "I got it. It's a car all right, Jack."

On one of the remote feeds controlled by Maanka Dak, a similar scene was shown through a light amplification system as a jet screamed overhead. Behind the blinding glare of the headlights were the fuzzy images of four faces, a driver and three passengers. The image was enhanced until the faces came into sharp focus. The camera controlled by Maanka Dak focused in on the driver, and a split-screen image showed a mug shot and stats on the driver, a human woman.

"Are you recording this?" Maanka asked over the audio system.

Amanda pressed the button to her feed and said, "Of course."

The data sheet on the driver showed her to be Mallory Brett, a hitter for the Cole organization based out of Baltimore. She was an expert in electronic security and was suspected in at least nine gangland slayings. She had never been charged with anything.

Sitting next to her was Rick Tomas, a knife and explosives specialist suspected in eleven individual murders and the deaths of thirty-one men, women, and children in the Covina Celinist Church bombing the year before. He too had never been charged with anything.

"Nice people," Jack Rovitch muttered.

The next face went up on the screen. It was Walter Rittenhouse, formerly of the New York advertising agency of Vernor & Price, former Washington correspondent for the *Atlanta Herald*, and former registered lobbyist for the Libyan government, currently public relations specialist employed by the NSA.

Jack Rovitch cackled just a little. "Now, Amanda, that's beginning to develop a bit of an aroma."

The fourth face came on the screen: Morton Lipscomb, former professor of communications at Georgetown, former media consultant to senators, cabinet officers, and even one presidential hopeful, currently media advisor to Central Intelligence. "Whew!" Jack said as he wrinkled his nose and mimed a horrible smell. "Well, the stink is getting there, but will it stick?"

The car pulled up in front of the dilapidated administration area, parked, and the driver killed the lights. The occupants sat silently for a long time, allowing Maanka Dak to adjust the sound pickups. At last Rittenhouse asked, *"Where is he? Aren't you two going to look for him?"*

Mallory Brett said calmly, *"You're here and you're*

alive. That's all we're being paid for. The orders from the doc are for you two to sit tight, but if you want to get out and look for that crazy son of a bitch on your own, you're welcome."

Again the occupants fell silent until Lipscomb muttered, *"You sure the Air Force understands everything?"*

"We're invisible," Rittenhouse said. *"We're not even here."*

"Almost," Jack Rovitch said, as though he were coaxing a reluctant lover. "Almost."

"Did you talk here at base security?"

"I'm not an idiot. I cleared everything with General Van Zandt at Air Force Intelligence. The base commander just takes his orders like a good little soldier. As far as Edwards is concerned, this part of the base fell off the planet."

"Ooooo!" said Amanda. "Sticky, sticky?"

Jack nodded, a grin on his face. "It is thickening up a mite."

"Did you deal with Van Zandt personally, or—"

"Are you two assholes going to talk all night?" Tomas interrupted Rick. *"The reason I ask is, if you plan to keep jabbering, me and Mall are going to go off in the shadows somewhere and wait until Dak wastes your asses. Then we'll come back and tell Doc Norcross things just didn't work out."*

"Norcross?" Jack Rovitch asked.

One of the video monitors filled with the image of and specs on Carrie Norcross, chief of neurosurgery, Walter Reed Army Medical Center, staff advisor to the Surgeon General, Director of MDQ. On another monitor appeared the data on MDQ.

"C'mon, baby," Rovitch begged. "More of a name.

There're lots of Doc Norcrosses in the world. Narrow it down for me. Lace it in. Sticky, sticky."

But the occupants of the car remained silent as the image changed to show another vehicle approaching the camp buildings. This one was a minibus carrying eight passengers, all of them hitters, all of them with ties to organized crime, all of them sitting grimly silent. The minibus stopped, two men got out, and the vehicle continued down the road fifty yards, where it stopped and let off another pair. They all carried automatic weapons.

"Carlo?" Jack whispered into his headset.

"What?" came the almost inaudible reply.

"Get your ass down here, don't show any lights, and don't make a sound. Got me?"

Carlo keyed his mike. As he was shutting down his operations atop the mobile unit, Jack faced Amanda. "Baby, we are in the middle of a gathering shit storm, and we got no umbrella. If I had any sense, I'd call it a day and get the hell out of here; and you know what?"

"What, Jack?"

"I got some sense. I say let's call it a day and get the hell out of here."

"It's just getting interesting, Jack," came Maanka Dak's voice over their headsets.

Jack held his hand to his headset and frowned at Amanda. "My mike isn't keyed."

As Maanka's laughter came over the headset, the sounds of helicopter blades beating the air filtered through the walls of the mobile unit. Amanda Reckonwith pointed at one of the video monitors. "Air Force."

Three DX-17 assault choppers flew over the roofs of the camp buildings, their powerful searchlights examining every street, window, and doorway. "Goddamn attack choppers! They're going to find us," Jack whispered. Suddenly a hand dropped on Jack's shoulder. He screamed, twisted in his chair, and held up his hands to guard his face.

"Jeez, Jack. You better switch to decaf."

"Carlo!" As Amanda giggled, Jack gestured angrily toward a bench built into the back of the mobile unit. "Why don't you get on the recorders, asshole, and see if you can stay out of trouble."

Jack turned back to the monitors, took a deep breath, and let out a ragged sigh as the choppers landed facing the camp's dilapidated administration building. Heavily armed men and women in civilian clothes piled out of the choppers and took positions around the building. One by one Maanka's light-amplified camera picked out the faces and flashed the particulars. The ones who came in by chopper were all federal marshals, except for a lone woman clad in trousers and heavy jacket.

A camera zoomed in on her face, and the data for Dr. Carrie Norcross appeared on the screen. "Ooooo!" Jack exclaimed, the images before his eyes overcoming his fears. "It stinks, it sticks, and sister does it ever smear. That's what I call some good shit. How high's it smear, though?"

Carrie Norcross strode toward the administration building, her face grim. She was flanked by four marshals armed with assault rifles. Amanda sat back in her seat and frowned.

"What is it?" Jack asked.

"A hunch. Maanka's setting himself up to be killed." She keyed her mike, knowing as she did so that it implied a control that was literally out of her hands. "Maanka Dak." There was nothing but silence through her headset. "Maanka, I know what you're doing."

"Then pay attention, Amanda. You know there won't be any retakes."

Jack Rovitch sat red-faced, his arms folded across his chest, glaring at the monitors. Amanda reached out a hand and shook his shoulder. "This is terrific stuff, Jack. What's the matter?"

"The matter?" He nibbled at the inside of his lips, shrugged, and shook his head. "The matter? I'll tell you what the matter is. There's nothing in this world that quite fills me with as much satisfaction as wrestling down the turnip and squeezing out a quart of blood, whether the blood's there or not." He waved his hand toward the screens. "There's something wrong with this. It's being handed to us. Everything down to and including the camera shots. It's all spoon-fed."

"We'll check it all out, Jack. We'll verify everything through independent sources. Everything by the book."

Jack continued glaring at the monitors, his head shaking, as Carrie Norcross left her bodyguards behind and entered the front doors of the administration building. "There is good shit and bad shit, Amanda. I'm getting a whiff of something that's maybe not so good."

The halls were thick with sand dust, the walls grimy and peeling. The lights of the choppers filtered through cracks and broken windows, showing the haze in the air. One of the monitors switched to show the interior of a cavernous room. Amanda recognized it as the Newcomer testing area where, years before, a much thinner Jack Rovitch had shown up with a mobile unit to delve into the sordid world of

Tenctonese sex. Those were the days when Jack was in front of the camera and was considered the mogul of muck. As Amanda studied the interior of the huge room, she remembered answering Jack's question, instinctively knowing what he wanted, and feeding him the slime he craved. He had hired her on the spot. At the time, she had looked upon it as the most thrilling thing that had ever happened to her.

In the back of the room a door opened and Dr. Carrie Norcross entered. She walked until she was standing in the center, waited for a long moment, then said, *"You wanted to see me, Maanka, in exchange for the data you erased. Very well, here I am."*

"And here is your data, Doctor."

A light went on a few paces away, revealing a stack of plastic boxes on the floor. Dr. Norcross went over to the boxes, squatted down, and opened one. After examining the disks inside, she took a disk reader from her pocket, inserted one of the disks, and viewed the tiny screen. *"I don't understand, Maanka. Why did you break out? I was less than a step away from obtaining your release. Now you've ruined everything."*

"Put a tic in your world plan, did it, Carrie?" came Maanka's sarcastic reply.

"Dak, you have simply no idea how far you could've gone. There was nothing—nothing—that would've been denied you. My God, the royalty trust fund on your inventions has current assets of over three hundred million dollars. And that's nothing next to what it could have been once the neural transmitter was perfected. You could've gone so far." She withdrew the disk and inserted another from another box.

"You mean, we could've gone so far, don't you, Carrie?"

Maanka Dak came walking out of the shadows. He

stopped twenty feet from Norcross, his hands at his sides. He did not carry any weapons.

"Is he crazy?" Jack blurted. "That woman's packing."

Amanda nodded as she adjusted a control. "He's one crazy son of a bitch."

Carrie Norcross's right hand stole into the pocket of her coat as she said, *"Everything may not be over, Maanka."*

"Enlighten me, Doctor."

"NSA has its own version of the federal witness protection program for national security assets. I'm certain I can get you in."

"Ah, me," Maanka Dak said, *"the life of a tract-house dweller for Maanka Dak, citizen at large. Three bedrooms, two baths, and a job assistant managing a Radio Shack in East Jesus, Utah, demonstrating discount plasma generators to holiday shoppers."*

"She's got a gun!" Jack said.

"Of course she has a gun," Maanka said, but the image of Maanka Dak facing Dr. Norcross didn't move its lips. Norcross gave no indication of having heard Maanka's comment to the mobile unit crew.

"More than you deserve, Maanka. Do you realize how many deaths have resulted from your actions?"

"Do you mean our actions, Doctor? I wasn't the one who bypassed China Lake's security to give all those toys to a psychopathic killer."

Her hand moved rapidly, withdrawing her weapon. She aimed and fired twice. Maanka stood there, laughing at her. *" 'The regimen I adopt shall be for the benefit of my patients,' "* he quoted from the Hippocratic Oath, *" 'according to my ability and judgment, and not for their hurt or for any wrong—' "*

She fired again, and the image of Maanka Dak

vanished. "What in the hell?" Amanda said as she looked in astonishment at Jack.

"Rather simple, really," Maanka said. *"It's an adaption of my high definition holographic imager. She was one of the principal supporters of my work in holographics. I didn't think she'd fall for it. She's probably under a great deal of stress."*

Norcross stood silently as three of the U.S. Marshals burst into the room and spread out, weapons held at the ready. *"He's not here,"* Norcross said, *"but he's close. That imager can't project more than a few feet."* She turned her head and pointed at one of the men. *"Get the others into the choppers and tell the pilots and gunners to stand by."* As he left, she pointed at the other two. *"Gather up these disks and take them to my chopper. Be quick about it. You don't have much time."*

The two men picked up the plastic boxes and carried them from the room. Once she was alone, Dr. Norcross stood next to the illuminated area, her weapon held uselessly at her side. *"I know you're recording all this, Maanka. I also know there aren't any outside feeds. We've swept the area, and whatever you have recorded is here or close to here. That means it will be destroyed within minutes."*

"Hey, Jack?" Carlo said. "What's she talkin' about, man?"

"Shut up."

The image of Maanka Dak walked into the light, leaned against a post and folded its arms. *"What's your point, Carrie?"*

She didn't look at the image as her gaze searched the darkness surrounding her. *"You have so much to offer, Maanka. Why throw it all away? For what?"*

"Well, as Amanda Reckonwith once said, I'm one crazy son of a bitch."

"Amanda Reckonwith?"

"She's a local TV reporter." The image of Maanka pointed toward the screen. *"She's watching us now."*

"Holy shit!" Jack exclaimed.

Dr. Norcross glanced in the indicated direction, but could see nothing in the dark. She shook her head and said, *"Not for long."* The doctor turned and walked quickly from the testing hall.

"Not for long?" Carlo repeated. "What's she mean, not for long?"

"Stuff an avocado in it, Carlo," Amanda ordered as she watched the image of Maanka Dak stand, pull a knife from its pocket, and draw the edge across the palm of its left hand. Pale Tenctonese blood dribbled onto the floor, then the image turned and walked back into the shadows, leaving the tiny splashes of blood behind.

"That was Maanka Dak himself," Jack said.

Amanda nodded. "One crazy son of a bitch."

The sounds of the choppers revving up beat upon the outside of the mobile unit, and three of the monitors showed the three choppers lifting into the night. One of them turned north and headed straight for the airfield, while the two remaining gunships stood off the administration area and opened fire with rockets. In less than a second the camp administration area, as well as all nearby buildings, were thoroughly engulfed as the interior monitors went blank. The exterior cameras showed the choppers continuing the attack. Dark figures ran from the flames into the safety of the shadows, only to be met by more rocket fire.

"My God," Amanda said. "Those're the goons that were dropped off to guard the area."

Jack looked at Amanda, his face ashen. "What about us? We got Carrie Norcross on tape for everything from mass murder to treason, but it's not going to do us much good if we're cinders." He jumped as the remains of a gas storage tank exploded, illuminating the desert for miles around. "God, please, God, please let me live long enough to get this on the air before Channel Seven."

There was another explosion, and the car carrying the unlikely team of Brett, Tomas, Rittenhouse, and Lipscomb vaporized while both choppers swung around and began searching out warm bodies on the desert. Each body found was burgered on the spot with computer-directed, high-density machine-gun fire.

"Loose ends," Amanda said. "Carrie Norcross is snipping off loose ends."

"Jesus," Jack Rovitch said. "Now that's what I call one crazy son of a bitch."

"Dammit!" Carlo shouted. "What about us? Aren't we a loose end? The biggest goddamned loose end that Norcross's got?"

Jack wiped his brow and stared at the monitors, glorious visuals awash with flames, audio heavy with thunder. "They got too much on their minds. We're not close. They won't notice us."

"With the silver mirror and electric-green paint job on this thing?" Carlo shrieked. "And what about those feed lines? They run right up to us. Let's pull the plugs and get the hell out of here! No lights, no nothin', just blow, split, vanish!"

Jack rose halfway from his chair and froze as one of the monitors showed one of the choppers heading east toward the mobile unit. "Uh-oh." He glanced at Amanda, then Carlo, then the door.

"Carlo's got a point. We got to get the hell out of here. That culvert down the road. Maybe we can reach it. Maybe the heat sensors can't read us through all that concrete and steel." He looked back at Carlo and Amanda. "Grab the tapes!"

The sound of the chopper blades pounded their eardrums as Amanda jabbed the ejection buttons on two recorders and screamed in frustration as the mechanism paused, verified, cycled, and pushed the bright red plastic case out of the panel. She grabbed the cassettes, saw that Carlo had a cassette in each hand, then she lunged for the door, knocking herself to the floor as she ran into Jack Rovitch's ample backside. Climbing to her feet, she said, "Jack? What is it?"

He pushed the door open all of the way with his foot, revealing the desert pocked with red and blue flashing lights. "Cops." She pushed Jack aside and stepped down from the door. There were more than a dozen police cruisers surrounding the TV mobile unit. All of the officers were standing outside their vehicles, their weapons at the ready. Facing them forty yards away was the Air Force gunship. The image held for close to fifteen seconds, then the DX-17 turned slowly and headed north.

"Too much," a voice said.

"You're right, Cap. The Air Force declaring war on the Los Angeles Police Department just wouldn't look good no matter what kind of spin they put on it."

Amanda walked over to the speaker. In the strobing red and blue flashes of the lights, she recognized him. "You're Detective Sergeant Francisco."

George smiled but continued looking toward the north. "And you are Amanda Reckonwith, queen of the Slagtown news beat."

"When did you cops arrive?"

"Five or six minutes ago. It looks like we were just in time."

"That's the honest damned truth," Jack Rovitch said from the door of the mobile unit. Carlo was peeking over his shoulder, and Jack stood out of his way. "G'wan. You don't need a green card. You were born here."

Amanda took two steps and came to a halt facing George. "You knew about this?"

"I suspected something. He had something I needed delivered to the hospital. It was part of a deal we made. The strange thing was, there was no way for Maanka to collect his part from me. I thought something like this might happen."

"And you just let it happen?"

George turned away, looked into the darkness for a moment, then faced the reporter. "I'm not really certain what's happened. Are you?"

"Dak's dead, a whole bunch of mob hitters, and a couple of spin doctors along with him. Dr. Carrie Norcross gave the order, and she's gotten away."

"I guess I got that part wrong," Captain Grazer said.

Amanda felt her eyebrows climb. "That part?"

Grazer nodded as he shifted his gaze to look after the departing choppers. "There was some data Maanka Dak had that Norcross wanted. You must know about it. Dak said the entire thing would be witnessed."

"Yes. There were some computer disks. Norcross had them loaded on her chopper."

Grazer nodded and said to George, "That's what I said. So why hasn't that chopper been blown to pieces? He took over my whole command center in a matter of minutes. Maanka Dak can sure rig something as simple as a altimeter switch."

George shook his head. "You don't understand, Cap. *Rekwi ot osia:* death to authority. Carrie Norcross alive and in front of a congressional committee will do more to kill corrupt authority than spreading her ashes all over the desert."

The sounds of distant sirens caused Amanda to look north toward the airfield. Tiny pinpricks of red flashing lights sparkled in the night. "The base fire brigade," Grazer said.

Amanda glanced down at the cassettes in her hands. "I don't understand something, Sergeant." She looked up at George. "How is this going to wind up in front of a committee? This is big stuff. Depending on where it leads, it could bring down the government, and I'm not talking about the mayor's office."

George nodded. "You could be right."

She held up the cassettes. "I've been in this neighborhood before. It's about now that some bureaucrat starts talking about national security and runs off with all our stuff."

"I wouldn't know about that, Ms. Reckonwith. The LAPD has no jurisdiction here on federal property, and in fact we should get going before that bureaucrat you mentioned starts yelling at us. The fire brigade and the air police should be here soon. Our work is done."

"The choppers don't look like they're coming back," Grazer said. He patted George on the shoulder. "Take it easy on the leg. See you at work in ten days. I'm leaving you Devlin to drive you back."

Captain Grazer gave a hand signal, got into his car, and drove off. One by one the officers got into their cruisers, turned off their flashing lights, and followed

Grazer's car back to L.A. In a minute there was only a lone car and officer left.

Amanda turned back toward the mobile unit and saw Jack and Carlo still gawking out of the door. "Tell me you got that. You got that, right?"

Jack and Carlo looked at each other, then looked back at Amanda. "Sorry," Jack said. "I'm still trying to get used to being alive."

When she turned back, George had opened his door and climbed into the passenger seat. "Sergeant Francisco?"

He pulled the door shut and hooked up his seat belt. "Yes?"

"Thanks for not letting us die."

"Thank Maanka Dak for that. He told us only two things: where you'd be, and to protect the First Amendment to the Constitution." He cocked his head toward the mobile unit. "Do you have a computer in there?"

"Sure."

"I'll bet you your next two smear campaigns against the LAPD that everything you need to put your story together is on your computer."

Amanda grinned widely. "No bet." George nodded at the driver, the car backed around and stopped as Officer Devlin saw Amanda Reckonwith waving at them. "Sergeant?"

George looked out of the window. "Yes?"

"Maanka Dak. What was he after? He's dead and he'll still be dead once the stink dies down. What was this?"

George frowned and looked thoughtful. "An apology," he answered. "It was an apology." He nodded toward the driver, and Devlin put the car in gear, turned on the headlights, and drove into the night.

Amanda looked toward the quarantine camp, the flames from dozens of buildings climbing into the night sky. The fire brigade was still miles away. "One crazy son of a bitch."

She turned, placed the cassettes beneath her arm, and climbed into the mobile unit. Before they reached the San Gabriel Mountains, Amanda Reckonwith was writing her copy.

CHAPTER 28

Buck held the withered plant in his hand and looked at Aman Iri as Malcolm Bone watched. "When I say this is gray-green and carries a pink and yellow blossom when it blooms, and that it grows an average of nine inches in height, I'm talking about this object. When I say that it is beautiful or that it is a flower, I'm talking, not about it, but about myself. The words 'flower' and 'weed' are not descriptions of real things; they are judgments, like 'us' and 'them,' 'black people' and 'white people,' 'good' and 'evil.'"

Aman Iri nodded, removed his straw hat and looked up at the burned walls of the garden. "And if I should send you out into the garden to bring me back a flower, what would you do?"

Buck smiled. "First I'd have to find out what you meant by the word."

"Sounds inefficient, troublesome. It might even make you look unintelligent."

"All of which are terms of judgment, *Hila*—" Buck paused for a moment, glanced at Malcolm, then grinned as he said, "—as is the term *Hila.*"

Aman and Malcolm both laughed. Iri nodded and placed a hand on Buck's shoulder. "I hear you had a bit of a misunderstanding with Malcolm."

Buck glanced at Malcolm, then looked at Aman. "Misunderstanding. That's a very kind word to use to describe a bigot's freakout."

The corners of the *Hila*'s mouth went down as he looked scornfully at Malcolm Bone. "Well, after all, he is a human. And try as we might, there are certainly distinct differences between humans and Tenctonese."

"Not differences that matter," Buck answered. "Besides, I saw on the news this morning about a couple in Santa Cruz, a human male and a Tenct female, who are part of an experiment to enable impregnation between humans and Tencts." He looked at Malcolm and said, "I apologize for how I acted. I also thank you for helping my father. He, and I, believe you saved a lot of lives with your advice."

"How is he?" Malcolm asked.

"He's taking a few days off until his leg heals and the *riana* runs its course. I don't know how much rest he'll get, though. The past few days have been pretty rough on the house, and my mom's got a platoon of carpenters in there doing repairs."

"Well, he can always come down here to the *vo*. It's a good place to sort out your circuits. How about his partner and the other officer? According to the Slagtown news, they're both heroes."

"That'll last until the Dodgers win another game," Aman said.

"In your dreams," Malcolm responded. Turning to Buck, he repeated, "What about Matt Sikes?"

"The operation with the *tivati urih* was a complete success. Dad said Matt was asking for chocolate chip cookies this morning. Ruma Kavit was released. After her wounds are healed, she's going back to do cops, as she put it. That's real hard for me to understand."

"Not so difficult," Aman said. "Every fear you refuse to face surrounds you. The only way to escape a fear is to face it. She's facing hers." He smiled at Buck. "Your father asked me to speak with her. What of Paul Iniko?"

"The FBI agent. He's still in the hospital, but they expect to let him go in a few days. I don't know what's going to happen to him. He's agreed to testify before the Senate Intelligence Committee."

"He's an Overseer, isn't he?" Malcolm asked.

Buck pursed his lips, raised his eyebrows, and smiled. "He once carried that title." He shifted his gaze to Aman Iri.

"What about yourself, Buck?" asked the *Hila*. "Where are you in your search?"

Buck glanced down for a moment. When he looked up again, his voice was strong. "I've gone back to high school."

"I thought you'd learned everything high school could teach you."

His eyes yellowed from embarrassment. Buck grinned and cocked his head to one side. "I found that I still have a lot to learn there. To begin with: how to be a teenager." He held his head straight. "Do you want to meet the additions to your collection you sent me to find?"

"Most assuredly."

"When you sent me for a yellow man and a black

man, it was within your instructions that they be women, wasn't it?"

Aman Iri frowned and nodded. "A yellow woman and a black woman would do."

Buck held out his hand toward the building. "They're awaiting your pleasure in the garden vestibule. Did you enjoy your skiing holiday?"

"Quite."

Malcolm jabbed Aman in the ribs and pointed at Buck. "He's got a mouthful of canary feathers."

"Don't be disgusting."

Once inside the vestibule, they were met by two men and two women, all in their late teens. Buck went to a dark-skinned male and said, "May I introduce my friend Theo White, my white man." He held his hand out toward a pale-skinned male. "This is my friend Victor Rojas, which means 'red' in Spanish." He held his hand out toward a tall athletic woman with bright red hair. "This is Patty Gelbe, which means 'yellow' in German." And finally, he held his hand out toward a dark-eyed creature with an elfin smile. "And this is my black woman, Mioshi Kuro."

As Malcolm Bone leaned against the door to support him in his laughter, Aman Iri removed his straw hat and said to Mioshi Kuro, "And 'kuro' means 'black' in Japanese?"

She nodded and giggled. "We have talked among ourselves, sir, and we can supply a Brown, a Gray, a Green, and we think, a Blue."

There was laughter. The joy of learning. The thrill of taking those first halting steps toward freedom of the mind. As they went in to eat lunch, Buck's friends decided the *vo* was a good place. They all made up their minds to return.

CHAPTER 29

LATE THAT NIGHT in a semi-private room in Mt. Andarko Hospital, Matt Sikes was propped up in his bed, his bedclothes pulled up to his neck, looking at George sitting in a wheelchair. He glanced at the door and said, "Partner, I don't think I'll ever be warm again."

In the next bed Paul Iniko took a sip of water and replaced his glass upon the nightstand. When he was finished he looked at the door, and then at Matt. "Do you notice any difference from before, sergeant? There was some question about brain damage."

"I can't do long division, but that's okay because I never could." Matt looked away from the door and faced Paul Iniko. "Are you getting along okay on only one heart?"

"Are you?"

"Just trying to be friendly," Matt explained.

"I'm doing just fine." Paul Iniko faced George.

"Now that you have those tremors in addition to the blindness, you really ought to be in bed. Dr. Rivers told you that."

"Muddy Rivers," muttered George. All three of them jumped as the door to the room opened revealing Dr. Liveit, the Tenctonese administrator of Mt. Andarko.

"You people seem nervous for being big time celebrities." He walked over to George's wheelchair and placed a hand on George's shoulder. "Especially you, sergeant. I've never seen Amanda Reckonwith's show so enamored of the police."

"Is it this one?" asked Paul Iniko.

"Well, of course, this one," said the administrator.

"Forgive me, sir," said Paul. "I was asking Sgt. Francisco a question."

"Sorry."

"No," answered George. "This isn't the one."

"One what?" asked Dr. Liveit.

"It's a game," said Matt. "George can't see very well, and he's trying to pick out voices."

"What a remarkable attitude. I—"

The trio jumped again as the door opened revealing a human nurse. She entered, a tray in her hands. The nurse was slim and quite attractive. "Matt," she said, "Cathy called to say she'd be in early tomorrow." She put down the tray and began preparing a hypodermic. "It's needle time again."

Matt stared at the woman for a moment, then smiled. "Anything to get my pants down, right, Linda?"

"Thrills are my stock-in-trade."

Matt raised his eyebrows at George. "What do you say, partner?"

"This one," answered George. The room filled with

explosions as both Sikes and Iniko fired their weapons through their sheets at Linda the nurse.

Dr. Liveit stood in shock, his mouth opening and closing like a beached fish. Sikes pulled down his covers and put on his slippers, his weapon still aimed at the nurse. As he struggled out of bed, Matt said, "Linda's blood is certainly pale for a human." He knelt next to her, thrust the muzzle of his weapon against her temple, and peeled off her mask. The face lifted off, revealing the features of Maanka Dak. Dr. Liveit sat down on Matt's bed.

"What in the hell is going on here?"

Matt's search of Maanka's body produced two automatic pistols. "That's what I want to know, George. What's going on? I thought this guy was feeling bad about what he did. Didn't he apologize?"

"Yes. But Maanka was apologizing for how he carried out his *vikah ta,* not the *vikah ta* itself. After all, he did take an oath."

Matt stood up, dropped the weapons on his nightstand, and sat next to Dr. Liveit. "So, partner, once the *riana* is all done, will you be permanently smart?"

George grabbed the armrests to the wheelchair and pushed himself to a standing position. "Each time I go through the changing, I will have an incremental increase in intelligence, that's all." He felt his way over to Maanka's body and knelt down next to it. He placed his fingers on Maanka Dak's face and felt down the front of the uniform, over the artificial breasts, down to the waistline.

"Maanka might have become an incredible mental power," Paul Iniko observed, "had he lived long enough to experience *riana.*"

"Yeah," said Matt, "what could he've become?"

George stood and tossed Maanka's pair of heart picks next to the guns on the nightstand. "He would've been an even crazier son of a bitch."

"George, are you all right?"

"All right," he answered. He lowered himself into the wheelchair, closed his eyes, and watched columns of green flame rise from a black hell to fill the skies above with billowing clouds of orange smoke. "Celine," he prayed in a whisper, "the last brother of the *Ahvin Yin* is dead. There are no more debts. Let the *Ahvin Yin* die as well."

Great blues and whites splashed onto the heavens, and then Nicto slept.

**THE INCREDIBLE STORY BEHIND ONE OF
STAR TREK'S BEST-LOVED CHARACTERS**

STAR TREK®

SAREK

A.C. CRISPIN

Pocket Books is proud to present SAREK, the
sweeping story of the life of Spock's full-Vulcan
father. Since his introduction, the coolly logical
Sarek has been the subject of endless specula-
tion. Now, finally, comes a book that spans
Sarek's life and illustrious career as one of the
Federation's premiere ambassadors as well as
his unpredecented marriage to a human
woman, and conflict with his son, Spock, that
lead to an eighteen-year estrangement
between the two men.

**Available in hardcover
from Pocket Books**

934